WHO KILLED
Walter Dobbs?

J.D. Tynan

Strategic Book Publishing
New York, New York

Who Killed Walter Dobbs?
Copyright 2008 All rights reserved: J.D. Tynan

Strategic Book Publishing
An imprint of AEG Publishing Group
845 Third Avenue, 6th Floor – 6016
New York, NY 10022
www.StrategicBookPublishing.com

ISBN: 978-1-60693-185-1 / SKU: 1-60693-186-7

Printed in the United States of America

Book Design: *Mark Bredt*
Cover illustrations: ©*William Berry;* ©*Mollypix*
                    -- Dreamstime.com

Dedication for Walter Dobbs

I'd like to dedicate this book to my mom, Kris, who has always been there for me. She's always encouraged me to do my best, not be afraid to fail and to love myself unconditionally.

Thank you
A special thanks to Mark for believing in me.

To Sergeant Ron Mason of the Portland Police Bureau and
Corporal Doug Rickard of the Vancouver Police Department,
thanks for answering my silly questions about police work. If I
chose to ignore any procedures it's only because I'm stubborn,
so neither officer is at fault for any mistakes I made. I write
fiction, so we'll just keep it at that! I truly enjoyed the time we
spent together.

To Tisha Woodard, for being a wonderful friend and excellent
editor.

To Linda, for keeping me going on a daily basis. Your
inspiration and friendship means the world to me.

To my husband Jim. Thanks for being there through good
times and bad. I'm happy to take this lifetime journey with you
by my side and I look forward to the good times ahead.

To James and Shea. Thanks for being who you are. The most
wonderful gifts I could have ever asked for.

www.JDTynan.com – www.JDTynanOnline.com

Other works by J.D. Tynan

Jill 9
Charlie Ford Meets Secret Agent Man
Charlie Ford Meets the Mole

One

Choleric: *adjective, meaning bad tempered, angry, or snarling.*

Wow! I always thought that word had something to do with the colon and an invasive procedure at a medical clinic. *Okay, so I don't know everything; who the hell does?*

I trailed my index finger along the black and white text. *And yet, cholera is a disease marked by severe vomiting and dysentery -- Hmmm.*

If you're wondering why I'm reading the dictionary, it's because my principal told me to. Actually, he told me to go look up choleric after I furrowed my brows at him and demanded he speak English. That was twenty minutes ago, and my blood pressure still has not dropped down to a reasonable one-twenty-over-seventy.

My desk is cluttered as always, but because it's Friday, and I have a blind date, I don't mind so much and I refuse to clean it off after being scolded for the last hour. It's my classroom, my mess, and my prerogative to be a sloppy pig. Principal Kensington has no power over me. I'm my own woman, my own entity, and my own person and yet day after day, I'm being pulled into his miniscule, yellow tinted office and being told to watch my attitude. Where the hell does he get off? Oh boy, thinking about Don Kensington is not good for my blood pressure. I can actually feel the vein in my forehead protruding through my lightly tanned forehead.

I need a massage -- or at least a couple of margaritas to calm my nerves.

I wasn't always that bitter, or perturbed about being told not to scream at my clearly brain-dead students, but damned if my life has been going well lately.

***

Lowlander and Bonks was the hottest spot on Friday night. Actually, it was the hottest spot any night of the week, because it's just about the only tavern without bare breasts on the entire Southeast side of Portland, Oregon. That's where I was living and had lived most of my life. I did go to college in Ashland, Oregon, and let me just say…Ashland has Shakespeare and that's about all. I was bored to tears for four long years. That probably had a lot to do with my bad behavior this afternoon. Not really. Boredom in college had nothing to do with my sour mood. Pain, anguish and heartache were to blame. I completely understood that my anger and disappointment needed to be dealt with in a more positive way, I just didn't know how.

Traffic was unbearable, but I did manage to flip-off only three people instead of four, like I'd wanted to, but something about the tinted windows on the low-rider pimpmobile made me think twice about gesturing to the nice young gangster wannabe who cut me off on Stark Street.

The parking lot at Lowlander's was full, as you can imagine, on a Friday at four-thirty. My student loans were still being paid off—even though I did graduate more than a decade ago. What can I say? Shit happens and unfortunately, it always happens to me. Anyway, I was about to explain why I was still driving the car I'd bought when I turned twenty-two. It was a bright red Volkswagen GTI and it was still running, even after hitting the one hundred and thirty-seven thousand-mile mark. It was dependable, not pretty and without a doubt, on its last leg. Now that I'm older, I do feel relatively ridiculous driving around in a college student's car. But again, I have more important things to worry about than what kind of crap-car I drive.

Up ahead on the right, I saw my opportunity -- a space was about to be unoccupied, so I crept up and turned on my blinker. I shoved my Foster Grants back onto the bridge of my nose and tapped my fingers on the steering wheel in time to Bruce Springsteen singing about dancing in the dark. I wonder if that song really has a sexual undertone to it. Most likely, it does. Why else would you dance in the dark, unless you were naked with a hottie?

Waiting. Patiently waiting for the old man in the white Oldsmobile to finally pull out, I closed my eyes and tried to tune out all the emotional turmoil.

When I reopened my eyes, I blinked at what I saw.

Unbelievable!

"I was waiting for that spot," I shouted out my window at the tall man in the Jeep Wrangler who had snuck in front of me and stolen my one-and-only hope for a parking spot. "Hey, I'm talking to you," I yelled louder, when he all but ignored me.

He shrugged, pulled a black comb from his back pocket, and grinned. "You snooze, you lose." He raked the comb through his hair and because of the horrible day I had, I screamed a couple of obscenities out the window and considered pulling a Kathy Bates and ramming his camouflage Jeep a couple of times -- but that would've meant that my poor GTI would have to go to car heaven and I couldn't afford that. Not now, not after my washing machine had decided to go ape shit and dump thirty gallons of water into my kitchen. The flooring alone was going to cost an entire measly paycheck to replace.

My best friend, Lily The Yoga Enthusiast, always told me to take deep breaths in and deep breaths out in times of sudden duress, so I did just that. I did that until I was calm enough to pull across the street and illegally park in the bank parking lot. My day had already gone to hell, so at that point, I didn't think getting towed would add much stress.

I straightened my purple and yellow sundress, applied a smidgen of lip-gloss, and shimmied my way out from behind the steering wheel. The temperature had hit eighty degrees on that fabulous day in May, so I left my yellow cardigan sweater behind and waltzed across the street with clammy palms, nauseated by the thought of yet another blind date.

The bar was established, filled with slobbering morons and already smelled like clove cigarettes and spicy Buffalo wings. Lily and Chad were glued to the bar, sipping microbrews, and watching the last inning of the Mariners' game. I could see from my position by the front door that the Mariners were up to bat, but I couldn't see the score and it wasn't until I turned the corner and headed toward the south end of the bar, that I knew my night was about to get much, much worse. Who could have guessed that sitting next to Chad, sipping a Corona and high-fiving my best friend, would be the ass-wipe from the parking lot – my blind date for the night. The first thing I noticed after I stopped seeing red and caught my breath was the black comb sticking out of his back pocket. Ugh. *I want to die!*

I had two options. Run out the door, call Lily, and pretend to have cholera, or saunter up beside the jerk and bash him upside the head with his beer bottle. I chose the first option and ran home, by way of 7-11 for a quick burrito and a bag of chocolate covered raisins.

Lily was disappointed that I wasn't feeling well, and she did apologize for Chad's ridiculous idea of setting me up with his second cousin Gil. Lily said that the man had no class and continually combed his hair every other minute. He wasn't my type anyway. He lacked a college education, proper shoes, and he ran his own limo company. Ugh. I should have never agreed to let Chad play matchmaker. Hell, I'd let him do that once before and after the last loser, I should've known better than to let him try again.

Lily and Chad were blissfully married and were, therefore, taking it upon themselves to find me a new husband. Little did they know that a new husband was the last thing from my mind. I'd sworn off marriage, or falling in love, and even decided that celibacy would be the best course of action at that particular juncture in my life. I wouldn't dare tell them that, though. Telling them would just make them try even harder to find me a Mr. Perfect.

Half the furniture in my house was missing. Not at all bad, in and of itself, because Ray had the worst taste in décor, but there were days that I missed him, and/or wanted to run him down with my Dad's tractor until his brains splattered from his eye sockets.

A tear dribbled down my cheek in honor of his abrupt departure, but I didn't let that stand in my way of watching *Sleepless in Seattle* for the thirteenth time in the past week.

***

When I woke up Saturday morning, my eye sockets actually ached from crying so hard and the pain behind my right ear just reminded me not to fall asleep on the remote control anymore. What can I say? I was suffering from a broken heart and nothing short of getting Ray back was going to fix the gaping hole that seemed to be eating me alive. Photos of Ray still hung on my refrigerator and although I know it's not healthy for my state of mind, I was still wearing my wedding ring. Some habits were harder to break than others.

I know I will sound completely pathetic by admitting this, but I miss everything about Ray. Even the way he criticized me for not dusting under the bed and, of course, the way he always left the cap off the toothpaste, and tried to school me in the proper way to use an iron. I know that most women loathe that about their husbands, but just for one minute if all those women thought about waking up alone every morning, I bet they'd see life a bit differently.

Ray wooed me at a young age when I was finishing my Master's degree at Portland State University. He was a great educator – actually the only professor I ever even contemplated sleeping with. I understand it's frowned upon, but we were fools in love and he was the sexiest man I'd ever seen. His dark nappy hair was practically non- existent, but he refused to shave what he did have because he was afraid that people would confuse him for one of the Trail Blazers. Yes, Ray Shirpa was an African American, six-feet-four-inches tall, and very nicely put together. I never really did get over my childhood crushes on NFL superstars like Walter Payton, Kenny Easley, and Jerry Rice and I guess it carried over into my private life. My father told me time and time again that Ray and I would never make it, or that we were too different, but like any other girl out there, I really wasn't interested in how my father felt about the man I loved. What mattered was that I fell hard and fast, like I'd been hit by a Greyhound Bus. Ray was strong and self-assured. He carried my books down the hall, gave me A's on my exams when I really only deserved B's and never once let on that he disapproved of the way I ate corn on the cob. He loved that I laughed at him when he played the saxophone in bed and he loved that I couldn't keep a straight face in church. It was one of those Pentecostal parishes and I couldn't help but laugh when the entire congregation closed their eyes, tossed their hands in the air and yelled, "Hallelujah," or "Praise the Lord," at the tops of their lungs. I loved Ray, though, and we worked well together to mesh our cultures and appreciate our differences – and well, I just loved Ray more than I ever imagined loving another person.

Everything about Ray made me swoon and where did that land me? Knee deep in divorce hell, with no happy ending on the horizon -- no money in the bank, no friends and because he left no indication that he was coming back, a huge void in my life. I didn't know how to move on. I didn't know where to go from there and I didn't know why, after eleven months of being without him, I was still wearing my damn wedding ring and could still smell him in our house.

***

The seniors that had actually passed my law class at David Douglas High School walked down the aisle in the gymnasium that afternoon. It had been a week or so since my last emotional breakdown. I stood on stage with a dozen other teachers and wished them well, shook their hands and helped pass out diplomas to the deserving graduates. I had a few favorites in my class, but the majority of students were the jock crowd who thought my class would be an easy grade. Boy, were they in for a rude awakening. First off, I'm not the most understanding of teachers and, secondly, there's not one easy damn thing about learning the law. I should know, because after I received my Bachelor's degree in Criminal Justice Administration, I went back to get my Masters. It was a difficult major and then, of course, I fell in love and was coerced into teaching like my husband did. He liked things his way and he wanted our schedules to match so we could have plenty of time together, and of course, made sure I still had plenty of time to keep a tidy home.

I should have known right away that it wasn't in my nature to be nice to spoiled rotten teenagers with acne and no sense of personal style. Each and every one of them looked as if they woke up, rolled out of bed, tossed a baseball cap on their greasy hair—sideways I might add—and forgot their belts. Either that, or they had lost twenty pounds overnight and that's why their jeans were hanging half way off their asses. It disgusted me. *Me,* who grew up in the age of Izod, Polo, and pants that actually fit.

The ceremony lasted exactly three hours, after which I was ready for a chilling shower and an appointment with the realtor who was selling my house. I'd put it on the market just three days prior, and to my surprise, I got three offers right away. It helped that I lived in a fairly beautiful neighborhood, surrounded by elm and chestnut trees. The house was older, but in fair shape for its age. The yard was huge and I think that's why it was so sellable.

"Angie," Bill, the sly real estate broker, said from behind his iced Starbucks' Caramel Machiato drink. "I think we should take the second offer. We need to strike while the iron is *hot.*"

He actually made a high-pitched hissing sound and touched his ass like it was on fire.

My god, I hate my life.

"I don't know," I said, still unsure. I was positive that I was making a huge emotional mistake by selling my home; but quite honestly, after my latest breakdown, I knew something had to give. I'd considered selling the house that Ray and I shared about seven or eight times in the past year, and now that it was down to the wire, I was having serious doubts. Mostly because I liked Ray's scent in the closet and I loved seeing our handprints in the cement patio that we built out back and, mostly, I didn't want my marriage to end. Feeble, aren't I?

With as much strength as I could muster and with all the courage I had in my soul, I lifted my chin from my chest, brushed the sappy tears from my eyes and grabbed Bill's gold plated pen. "Where do I sign?"

His eyes lit up like it was the Fourth of July and I was about to be a couple of hundred thousand dollars richer — thanks to Ray's mom who died the year after we married. Her only last dying wish was that Ray and I have the house that she and her second husband had recently paid off. It was a good inheritance and one that I figured we'd pass on to our own kids someday. Ray had a different idea, but surprisingly when the lawyers did their thing, Ray didn't put up a fight. It was the only thing I got in the divorce, most likely because Ray felt guilty for his mid-life crisis.

The minute Bill left, I felt so brave that I actually picked up the phone and dialed the love of my life. My hands were shaking. It felt as if someone had a stranglehold on my larynx, but it needed to be done.

"Hola!" A very young, Latina voice purred into the phone.

I gagged, wheezed a bit and then lay down on my hardwood floor and lifted my legs to encourage the blood to return to my brain.

"Hello," she spoke again. "Who is there?"

I envisioned what she looked like, although I never did see her. I recognized her voice, though. Only the last time I heard the Cuban harlot's voice, she was moaning and squealing and screaming out, *"Oh Papi, you're so BIG!"*

I felt vomit surge in my throat at recalling exactly what she said after that. If I weren't a noble, self-controlled woman with high morals and a sense of what happens to cold-blooded killers, the bitch would no longer be breathing.

"Can I please speak to Ray?" I asked through clenched teeth.

"May I ask who is phoning?"

My guess is that she doesn't speak English all that well, or perhaps, she just hasn't finished high school yet.

Oh, that was cold of me. Ray was a two-timing, cheating, piece of dog crap, but he was not a pedophile.

"Angie," I said and heard her gasp and quickly mutter something in Cuban, or Guatemalan for all I know. There was a moment of silence, followed by the sound of a door slamming.

Ray cleared his throat loudly before he spoke. "Hello, Angela."

My heart clenched and throbbed hard in my chest. I was still lying on the floor with my feet dangling above my face. "I sold the house," I said without a hint of emotion.

"Oh," he said.

The silence was unbearable as was the pain radiating through my thorax.

"I just thought you should know." Woman of few words that was me. At least when I spoke to Ray. When I spoke to normal people—people that I didn't want dead—I was usually a bit more outgoing. *How could I ever let myself love someone that much? So much that it was literally killing me now that he was gone. Was I a fool to think that marriage was forever, or did I just have rotten luck?* I didn't know. All I knew was that I still loved the sound of his voice.

"How are you, Angie?"

"I'm good." I bit down on my lip and wept quietly. There was a good moment or two of silence before he spoke again.

"I'm so sorry, Angie," he said in his sultry, deep voice that sounded so incredibly sexy – an amazing cross between Barry White and Luther Vandross. "I never meant for this to happen, Baby and I know you still don't understand – but something happened to me after the heart attack. I changed, Baby and I never, ever meant to hurt you…"

Hearing that just made me wail harder. His heart attack happened about three years ago and was the beginning of the end for us. Four days before his fifty-second birthday, he woke up, mowed the backyard, and dropped onto the lawn like a lifeless crash-test dummy. I'd never felt such fear in all my life.

"I have to go," I said, but I really didn't want to hang up. What I really wanted was for him to tell me that he still loved me – that he was wrong for leaving and marrying the slut and, yet, that didn't happen. Instead, I heard the baby crying in the background and that sent me over the edge, as if I wasn't already there. "I'll send you my forwarding address when I find a new place. Goodbye, Ray."

The details of my life for the next half hour were a bit sketchy. Blood was pounding in my skull. I couldn't seem to feel the tips of my fingers and although I've never experienced a massive stroke, I was sure that I was having one. I remember hearing the neighbor yell at his stepson – who just happened to be my favorite student – and when the old man started in about how lazy and retarded Dale was, I lost it and flung open my screen door with fire in my eyes.

"Hey!" I screamed like a deranged lunatic from my front porch.

Walter and Dale were standing in their driveway on the other side of an older model Mercedes sedan. The only thing that separated my lawn from his was a three-foot white picket fence and a couple of purple azalea bushes. I don't think I was all that angry with Walter, I just think I needed to let off some steam before my eyeballs popped out. "Dick-face. Why don't you take a long ass look at yourself, there, Tubbo?"

Just imagine a giant hairy white beer belly with a big mouth. That pretty much described Walter Dobbs.

Dale, on the other hand, was the epitome of a world-class scholar. He was quiet, reserved and usually spoke in class only when I specifically asked for his input. Most of the time, he wore brown-rimmed glasses, striped Izod shirts that were two sizes too small and faded jeans. Today he was lacking the shirt due to the heat. Sure, he looked like a classic bookworm and barely had any meat on his bones. I never saw him do yard work, or even wash his new Toyota, but he was as smart as they come and a very conscientious young man. I'd known him since the day they moved in just over five years ago, when he was just an acne-faced pre-teen. Every summer, I paid him a few bucks here and there to mow my lawn and when he did, he usually did a piss poor job. But he, under no circumstances, deserved to be called a worthless turd.

There was a time in my life when I would have shown restraint in a situation like this one, but I went with the rage inside me and hurried across the front lawn to get in Mr. Dickhead's face after he ignored my warning to lay off his kid.

He called me a dirty 'C' word before I even reached the fence and then I tossed my hands in the air and muttered a few obscenities myself. It's a good thing that Dale had recently graduated, because it would have been awkward as hell if he were to come to class knowing that I once called his step-dad an overgrown genital wart.

The insults continued to fly and soon the entire neighborhood was out on their lawns, casually trying to eavesdrop by pretending to get their mail, or by watering their rhododendrons.

"And how about getting a leash for that rat-shit piece of fur you call a dog." I grabbed my red garden shovel and began frantically waving it in the air. Lately, it had been my weapon of choice with which to extricate dog feces from my vegetable patch. "I swear to God if he shits in my garden one more time, I'm gonna start up a crap collection and smear it on your Mercedes." I glared hard at Walter, and waited for his reply, but instead, he backhanded Dale for not moving fast enough. I think I cleared the fence in less than two seconds. I was a champion hurdler back in high school, and was happy that I still had agility in my thirties. I still had my garden shovel in one hand and my other was clenched into a tight fist.

"You touch that boy one more time and I swear to God, I'll kill you myself!" I screamed, nearing glass-breaking caliber, and that's when I felt a hot hand on my shoulder. I spun around so fast I nearly got whiplash. "Jesus!" I shouted at Chad, whose mouth was still agape from hearing me threaten death.

I turned as Walter hurried past me, en route to either calling the police, or most likely pouring himself another twelve-year-old Scotch.

Lily was in my front yard, trying to catch her breath. I had forgotten that I had invited them for a celebratory drink. They lived just four blocks away so we usually walked en route to visiting one another.

"What the hell is wrong with you?" she shouted at me once we were safely inside my house. I dropped the red-handled shovel and collapsed onto the couch. "I think you have some serious anger issues."

"Ya think?" I groaned. My heart was beating so fast; I thought a Quiet Riot concert was playing in my chest. "I don't know what's wrong with me lately."

Lily sat down and tangled her fingers into my blonde hair. The style I'd recently chosen worked wonders for my round face and was just starting to grow out and extend past the tops of my shoulders. It was still slightly layered, but it was thin and very fine, so most of the time, it just hung down into my eyes. The color was mostly my own, but every so often I liked to throw in a bit of dark brown to accentuate the blonde. I have deep brown eyes like my mom, and a mirror image of her upturned nose that makes me look pretentious, although I'm not. Most of the time, I'm perfectly happy, sporting a warm smile and kind eyes. I even had faint laugh-lines to prove it. I also have a bit of a weight problem. The problem being that I just can't find a weight that I'm comfortable with. In high school, I was way too thin, so in college, I ate like a frat-boy and gained more than enough to fill out my large frame. Right before grad school, I lost a bit and thought I looked too thin again, and now, I have overcompensated in my thirties and was packing an extra twenty pounds that I put on when Ray left. I still looked good, wore a reasonable size fourteen, and visited the gym at least twice a week. My height of almost five-eight helped out in that department because I could carry more weight than someone like Lily for instance. Lily was a waif – a tiny redhead, with no boobs and well-defined cheekbones.

Speaking of boobs, I had great ones and up until Ray had his heart attack, they were the only breasts he ever looked at.

I know what my problem is. I'm angry. I'm so angry that I'm like a ball of pent-up rage. An inferno of hate and disappointment—a tornado of fury—a time bomb just waiting to be blown into orbit.

"You're not yourself these days, Ang." Lily played with my hair and that actually calmed me down some. I'm not a lesbian or anything, but it felt amazing to be caressed and loved. "I've never seen you act like this and I've known you since your terrible-twos. What's wrong with you?"

I sniffled before rolling my head to look into her blue eyes. "I heard the baby," I said. "I called Ray to tell him about the house and *she* answered the phone, Lily. I heard the baby cry…that was supposed to be me for Christ's sake!" I swiped viciously at my eyes, outraged that I was again so damn angry. It was a vicious cycle. *Damn it!* "That was supposed to be *my* baby."

Chad appeared distraught, as he usually did when I bawled, and continued scanning my latest issue of *Better Homes and Gardens*. Lily looked sympathetic to my pain, but she had no idea about the hell I was going through – the inner turmoil of having the one person I loved and trusted most up and decide that he needed more from life.

Before his heart attack, things were wonderful. We talked about having children and moving to Vancouver, buying a minivan and working on a plan so that he could retire. Ray was almost nineteen years my elder, so when death stared him down, he stared right back and decided he wanted someone younger than me – someone who made him feel young and virile and steadfast. Suddenly, he didn't want to think about retirement. He wanted to climb Mt. Kilimanjaro and eat raw oysters for breakfast. Doing things we normally did just wasn't enough for him anymore. Crossword puzzles in bed were boring, as were walks in the neighborhood at sunset and sipping apple martinis on lazy Sunday afternoons. I'm not saying we were a boring old married couple, we were happy…comfortable…in love. Or so I thought up until that day I caught him in an adulterous act. I should have known that someday it might happen. After all, he seduced me when I was a student. What made me think he wouldn't do it again someday?

"How about dinner?" Lily said enthusiastically, bringing me right back into the painful present. "A celebration for finally selling this place and moving on." She stood up and extended her dainty hand to me. "Come on, Ang. I have a feeling this is the best move you'll ever make."

***

Three weeks after what had been hailed as the *Walter Dobbs Should Die Incident*, I was still packing boxes when the movers arrived. I'd found the perfect house across the Glenn Jackson Bridge in Vancouver, Washington—far away from the neighborhood that Ray and I once thought about moving to. My motivation for leaving Portland was to leave my old life and its bad memories behind.

The summer sun beat down relentlessly as I filled box after box with the remnants of my shattered life.

I can happily say that I hadn't threatened any more neighbors with bodily harm; I diligently paid attention to whom I flipped off in my car and I actually had a blind date lined up for dinner. Again, it wasn't my idea, but Lily insisted that if I didn't get laid soon, my head might explode. Whatever. I was still on a mission of celibacy until death.

I had several errands to run before said date and not a lot of time to do them if I was going to make it to the restaurant on time. It took me three minutes to get my car started and once it started, it took me another six minutes to get to the U-Haul store to pick up more boxes. I loaded my backseat with as many boxes as would fit and then I turned on my blinker and was about to merge into traffic, when a carload of ditzy blonde teenagers barreled out in front of me and clipped my fragile bumper.

"Hey!" I screamed and honked, but they kept on driving, Blonde Barbie hair flapping in the breeze. The driver was on a cell phone and Nelly was belting out that obnoxious song about getting hot and naked. Needless to say, since I'd been a good girl lately, I felt the sudden urge to track the *ho's* down and beat them senseless with a cell phone.

Not really, but someone was going to pay for my bashed-in bumper.

I sped down Glisan Street, honked my horn wildly and when I finally caught up to them, I screamed out my window for them to pull over. That's when I noticed the blip of a siren and then, of course, there were lights flashing in my rear view mirror.

The convertible full of delinquents got away, I pulled over, ripped off my seatbelt, and did the unthinkable.

I wrenched open my door and walked swiftly toward the officer in blue.

"They hit me! Why the hell are you pulling me over? They hit me!" I shouted and planted my hands on my hips. Dirt, sweat, and grime trickled down my forehead. My hair was pulled up tightly in a scrunchie. I must have looked like a white-trash trailer hag.

The officer removed his mirrored sunglasses, stepped toward me in a menacing fashion, and glared. "Get back in the vehicle, Ma'am."

He looked about my age or even older, so it pissed me off that he called me *Ma'am.*

"Excuse me?" I said fiercely and began waving toward traffic. "Did you *not* hear me? They *hit* me!" I started walking around the front of my car to show him the gash. It wasn't as bad as I feared and that happened to be a bad thing, because I didn't have a leg to stand on.

"Ma'am," he said again. "Let's see your driver's license and registration."

"Umm," I mumbled, visualizing my wallet and checkbook on the kitchen countertop. "It's at home," I said sheepishly. I felt about two inches tall.

He looked down at me, planted his hand against his expandable baton, and asked me to kindly get back in my vehicle.

I did and then I was given the biggest ticket I've ever gotten. When I balked about the three-hundred-and-fifty-dollar fine, I was issued another ticket for a burnt-out brake light and then after I got out of my vehicle to try to explain myself further, I was handcuffed, tossed into the backseat of his car and taken four blocks up the road.

I guess I may have gone too far when I pressed my finger against the buttons of his nicely ironed uniform.

Needless to say, it was my first time riding in the back of a cop mobile and, because of my latent anger, I figured it wouldn't be the last. Someone was going to have to die and Officer Dick Weed seemed like a great place to start. I stared at the back of his head the entire time and envisioned doing some serious bodily harm.

Hi, my name is Angie Shirpa and I'm a rage-o-holic!

The drive seemed excruciatingly long, but really it was only a matter of blocks to the East Portland Police station. We pulled into a secure garage. The corrugated metal door closed behind us and all eyes were on *little ol' me* sitting in the back of the cop-car like a common criminal.

To my surprise we bypassed the booking station and when I was finally set free of my cuffs and told to sit down, I was greeted by a lovely man named Sergeant Leo. Sergeant Leo reminded me of the Cowardly Lion, curly red hair, and all.

Sergeant Leo and I had a nice long chat. Well, it seemed long to me, but in reality, it only took him three minutes to issue me an ultimatum for a new road rage program the city of Portland was implementing. The gist of it was, I would agree to take the road rage classes every Tuesday and Thursday for six weeks and my tickets would all go away, my arrest would be revoked and my insurance company would never be the wiser.

Well, geez, let me think about that!

***

I made it back home just as the movers finished loading the heavy stuff into the truck. I took a quick shower to ease my pain and get the undesirable police-station-aroma from my pores. I couldn't believe that I once wanted to be a police officer. I still did in fact, in some capacity, but not a street beat cop. I think I'd rather prefer behind the scenes, or maybe even IAD. *Yeah, the cop's cops.*

I pulled my hair into a bun. It was far too hot to wear it down and far too hot to be wearing much clothing, so, again, I put on the only sundress I owned and slipped into my Birkenstock sandals. My mascara tube was almost gone, so I did the best I could with what I had.

The restaurant Lily picked was a new one on the Vancouver side of the Colombia River. They served clams, oysters, shrimp, and the perky tone of the atmosphere bordered on nauseating. Waiters and waitresses were wearing Lobster aprons and singing "Happy, Happy Birthday" to a seventy-five-year-old man at the top of their lungs. You'd have to hold a gun to my head for me to do something that humiliating now, but I did do it often while making my way through college.

I'd arrived before my date and somehow that unnerved me slightly, because I couldn't check him out before getting sucked into hell.

Lily and Chad were already sharing a shrimp cocktail when I pulled up a chair to join them on the outside patio.

"Sorry I'm late," I said and grabbed a big prawn as I sat down, ducking my head under the big red and white umbrella.

"You're not late," Lily said. "We're just early. The house was too hot and the air conditioner is on the fritz."

"Well," I said after the prawn was en route to being digested, "thanks to a certain unyielding prick with the Portland Police Bureau, I was detained for quite some time this afternoon." Then I raised my hand to shade my eyes from the magnificent, still bright sun. I told them the entire story from beginning to end. They were both stupefied, but most likely relieved that I didn't manhandle the poor officer. "So, where's this super-stud you've been dying for me to meet?"

Lily and Chad both smiled and glanced above my head and I knew that I'd just stuck my foot in my mouth. My date must have been standing behind me. I saw that was the least of my problems when I turned slowly and cringed seeing his familiar scowl. My heartbeat quickened, sending a shiver across my balmy skin. "You've got to be kidding me," I growled to the man standing at my right. I couldn't help the evil glare.

He looked a bit different out of uniform. I had to admit that I did let my eyes wander south and although no man is perfect, Officer Dick Weed did have an unbelievable ripple to his chest. I gulped and quickly snapped out of my momentary lapse of self-indulgence. My eyes narrowed, I almost smiled, but the ride in the back of his cop car had put me in a less than friendly mood. "You're Scot?"

He finally relaxed his facial muscles and grinned down at me. Then he did a quick male bonding handshake with Chad. Chad was a firefighter and obviously knew his fair share of cops. Why on earth did I happen to get hauled into the police station by the one cop they were so hot to fix me up with? I can tell you why. Because my life sucks, that's why.

Not that it mattered much. Celibacy rocks!

"Scot, this is Angie…but why do I have the feeling that you've already met?" Lily said as the light bulb went off in her head. She actually giggled like a girl and sat back down in her chair, glancing at me for only a quick moment before giggling again and turning to hide her amusement.

Scot immediately caught onto Lily's chuckles and relaxed into his seat. The sun did wonders for his smile, except he looked devilish beyond a shadow of a doubt. It was a good thing that he wasn't a good-looking guy, because that smile of his could do some damage to a girl's quest for celibacy. His hair was almost black, except for the little bit of gray on his temples that shimmered slightly when he turned to engage in conversation with the waitress. I noticed right away that he was polite, but not obnoxiously flirtatious.

Ray was obnoxiously flirtatious at times, because he was damn good looking and he knew it. Perhaps I didn't have to be celibate after all. I could only date guys I'm not the least bit attracted to.

"Did she tell you that she touched me?" Scot turned after saying "thank you" to the waitress. I could sense a hint of a smile in his remark, and yet his lips were flat-lined against his tanned skin. He was probably a handsome man in his youth, but his nose was slightly crooked, like it had been broken a few times and he had a small scar just above his full lips. Not that I was looking or anything. He had kind eyes too and I liked that he didn't ogle the waitress's young ass as she walked away.

Lily and Chad both gasped in awe.

I shrugged. So, okay, I did leave out that very pertinent piece of information. So what? I touched him. I'm sure it wasn't the first time.

"No!" Lily finally chuckled. "She's not herself lately." She must have felt somewhat compelled to apologize for my bad behavior and thus broke the very important Best-Friend-Code-of-Conduct by going on and on about Ray and his mistress.

If I didn't love her so much, I would have thrown my fork at her forehead.

"I can't believe this," I groaned and looked away. I muttered a few choice obscenities and then turned to find Scot gazing right into my eyes. He had a smirk on his face and he actually looked sincere.

"I'm sorry," he said.

"For what?" I groaned and rolled my eyes. Like I didn't know.

I know she tries hard and loves me like a sister, but sometimes Lily can get carried away with telling complete strangers about my marital woes. She had single- handedly made me look pathetic.

"That must have been hard," he continued.

I narrowed my eyes at Lily and silently sent her a message that meant business. I should have known that she would bring up Ray and for all I knew, she had probably told Officer Dick Weed that I hadn't "done it" since Ray left and she's worried about my sanity. I should have, right then and there, stood up, and professed my plan to remain celibate until the day I die. I didn't do that. Instead, I gulped down my entire margarita and headed to the bar for another.

Scot met me in the lounge after I'd downed two more ounces of frosty tequila.

"I have one of those, too," he said as he twisted a pink straw with his big hands. The man was probably six feet tall. He was decidedly muscular and his jeans were a bit too snug for my taste, but he wasn't completely turning me off.

"One of what?" I asked, as if I didn't know. I was sure he was about to tell me his divorce sob story, so my eyes had already begun to glaze over.

"A best friend who is hell-bent on marrying me off," he said as he motioned toward Lily and Chad. "I only agreed to come because I figured you're probably in the same place I am and we might have a chance to vent about our best friends who just can't take 'no' for an answer."

I felt my lips tug upward. My God, I almost smiled.

"Really?"

He shrugged. "Well, that and Chad said you were hot!"

I blushed hard. I was not hot. I was okay in the *bod* department despite my size fourteen physique. I had curves and muscles covered with slight cellulite. Hell, I was thirty-three and cellulite or not, I still looked darn good. I had a nice face, great skin, but no one in their right mind would have described me as hot! Hot constitutes someone twenty-seven and younger. Chad must have been three sheets to the wind when he coerced Scot into meeting me.

He winked and left me at the bar, alone and baffled.

I turned to see our very pretty waitress admiring his backside as he sauntered away. "He's adorable."

"Excuse me?" I said with uneven brows.

"That guy. He's cute."

"Really?" I tilted my head to see if the angle made a difference. I just wasn't seeing it, but then again, I was still seething over the fact that he cuffed me and hauled me into the cop-shop. I don't think I'll ever be able to look at Officer Scot King again without remembering that incident. Even if I did somehow unexpectedly find him attractive – which isn't likely, because celibacy rocks! I just don't see how I could simply forgive and forget.

I played nice at dinner. I had crab legs, another gallon of margaritas, fried oysters and then I split a slice of cheesecake with my friend Lily. I'm not one of those women who only order salad when I'm on a date. I'm the opposite. I eat when I'm nervous, upset, bored, irritated, sad, mad...*oh hell, I just love to eat!*

After dinner was over, Scot smiled warmly, did another small hand ritual with Chad, and then turned to me as he grabbed his faded denim jacket.

"It was very nice meeting you, Angie," he said and then he said goodnight and left in his big, fancy blue truck. I think I may have drooled as he drove off, but then again, I was probably just drunk. His abrupt departure had my head spinning. Okay, so I wasn't all that nice to him and I'm sure he wasn't impressed with my bout of tears halfway through the entrée, but I figured from his warm smile that he was enjoying himself.

Lily and Chad drove me home and after finishing off the last of the peanut butter, I crawled into bed and turned on the late show to ponder why I was so intrigued by Scot's departure. The more and more I thought about it, the more and more I tightened my jaw. The evening wasn't a complete bust, but I couldn't have cared less that Scot had muscles, good teeth, and a fantastic pick-up truck. I'm in my thirties and that crap doesn't impress me anymore. Besides, I've sworn off men, sex, and relationships altogether. My life was on a different track now. I had wounds to heal, a house to move into and a career to salvage. The funny thing was, for the first time since Ray left, I wasn't all that scared anymore. I was beginning to feel somewhat back to normal.

Two

By the time I wanted to plant some flowers in my new yard, the sun was almost down and for the life of me, I couldn't remember seeing my garden shovel anywhere when I unpacked. I didn't remember packing it either, but that made no difference because Lily and Chad helped me pack, along with Rex and John from American Van Lines. *Oh well.*

I had some iced tea instead and stared out over the rose bushes, across the street and into my neighbor's front window. They had toddlers, three of them, and each time I saw one of those little boys run around in the yard, my uterus clenched in time with the rapid beating of my heart. I'd only been living on Vine Maple Drive for seven days, but I felt as if I'd been there forever. My move had prompted many changes in my life, but none as big as the make and model of my car. Yes, I finally did it. After putting a huge chunk of money down on my new ranch style home in Vancouver, I took the GTI to the auto graveyard and said hello to my very own SUV. A well equipped Ford Expedition with running boards, fog lights and even a third row seat just in case I suddenly needed to take a Boy Scout troop on a field trip. I was actually hoping for an SUV that came with a baby, but apparently, it doesn't work that way.

Lily thinks I'm insane for wanting to make a go of motherhood alone, but I think it'd be a wise choice considering my age and my decision to keep men out of my life. She thinks

I'm insane for that too. I finally told her that the setups had to stop because they were ruining my life and keeping me from wallowing alone in my misery. I know I have a long way to go, but being a mom would make the time pass much more quickly. Someday, perhaps when I'm sixty and ready to have a man wait on me hand and foot—then I'll consider dating. But I can't wait until I'm sixty to have a child. In fact, I can't wait until I'm thirty-five to have a child. It's either now or never, so come hell or high water…I'm taking the plunge.

I just haven't figured out the details yet, but give me time. Just give me time.

***

Tuesday night, I did what I was supposed to do and drove into Portland at seven-thirty to attend my first road rage awareness class. The classroom at Mt. Hood Community College looked a lot like my classroom at David Douglas, except it was filled with deviant drivers, all of whom looked as if they'd cut out my tongue if I said *hello* in the wrong tone of voice. Not taking any chances, I just nodded politely and took a seat behind a very muscular biker-dude with naked ladies tattooed on his massive bicep. He actually looked the friendliest out of everyone in the room.

"Hello," a tall gangly man said from the doorway. "Is everyone ready to confess their sins in front of the class?" He stepped into the room and closed the door tightly. "By the way, if you're late…you will not be invited back. I'm always on time, that means you will be too."

Grumbles erupted from the room and then we heard a knock on the door.

"Ignore it," he said and then opened his briefcase on the desk as the door rattled continuously. There was a moment of alarm when we heard a bout of extreme obscenities and then it just got eerily quiet. "I'm Officer Tony Little. Welcome to Road Rage 101."

I think he was trying to be amusing, but since he'd just confessed to being a law enforcement type person, he got snarled at by the majority of the group. I was one of only two women in a group of seventeen scoundrels. The only other woman in the group looked as if she was on her last gram of crack cocaine. Scary looking woman.

"You first," Tony said to a short man in the front row. "Why are you here?"

The man cleared his throat and stood up when Tony told him to. "I ran over my neighbor's garbage cans."

"And why did you do that?" Tony leaned against the desk and crossed his arms in front of his chest. He was in plain clothes; faded jeans, a dark red Polo, and a worn pair of Nikes.

The man shrugged. "I dunno."

Tony expelled an exaggerated gush of air from his lungs. "People, people, people." He finished his headshake. "You're not on trial here. We're trying to get you to be openly honest about why you'd do something destructive and put others at risk. This program won't work if you don't tell me why." He scanned the room and when he locked gazes with me, he grinned. "You."

"Me?" I groaned and stood up.

His smile was unnerving. "Are you Angie or Gail?"

"Angie," I said with great disdain. I was hoping for some kind of anonymity. I didn't want the class knowing my name. What if a serial killer was among us? What if...

"Angie, tell us why you are here."

I inhaled smoothly and wiped the sweat from my brow. "I chased down a convertible of blonde bimbos because they swiped my bumper and then failed to pull over and exchange insurance information with me."

Tony smiled. "See, that wasn't so bad, was it?" He beamed and looked down at what I am assuming was my traffic report. He spent a few minutes of silence and then he looked up at me again, just as I was sitting back down. "Was there a reason you went after the officer with malicious intent?"

I was so infuriated, I'm sure my face reddened to a deep crimson and, of course, the vein in my forehead must have protruded slightly.

"I did not... I was trying to...he was making me mad."

What can I say? I was so pissed that I couldn't form a whole sentence.

Tony laughed and handed out a sheet of paper for all of us to write on. He stopped in front of my desk and simply said, "You poked him in the chest with your finger…that's a big no-no."

"Arrggh."

We finished up our assignments of writing down our crimes and explaining what we could have done differently. Mine was a long list of the same sentence written over and over again like a kid writing a mantra on an elementary school chalkboard. It simply read, "I will never poke another policeman for as long as I live." Over and over again, I wrote that same sentence and when Tony came to retrieve it, he chuckled.

"What's so funny?" I snarled.

"Nothing," he said. "I'm just wondering if you're always this cute, or is it only when you're mad?"

I blushed slightly and slid down into my seat to escape his gaze. He smiled, winked, and then left me to deal with a scuffle between the crack whore and her pimp. When the tiff was settled, he came back and leaned back against the desk in front of mine. He stared at me for a few minutes, all the while sporting an unholy grin that made my toes curl.

"So, what do you for a living, Angie?"

"I teach Law and Political Science at David Douglas."

"Really," he said, his smile growing. He leaned forward as if entranced by my career choice. "I went to Douglas. Class of eighty-five. I always wanted to be a teacher."

"It's hard work, especially these days," I said as I squirmed in my seat. The rest of the class was behaving, which was a bad thing because Tony Little seemed to be getting quite comfortable right where he was.

"You married?" he asked.

"No," I answered back, while fidgeting with my ring finger. I'd finally taken the damn thing off when I sold my house. Now all that remained was a white ring around my finger, where the sun hadn't shone for the past nine years.

He just smiled again and then tapped his knuckles on my desk. "Good." He winked and left me alone.

At the end of our ninety minutes together, he said goodnight, tucked his briefcase under his arm, and grabbed his cup of coffee.

Not bad for my first night. But honestly…it was a big joke and I didn't plan on ever going back!

***

An entire week went by in which I did absolutely nothing of importance, except doctor the Ph of my soil and clean out the gutters. The house was a one-level ranch style, ten years old. The roof was brand new, but the inside needed some work. The exterior was the color of sand and had burgundy shutters on the windows, giving it a stylish look that fit in with all the new construction that was going up around me.

On that particular morning, I woke up with puffy eyes again. The funny thing is that I really don't remember crying before I fell asleep. I do remember watering my lawn, weeding the front garden and then digging through the one box of photos of me and Ray. The rest is just a big blur.

I scurried to the kitchen for a Diet Pepsi and a glance at the clock. The hardwood was cool under my bare feet, which I loved. It was invigorating. I usually loved summer vacation, but lately I hadn't really wanted to crawl out of bed. There really wasn't any reason to. I had no job to go to. My freezer was full of Lean Cuisines and I had enough Kashi and soymilk in the pantry to last me until December. What more could I need?

After finally showering and pulling on my black shorts, I breathed in my first breath of fresh air as I opened the back sliding door and stepped onto my patio. My house was in need of many repairs. Lights needed to be rewired, paneling needed to be replaced and I think the carpet in the bedrooms was ready to be ripped out. All I needed was a big strong man and life would be good…

I knew what was going to happen. As soon as the thought popped into my head, my eyes stung and I felt the familiar tingles of my tears. It was almost as if Ray were dead. I mourned him daily, but mostly I just tried to remember how he smelled.

***

Later that same afternoon, I somehow ended up walking a couple of miles up and down my neighborhood streets, wondering why I'd been dealt a crappy hand. I eat my veggies, take my fiber supplements, go to church on holidays and I even donate an hour or two every month to the soup kitchen in Portland. I'm fairly sure that heaven is awaiting my arrival, and yet I'm still so angry that I can't even crack a smile. I used to smile. I used to smile a lot, in fact, my old high school guidance counselor nicknamed me Guy Smiley back in the good-ol' days.

I sighed and decided at that point that I was going to stop feeling sorry for myself. I'd had enough. Ray is gone and that's that.

I can tell you right now, that didn't last long because as soon as I rounded the corner and saw my neighbors lifting their kids into the minivan, I saw red. Red that immediately turned into a gnarly shade of green.

Jealous does not even begin to describe how I felt at seeing that happy family. From the way I was going, I was going to endure each of the seven deadly sins by nightfall...then where would I be? Still single, still angry, and still horribly sad that Ray married a Puerto Rican ho!

***

When I finally made it safely back into the house, I made tomato soup for dinner, a grilled cheese sandwich followed, and then for dessert I had another grilled cheese sandwich. Yep, gluttony had set in and I felt bloated, so I thought I'd take another walk before another deadly sin kicked into high gear. The crickets and frogs were fairly silent for some odd reason and the clouds above looked ominous, almost like the world sensed something was amiss. I, unfortunately, wasn't that in tune with Mother Nature's warning because after a mile around the neighborhood, I turned the corner and was mortified to see two police cars out in front of my house. As I approached, I noticed two men in plainclothes at my door and even from a safe distance they didn't look all that friendly. For just a split second, I wanted to run. But then, again I'd done nothing wrong. Of course, then my mind began reeling about the fact that I'd skipped an entire week of road rage classes and I knew they were coming for me. *Ahhhh.*

I slowed my steps, reined in my fear, and then laughed in my head about what a wild imagination I had.

As I stepped foot into my yard, the men converged on me. It wasn't fun.

"Can I help you?" I swallowed hard and looked directly at the only officer who was shorter than I was. It was the only way I could keep from falling to the ground and begging for mercy. He looked nicer than the tall guy with a black goatee and sinister dark eyes.

"Angie Shirpa?" The taller scary guy asked.

I nodded, and for some unexplained reason I started babbling about how I wasn't really Angie Shirpa anymore, that I had changed my name back to my maiden name. "It's Harrington actually." I fumbled with the zipper on my sweatshirt and kicked the tall blades of green grass. "My husband left me for one of his students. They had a baby and moved to Bend and so I didn't want the reminder for the rest of my life." I continued rambling. "Anyway, I'm so sorry about the class thing, I was...well, I.... okay..." I groaned in defeat. "It was lame, okay. I don't see how confessing our motives to a class full of strangers was going to help the police figure out why road rage happens." I shrugged at the officers who were then staring at me in wonderment. "I think road rage happens because people are morons and a fair amount of the population doesn't know how to drive properly. I mean, I bet each one of you has wanted to literally drive someone off the edge of a cliff at one point...or maybe blow some idiot's tires out with those big guns you carry." I actually chuckled and wiped the sweat from my brow at that point. "I just don't see how that class was going to help me, but I'll gladly pay the fines...I mean, I'd never try to skip out on my obligations."

Yeah right!

The shorter blonde officer held up his hand to halt my ranting and shook his head with a scowl.

"Whatever," he barked and then the taller guy relaxed his stance and smirked at me. Apparently, he thought I was amusing.

"Miss Harrington, we're here to take you in for questioning in the death of Walter Dobbs."

"Walter Dobbs?" I said with a slightly confused expression, and then I felt the blood pool in my feet. There was not one viable drop north of my ankles and I felt my knees buckle. "What? Walter is...*dead*?" I gulped loudly and inhaled. "I...wha...I mean..." Again, I couldn't form an entire sentence.

"Would you please come with us?" The shorter man asked, but it wasn't really a question. His hand was hot on my upper arm and he was dragging me toward an awaiting police cruiser. Hello! I was about to take my second ride in the back of a cop-mobile, but this time, I wasn't cuffed. I was simply asked to step inside the vehicle and go with them to answer some questions.

"Wha...?" I grunted and then the door slammed in my face.

I'd just like to say that being in the back of that police car wasn't the only time in my life that I felt truly scared. I felt truly afraid when I rode my first upside-down roller coaster at Magic Mountain. I felt truly terrified when I learned my father had been shot by a drug lord. I felt scared the first time I had sex in college. I also felt truly scared when Ray had a heart attack in front of my eyes and now I felt truly scared that, maybe, somehow, in my bouts of rage I had done something stupid.

That thought kept me alert as we headed over the Interstate Bridge and into Portland, even though it was after ten and ten is usually when I close my eyes for the night. I was wide awake and imagining all sorts of wild scenarios. I thought about the fact that I hadn't seen Walter at all since the day after I threatened to kill him in front of the entire neighborhood, but mostly I thought about the fact that these police officers were treating me like a common criminal. I'd done nothing wrong. Sure, I threatened death at one point, but there's no law against that. Is there?

"Hey," I yelled at the handsome driver. I don't know what it is about cops, but *goddamn* they look good in uniform. "Do you know anything about this? What happened to Walter?"

He didn't respond, so I asked a couple more times before he turned his head slightly and told me, in so many words, to shut the hell up.

Okay. He didn't have to be so damn rude.

The police station that I was taken to was on the outskirts of Portland in the Parkrose neighborhood, very close to where I used to live. Three detectives, I'm presuming, met me when the car stopped.

"I'm Detective Jessup, and this is Detective Smalls. That's Litchfield."

"Hi," I said cordially. Detective Jessup was the tall scary looking guy. Litchfield was the short blonde one and Detective Smalls was a really ugly redhead with a really bushy handlebar mustache. "Can you please tell me what is going on?"

"We'd just like to ask you some questions about Walter Dobbs and the last time you saw him."

The door was held open by Detective Jessup, who seemed to be the only one at ease. Somehow, the scariest looking cop, had turned into my ally. Or so I hoped!

"Sure," I scurried down the hall and was shuffled into a small room that looked nothing like an interrogation room from television. It was small and perfunctory, about the size of my walk-in closet, but the lights weren't scalding my forehead and my chair was actually quite comfortable once I sat down.

Three pairs of beady eyes were staring me down and all I could do to keep from passing out was to remind myself to breathe. I was actually happy that I hadn't been busted for skipping road rage class. Perhaps I'd get away with it after all.

I fully understood that I was in deep doo-doo when they asked me if I wanted to call an attorney, but since I knew that I hadn't done anything wrong, I was fairly adamant about just getting down to business.

"You're sure?" Smalls asked between sips of coffee. I know this is a horrible cliché, but he *was* a double-fisted donut guy. He had one smashed against his white Styrofoam cup and another held tightly in his left hand. They looked stale. Obviously, they weren't Krispy Kremes.

"I'm positive," I said with my head held high. My hair was still pulled tightly into my scrunchie, my sweats were smeared with grass stains and mud, and the only makeup I had on was the smeared mascara under my eyes from my crying bout earlier that evening. I must have looked hideous.

Detective Litchfield started. "When was the last time you saw Walter Dobbs?"

I swallowed with difficulty and grinned. I hoped my grin wouldn't be misconstrued as a psychotic episode. I was just trying to show my sincerity at what I was about to confess. There was no use trying to beat around the bush. They had me there for a reason, so I wasn't about to lie about the fact that I had stood in the man's driveway and threatened to kill him in front of at least fifteen neighbors.

"The last time I saw Walter was when I threatened to kill him if he touched his kid again." I looked directly at Detective Jessup. "I saw the back of his head as he walked into his garage and that's truly the last time I remember seeing him."

There were a few snickers, most likely from the two detectives that thought I was innocent. Detective Litchfield didn't look amused.

"Want to tell us about that?" He eased back and rested his very ample butt against the countertop behind him. His arms were crossed tightly in front of his chest and he reeked of Old Spice and cigarette smoke.

"Nothing to tell, really," I said with confidence. "He was screaming at Dale and I'd just had a rather intense chat with my ex, so my blood was boiling and when I heard him tell Dale he was worthless and retarded, I lost it. I screamed at him and called him an overgrown genital wart and when he turned around and smacked his kid, I threatened him. It was nothing," I said with a sigh. "That's all I know."

Detective Litchfield glared hard at the chuckling officers behind him and then left me alone.

***

Two hours later, I was finally released. I wasn't being charged as of yet, but I was being told time and time again to stay in town and to call my lawyer.

Little secret among ordinary people—we don't have lawyers! We hire them when we get served with divorce papers, or when we want to sue our fellow Americans over stupid crap. The last lawyer I hired wasn't even a real lawyer— he was my cousin Chris, who was just a law student. I couldn't afford a real lawyer, and why would I need one? I had done nothing, and I repeat, *nothing* wrong.

"Hey."

I turned around when I heard a deep voice behind me. Officer Scot King was standing just feet from me, dressed in full uniform. A tightly wound newspaper was held in his hands. He looked almost as tired as I felt.

"Hey," I said with a sigh. If I weren't so happy to see a familiar face, I would have wept. "What are you doing here?"

Stupid question.

He chuckled lightly and rocked back on his heels, before cocking a brow at me.

"You want a lift home?"

"No," I said sternly. "I'm not getting into the back of another cop car for the rest of my life, thank you very much." My jaw clenched slightly, then I felt my cheeks flush because it was the second time Scot had seen me mimicking a disheveled trailer hag.

"I just finished my shift. I can take you home in my truck. Really, it's not that big a deal," he said before smiling again. "Unless you'd like me to call someone for you? Your parents, Lily -- or perhaps your lawyer?"

The mocking tone of his voice made my cheeks dimple slightly, but still, he was not going to get a smile out of me. Not now, not ever! Instead, I rolled my eyes and shifted uncomfortably in my sneakers.

"Fine," I grumbled.

He smiled, walked down the hall, and disappeared behind a door that I presumed was a locker room; because I'd seen numerous men exit that same door with street clothes on. I waited, and waited and drank almost an entire cup of coffee before Scot emerged from the door. His uniform had been traded in for a pair of khaki shorts, a white tee shirt advertising a local auto body repair shop and black and white Nikes. When he walked toward me, I noticed the wet hair. The guy actually had the nerve to keep me waiting in hell while he took a damn shower. I forgave him once I sniffed the air and the most amazing scent wafted toward me. I inhaled again because it smelled so good; like soap, mixed with a man's scent. Much like Ray's, but sweeter, not as musky.

"You ready?"

"Yeah." My eyes stung from the sensation of my eyeballs popping out of their sockets. Scot cleaned up nicely and thanks to those damn pheromone things, I was actually having a sinful thought. I hadn't had sinful thoughts in years, not about a man anyway. Sure, I had sinful thoughts about marbled caramel cheesecake and huckleberry ice cream, but not for men. Men were the enemy. Celibacy Rocks!

I quickly caught up to him and when we made it outside the building, he pulled a set of keys from his shorts and beeped the locks open on his truck.

He opened my door for me, which did nothing to squash the nice damn feelings I was having.

"Thanks," I said as I climbed in. I know I'm tall and all, but I literally had to *climb* in. Ford knows how to make trucks and his truck reeked of testosterone. When he climbed in beside me and turned the key, *Loverboy* resounded from the speakers and I think my nipples contracted to the bass that was booming in my ears. He immediately reached over and turned it off. That's when he finally inhaled sharply and actually looked at me. His eyes were dark, somewhat narrowed and filled with what seemed to be genuine compassion.

"You okay?"

He hadn't made a move to put the truck in gear and I was in no mood to have this discussion with a perfect stranger, let alone a cop.

"Fine," I lied and stared out the window.

From the corner of my eye, I saw him shake his head and bite his lower lip. He didn't say anything; he just quickly exited the parking lot and turned right toward the bridge that led to Vancouver.

The only sound that was made was by my voice directing him through the streets of my neighborhood until he pulled into my driveway and put the truck in park.

"Are you sure you don't want to talk? It might help."

"Thanks, but I've said all I have to say to the cops tonight." I made a move for the door and his right hand caught my left wrist before the door opened fully. I turned to see him, gazing at me with his big, soft brown eyes. I felt completely vulnerable and scared out of my mind.

"I heard you skipped out on class last week."

I glared hard and wrenched my wrist from his grasp. That seemed to be the least of my problems at that point.

"It was a stupid waste of time."

"You're in big trouble, Angie. I'm just trying to help."

"Why?" I groaned. "You don't know me, you certainly don't want to date me, so why would you care?"

"Fine," he said while placing both hands on the steering wheel. "See you around."

"Thanks for the ride," I said as I got out. I didn't look back as he drove off, but from the loud sound of the engine revving, I knew I'd been a bit short with him.

***

The next morning, I had breakfast plans with my dad at their vineyard in Dundee, Oregon. The drive was almost two hours long, the air was hot and sticky, but when I finally pulled my SUV into my father's garage, I felt as if I'd come home. *This is exactly what I need.* A weekend with my parents, a lot of wine, and some good old-fashioned love.

"Dad," I said with a tearful gulp. "I think I'm in big trouble."

My father smiled at me with the most amazing, loving smile and then he pulled me into his arms and completely ruined my new yellow blouse by smashing me against his grape stained apron.

He looked down at my speckled chest and roared with laughter.

It takes a special man to make wine: A jolly man with an exceptional talent of seeking out perfection: A man with a zest for life and an exuberant energy for long daunting days in the hot sun. That was my dad. His hair was mostly gray now, but in his youth, it was thick, wavy and the color of dark chocolate. He was still slender, but had added muscles in the past few years since he'd bought the vineyard and started laboring more with his body than just his mind. In his past life, he was an agent-turned-consultant for various law enforcement agencies up and down the west coast, thus my interest in Criminal Justice at an early age. I wanted to be just like my dad.

"What's up, Ang," he said as he slung an arm around my shoulder. "You don't look so good, Pumpkin." Tugging me toward the private stock, he pulled open a bottle of his select Merlot and poured me a glass. In my father's eyes, wine was a cure-all.

"Dad," I groaned. "It's ten a.m."

"So, think of it as grape juice." He nudged my arm until I tilted the glass to my lips. "There, now what's up, Pumpkin? Tell your old man all about it."

Where do I start? I mean, really. My father knew nothing about my anger toward Ray. If he did, Ray would be dead—

dangling from a tree by his testicles somewhere in the back forty acres, naked and decaying. That's how much my father loved me! My decision to keep my father in the dark about the details of my divorce sometimes made it difficult for me to explain my foul mood.

"Remember my neighbor, Walter Dobbs?"

"No," he answered, sipping from my wine glass. "Can't say that I do."

"Well, he's dead and the police think I did it."

My father scoffed, blew out an exasperated breath, and then turned ghostly white when he noticed that I wasn't just playing.

"What? How... I mean...what's this...Shit!" He raked a hand through his hair and now you see where I get it. Undecipherable gibberish runs in my family.

I placed my hand on his and gave it a little squeeze. "Dad, please don't lose it on me. Not now. I need help."

He downed the rest of my glass of Merlot in seconds flat and then poured himself another. "Tell me everything," he said and I did.

***

By the time, we finished our second bottle of wine, I was slurring the last part about being told not to leave town and to call my lawyer.

My father was half stunned, half drunk.

"I'll call Reese and we'll just see about this crock of bullshit!" He furrowed his dark brows and stood up. He wobbled a bit and sat back down. "Who's this little prick who took you in for stating your piece, anyway? I'd like to have a word or two with him."

I had to tell my dad all about the bimbos hitting my bumper and Officer King taking me into the station because I knew my father would find out anyway. He'd use his agency connections and have my every move choreographed down to the time I took a poop every day, just to show that I didn't have *time* to kill Walter. That's how the man works. He's thorough and incredibly attentive when it comes to his Pumpkin—that would be me.

"He's no one of importance," I said with a slight flush. I could still smell Scot. *Odd!* Usually when I thought of manly smells, I immediately thought about Ray. Hooray for me. *I'm making progress.* "I think my little traffic school violation is the least of my problems. What do you think, Dad? Do I need a lawyer, or are they just being thorough?"

"I think I need to make some calls, Pumpkin," he said as he kissed the top of my head. "Come on into the house and I'll make some coffee."

Coffee turned into toast, which turned into full vegetable omelets and fresh sliced peaches. My father made his calls, downed a pot of coffee, and then made more calls. Of course, I just paced the kitchen floor and waited for him to return from his den. The hardwood floor in the kitchen soon showed signs of my frantic pacing as it began to scuff beneath my tennis shoes.

The minute the door creaked open; I dropped my fingers from my lips and pretended that I hadn't been caught biting my nails.

"Well?" I said loudly. "What did you find out?"

"You better sit down, Pumpkin."

I sat down on the center barstool and waited with bated breath as my father poured himself another cup of coffee. He no longer looked relaxed; every muscle in his neck and jaw seemed to be standing at attention. It was if he'd regressed back ten years and was wearing that same scowl that was always present when he worked for the Feds.

I knew something dreadful had happened, I could feel it in my tired, angry bones.

"They have the murder weapon, Angie."

"So," I said, waving my hand at him to hurry his explanation along. "And?"

"A red-handled garden shovel," he said.

Emotionally, I felt drained. Physically I felt nauseous, but oddly at the same time, I felt the urge to burst into laughter.

"My garden shovel?" I said through the hysterical laughter. "Someone killed him with *my* garden shovel. Is this some sort of sick joke?" My laughter quickly gave way to blatant anger. "Holy crap!" I screamed. "Someone is out to get me." Then came paranoia. "That's got to be it. Why else would they use *my* shovel? I'm being framed…oh my God! This isn't happening! This is something out of a frickin' movie, Dad. What the hell?"

I broke down into long drawn out sobs and had to lean forward to keep from passing out. My father embraced me, rocking me until I could inhale smoothly and was no longer trembling.

"It's going to be fine. They don't have a motive…except for your death threat," he chuckled nervously, "and they really can't take that seriously. It's going to be fine. Reese will be here in an hour and everything will be just fine, Pumpkin."

Great! *Everything was going to be fine*? Then why the hell did my father call his old buddy from Nam? Besides major holidays, he usually only called Reese "Bulldog" Mathers in the direst of circumstances. The more I thought of poor Walter Dobbs being murdered with *my* garden shovel—the more dire my predicament seemed.

***

After a long hot shower and a couple of Advil, I was ready to face not only Bulldog, but also my mother. She came home, bouncing into the kitchen just as I downed the third painkiller. "Darling," she said and gave me a quick peck on the cheek. "You should have come by the church. It might do you some good to cleanse your soul once in a while. It's good for the complexion."

My mom! What can I say about Katherine Harrington? For one, she lacks height. She may be five-foot-four, but that might be pushing it. I definitely got my height from my strapping dad, because Mom is a waif, like Lily. She has blonde hair like mine, and I already mentioned the upturned nose that makes us look pretentious, but in Mom's case, it's somewhat true. She dislikes dirt, worms, weeds, and pretty much everything to do with the vineyard. Her passion is Jesus Christ and always has been. My mother's cure-all for everything is God—my father's is wine—that's probably why they are still married. She prays for his pickled liver and he drinks wine to shut out the word of God. I had to agree with my father's way of life more than hers. I think if God were a woman, she'd be my mom.

"Hi, Mom." I kissed her cheek and watched her sashay across the kitchen to kiss my dad. Dad grabbed her butt as she pulled away and blushed. The woman truly is a thing of beauty and I don't hold her faith against her. Just like she doesn't hold my lack of faith against me. My senior year of high school we had it out and from that point on, she wasn't supposed to criticize me for not going to church weekly. She still does it, of course, but she's technically not supposed to. I let it slide now that I'm older and more tolerant of her spiritual mumbo jumbo. I knew the news of my dilemma would send her running for the altar, so I just smiled and glared at Dad, silently warning him not to say a word.

"What brings you by?" she asked

"Just haven't seen you in awhile, I guess." I crossed my fingers and then jumped out of my skin when the doorbell rang. I knew it was Reese. Even the way he rang the doorbell reeked of International Espionage. Bulldog Mathers was my father's superior in Vietnam. They were both officers then, both highly decorated, but Reese didn't have a wife at home, so he outranked Dad because he was willing to do some rather risky operations. Dad did them too, but he wasn't on a suicide mission like Reese. Reese was a Bulldog and looked the part. Now that he was fifty-something, he just looked meaner. He still had the rolls of scruff on the back of his neck and, my God, his biceps had grown since the last time I saw him.

"Bull!" my father shouted and growled before marching across the room to engage in a male bonding handshake like no other. "It's been a while."

"Baby girl," Reese said as he narrowed his deep brown eyes on mine. "Didn't your pop teach you anything about covert ops? If you wanted the old fucker dead, there's better ways than slicing him open with a garden shovel." He roared with laughter and pulled me into the air by my armpits. He outweighed me by at least eighty pounds and was even taller than my father. His embrace was almost painful.

"Very funny," I groaned when he put me back on my feet. I rubbed my sore ribs and sank down on the couch. "And watch what you say in front of the urch-chay ady-lay" My Pig Latin was fairly rusty, but both men grinned and then got right to business. Reese was a lawyer, among other things. I hated to speculate what those other things were, but I was positive that he still worked for the government, if you know what I mean. I once caught him and my dad talking about an op that went down in Colombia when I was still in high school. After hearing that bit of information about my Uncle Reese, I took it upon myself to research everything I knew about Colombia, drugs and something called cartels. I became obsessed with the military, my father's past, and Uncle Bulldog's secret life.

"So, did you do it?" Reese asked me with a straight face. He was amazingly unwrinkled for his age and his jet black hair was barely graying.

"No!" I groaned. "I did *threaten* to do it and I guess I was holding the said garden shovel at the time, but I didn't do it. I had no reason to do it."

"So, why the hell didn't you call me when they first picked you up and why did you answer their questions?"

I moaned, groaned, and dramatically plopped face first into the leather couch cushions. "I didn't do it!" I bellowed.

When I finished my tizzy fit, my father and Bulldog were shooting the breeze, talking about Pinot Noir and the new Harrington Select label that was coming out in the fall. "Hello," I said.

"Hello," they both mocked back. "So, who's this prick who gave you a ride home? Can you trust him?" Bull asked, his tone more serious.

"He's no one!" I shouted and stood up. "Look, Bull. I think it would be best if we concentrate on a little thing called a defense."

Both of my elders cocked their eyebrows simultaneously, then dismissed me again and engaged in conversation as if I weren't even in the room.

"When did she get so angry?" Bull said with a slight headshake. "She was such a sweet little girl – happy! That's what's missing. She used to be happy and smiled all the time. What happened that made her so damn angry?" Bull continued and my father just shrugged. They both continued staring at me as my jaw dropped a couple of inches. "What a smile she used to have, huh, Mitch? That girl of yours used to light up the room with one of her beautiful smiles. She looks old too. Frowning tends to do that to you, don't you think?"

I growled and clenched my teeth together to stop the giggles. I bit my tongue, wrapped my arms around my chest to halt the onslaught, but the giggles came anyway. Followed closely by tears, of course. My father chuckled, gave me a swift kiss on the temple, and then retreated to get the plate of double fudge brownies from the kitchen.

Bull pulled me into his arms and gave me a squeeze. "Are you ever gonna get over that cocksucker?"

I whimpered and wiped the tears from my eyes. Bull and I shared a huge secret. He was the only one I had told about Ray and the Honduran ho. He was the only one who I trusted not to tell my secret—that and I was silently hoping he would *take care* of Ray. Just kidding. I wouldn't wish death on anyone! Geez.

We talked for a couple of minutes about my rage, anger, and newfound idea to keep men at arm's length. He shook his big burly head at me and ran his hand over his Marine boot camp hairdo.

For the first time in my life, I realized just how much he looked like Ray. Well, Ray and Denzel Washington. *Wow*, I shook my head and finished listening to his speech.

"That's no way to live, Sweetheart. The best revenge for you would be to find another man, a better man than Ray, and live your life as best you can. Find true happiness and someone who makes you smile again."

He was right, and it was amusing to hear a man like Bulldog talk about true love and happiness. It was almost surreal to hear him go on and on about finding that perfect someone out there for me, the future father of my babies. He was secretly hoping that I would marry his son, Eddie, but Eddie was even scarier than Bull. Eddie lived for war and was currently somewhere in Afghanistan hunting terrorists in underground caverns. That wasn't someone I wanted to settle down with, even though Eddie is sexy as hell. Eddie was my first kiss. I was thirteen years old when it happened and, boy, he could kiss. Not like Ray could, though.

Damn.

"How's Eddie?" I asked Bull to change the subject and get my mind off you know who.

"Higher than life, baby girl. I'll tell him you said hello." He winked and then his attention was on the plate of brownies.

***

We took a long walk around Harrington Vineyard. I love fresh grapes. White, green, purple, Concord, it mattered not. Just being away from the hell of my life was putting a smile on my face. Well, that and all the wine I was drinking. Our walks along the unbeaten path usually included drinking straight from the bottle, which we were doing. The three of us; me, Dad and Uncle Bull. Shooting the shit, talking about how I was going to handle my legal woes and how Bull was going to make it all go away. I liked the sound of that, but I knew I wasn't out of the woods just yet. I wanted to be involved. I wanted to help Bull find out who killed Walter, to clear my own name.

"I don't think so," Bull laughed and sloshed the red wine into his mouth. He normally was not a drinker of fine wine. In fact, before my dad bought the vineyard, I never saw him drink anything except coffee and water. His body was a temple and he still looked good, despite his age.

I took my gaze off his fine bare chest and wiped the excess wine from my lips.

"Why the hell not?"

"'cause you're a girl, that's why."

Okay, so Bull wasn't perfect and he had three failed marriages to prove it. He was old-fashioned, that's all.

"Bulldog Mathers!" I shouted and stopped walking. "You're a chauvinistic, pigheaded, macho motherfu…"

My father kindly planted a swift smack on my hiney before I could finish my sentence.

"He's right, Ang," my father said in agreement with Bull. "You're a high school teacher, not a cop and you have no business poking your head around a murder investigation. Let Bull do his thing and you just concentrate on going to your road rage classes and playing nice with the Portland Police."

Playing nice with the police? Is that possible? I was angry with so many of them. How could I possibly play nice?

Both men were chuckling obnoxiously and that's when I yelled at the top of my lungs and headed back down the hill. I found my mother on the back deck saying a rosary when I got back.

"Sit down. You can help me," she said, patting the vinyl chair beside her, all the while, mumbling a Hail Mary under her breath.

I rolled my eyes, but since I hadn't said a Hail Mary in years, I decided to help. It couldn't hurt.

The one thing that always bothered me about my mother was that she never cried in front of me. Not when her mother died a couple of years ago and not when I came home in tears after I found Ray with the ho. I expect that someday she'll break down and confide in me that she has no tear ducts, but until then I still have hope that she'll stop hiding behind the rosary and get real with me.

"How's Father Ashley?" I asked when we were all through. My mom has been Father Ashley's personal assistant for almost four years.

"He's doing well. How are Lily and Chad?"

See, my mother did it again. I try to talk about something personal with her and she turns it around.

"They're great. Still decorating their house. Lily's still teaching at Parkrose High and she said they're ready to start a family." I answered, and then thought I'd try once again. "Is he doing okay since the stroke?"

"He's good," she said with pursed lips. I know she's in horrible emotional pain because of the father's brush with near death. "I think you should start thinking about moving on. Ray's been gone almost a year. How long are you going to keep waiting around for Mr. Perfect to fall into your lap? You're not getting any younger, Angela. Men will stop looking at you once you turn forty."

"Thanks, ma," I groaned and leaned back in my chair. Covering my eyes with my hand, I gazed into the backyard just as the men made their way through the thicket. Dad had such a joie de vivre about him and my mother was such a stick in the mud. It made me wonder how they really made it work all these years. They are so different, yet when they are together, the air is alive with electricity. "Are you still happy with Dad? Do you ever get bored in bed or think you made a mistake by marrying him."

My mother clumsily dropped her rosary onto the patio and glared at me with blushing cheeks.

"I was just asking," I said in apology. "Touchy, touchy!"

She stood up and flattened the wrinkles from her sundress. "You need to go to church, young lady."

Don't I know it? I just asked my mother how her sex life was. What the hell is wrong with me?

Three

Another argument ensued after dinner, around the bonfire out back. This time it was my father who started in on me.

"You can't wait around for love. You have to make it happen. You have to get out there and search high and low until you find the perfect person for you."

He exhaled his cigar smoke and prodded Bull to get in on the action. "Isn't that right, Bull? Angie can't wait around any longer. Time's wasting. I'm not getting any younger and I want grandkids…lots of them."

I love my dad!

"I've actually been thinking about that a lot lately, Dad." I inhaled the Cuban rather smoothly and then quickly exhaled before I turned green. "I'm thinking about just doing it."

Both men choked on their smoke and wheezed hard a couple of times. The looks on their faces were priceless.

"Doing what?" they both asked simultaneously.

"Getting pregnant."

Bull laughed, and my father, God bless his soul, clamped his hands over his ears and began humming loudly to drown me out.

He continued on that way until we were all in tears from laughing so hard.

Okay, so maybe it wasn't a good idea to tell my dad that I wanted to fornicate with a perfect stranger just to steal his seed.

***

The next morning, I got up, said goodbye to my parents and went home. The drive was nice at seven a.m. and when I finally pulled into my driveway, I felt like someone had a stranglehold on my throat. I wasn't okay with Bull's plan to fix my little situation. Sure, I wanted his legal help and his counseling, but I wanted to do something wild and crazy. I needed to do something out of the norm. This was my one and only chance to play detective and I was going to take that chance...now. All I needed was some help.

I turned off my ignition, entered my house, and immediately called Lily. I relayed my ingenious plan for her and Chad, and they both happily agreed.

Thank goodness for best friends.

***

Later that day, I did some serious reconnaissance of my own. When I had called Lily to implement the plan, she had informed me that Walter Dobbs was being buried today. His funeral was held at the Lincoln Gardens Memorial Cemetery on the north side of Portland. I wasn't sure if Madeline and Dale would be upset by my presence, so I opted to wear a baseball cap, sunglasses, and a long black overcoat that I found in the back of my closet. I think I bought it for my grandmother's funeral ten years ago, so it seemed fitting for another funeral.

The sun was hot, I was sweating like a pig, and I stayed on the outskirts of the processional as they marched up the hill and gathered around the huge grave. I recognized a few neighbors, Dale and Madeline, and of course the detectives, Smalls and Jessup, who were acting just like I was and sitting back to watch. When the preacher finished his prayer, he handed Madeline what looked like a small crucifix and then everyone tossed red roses on the casket. I almost wept just because I felt their loss, but I was really weeping because I'm a big sap and funerals make me cry.

When the crowd began to disperse, I took note of every person and what they looked like, just in case I needed it someday, I guess. Then I snuck back down the hill and crawled under the bushes to get to my car, which was parked another two miles down the street. I wasn't taking any chances.

***

The following evening, I got behind the wheel of my SUV and followed my conscience all the way to Mt. Hood College, where the road rage class awaited me. I was the first to arrive and not at all surprised that our group of seventeen had dwindled down to eleven. The biker dude with the naked lady tattoos was still present, as was the spindly guy with thick glasses. The crack whore was gone, but her pimp was still sitting pretty at the head of the class.

I remained in the back row, tapping my pencil on the desk until Officer Tony Little entered the room and narrowed his eyes on me.

He marched straight back without as much as a hello and sat down on the desk in front of me, his eyes never leaving mine.

"So, you decided to come back," he said with a smirk. "I didn't ask you back, now did I?"

I hadn't thought of this scenario. He once said if we were late, not to bother coming back...well, I was over a week late. *Oops!*

"I can explain..." I started to say, but he smiled and stood up.

"We can talk about this later."

He walked back to the front of the classroom and sipped from his thermos lid.

Soon everyone's eyes glazed over as he went into detail about the law and the right way to handle anger. Taking deep breaths, counting to ten, clenching our fists a number of times. I've tried all of that, and I'm sorry to say that nothing short of punching Ray in the cajones was going to make me feel better and even then, I didn't know if I could just put aside my anger and disappointment. Honestly, I think I may just stay angry and bitchy for the rest of my days and die a lonely old spinster who lives with twenty-three cats.

"Am I making any sense?" Tony said when he was suddenly two feet in front of me. I'd been daydreaming about cats and how I'd be able to provide for them on my fixed income when I'm eighty. "You have a great deal of making up to do." Tony winked at me and went back up front. This time, he engaged the entire class with his question.

"What's the one thing we are trying to accomplish with this class?"

"To bore us all to death." Someone in the front quipped.

"To stop road rage," I said under my breath, while doodling on my legal pad.

"What was that?"

"To stop road rage, duh."

Tony laughed, as did the entire class. I felt as if I'd regressed back to junior high and was once again the class clown. "Take five," he said and met me by my desk, as I was about to escape to take a bathroom break. "You're a spunky one, aren't ya?"

From the first time I ever met Tony Little, I had a strange feeling that he was coming onto me. I don't know if it was the smirk he always gave me, or the way he bounced his brows at me when he winked, but something told me he was interested. And that was utterly disgusting because he had a wedding band on his left ring finger. *Men!* You can't live with them and, apparently, you can't kill them with a garden shovel.

He actually reached out and played with the tips of my hair. I had opted to leave it down because after a week spent wearing ponytails and buns, my scalp was starting to ache. I had curled it too, and put on mascara, and my sundress. Okay, so I knew from previous experience that sometimes I can use my feminine wiles to get away with stuff and I thought if I looked pretty tonight, Officer Tony might forgive my absences. There, I admit it. I'm a ho.

"I like your hair down." Tony winked at me and I said a prayer to God, begging his forgiveness. "So, you want to talk about why you weren't here last week."

I blinked a couple of times because he was making me nervous with the way he was watching my lips move. I had a difficult time swallowing because I was about to lie. Another silent prayer to God.

"I...well...you know.... okay," I groaned. "I thought it was a waste of time."

"And now?" he chuckled.

"And now, I've seen the error of my ways."

"Well, I usually don't forgive and forget, but if you were to do me a very special favor, I think we can work something out."

I didn't like the tone of his voice, or the devilish smile he gave me and I really am not a ho in the sense that I was not about to give out sexual favors to save my ass.

"Uhh," I tried to speak, but I couldn't. I wanted to yell, to scream "sexual harassment," but I didn't. I just stared at him with wide eyes as he jotted down what looked like an address on the back of my paper.

"You come over for a barbecue tomorrow night and I'll forget all about your bad behavior."

"I...I mean, I don't...."

"Pretty please," he said with a downward smile. "It's just a few friends getting together for a barbecue. It won't kill you to get out and have some fun, now will it?"

Oh boy. What kind of fun are we talking about?

"Uh, okay," I said as I twiddled my thumbs under the desk.

He turned with a quick glimmer in his eye. "And wear your hair down."

It was pure and simple extortion. That's what it was and I was actually going to go on a date with this man to get myself out of trouble. My God, my mother is right. I needed to go to church.

***

I could barely sleep after eating a pint of ice cream and wallowing in my latest sin, but I did manage to finally close my eyes around the three a.m. mark. I slept for seven hours and when I woke, I got right to work. Lily met me at our usual coffee bistro near my old house. It was the one thing I missed about my old neighborhood. They made the best mochas ever.

"Hey," Lily said with smile. I love her smile and, honestly, I miss smiling myself. "So, what happened last night?"

"Well, let's see." I sipped some heavenly coffee and sighed. "I was right about him liking me. The perv actually blackmailed me into a date—in return he said he'd forget all about my absences."

"That's sexual harassment. He can't do that," Lily's face reddened to the same shade as her hair. "You need to tell someone. He can't get away with that!"

"He's a pig," I growled. "But, he's the least of my worries, don't you think? What did you find out for me about Walter Dobbs?" I quickly changed the subject to something more important.

She pulled a notebook from her red and white shoulder bag and flipped it open. A pen was dangling between her lips and she looked excited about being my investigation buddy. "His business was in financial peril. Dobbs and Hopper Bail Bonds near the Multnomah County jail, do you know the place?"

"The guy was a bail bondsman?" I was flabbergasted. "A hundred people probably wanted him dead. That's about the sleaziest job you can have, isn't it?"

"Besides being a road rage class instructor." She cocked her brow at me. "Yeah, I guess bail bondsman would be the next sleaziest. According to his business partner Walter was in some pretty serious financial trouble. He liked to gamble, bet on horses at the track and—cheat on his wife."

"Excuse me?" I choked on some hot coffee.

"Chad had to get his partner pretty plowed to admit that one, but apparently, the man was no saint."

"Eew. He was disgustingly ugly. Who in their right mind would touch him?"

"Dancers," she said. "He frequented a number of places, but his favorite was The Dancing Beaver on Stark Street. Had himself a few too many lap dances there."

"Gross," I groaned. "I think I'm going to be sick." I leaned back in my chair, closed my eyes to think of something pleasant, but all I could see was fat, old Walter Dobbs flicking sequined titty-tassles with his tongue. "So, the cops are stupid? Is that it? They haven't checked into any of this yet?"

"He'd only been dead eight hours when they picked you up. Apparently, they are not only stupid, they're lazy too. Three or four neighbors told them about your threat and they went running to your place. Well, of course, that and they had your garden shovel to go on too."

"Yeah, the garden shovel. How the hell did that happen?"

"Where'd you put it after you screamed at him?"

"I don't remember. I can't remember if I still had it in my hand, or if I dropped it in his driveway when Chad grabbed my shoulder. It's all just a big blur." I felt my head swell with blood. The muscles in my neck tightened and I desperately tried to remember where I'd last seen my damn shovel. "It doesn't matter. I kept it outside anyway. Anyone could have grabbed it from my garden bucket at any time." *But why? Why would someone use my shovel? It's really creepy to think that a killer actually set foot on my property.* "It was probably the neighbor on the other side of Walter's," I said with wide eyes. "Mrs. Talbot was always bitching about him leaving his stinky garbage cans too close to her rose bushes. She kept insisting that the stench was killing her flowers."

Lily laughed at me and finished off her scone. "That's a motive for murder?"

"It's a lot better than no motive at all. I mean, what would I have to gain by killing him. I barely knew him."

"Yeah, but you were the only one stupid enough to threaten to kill him in front of the entire neighborhood. Sometimes, your mouth gets you in trouble, Ang."

"Don't I know it." I attempted a smile and thumbed through the rest of the information that Lily and Chad were kind enough to gather for me. I would have done the majority of it myself, but I had class to attend last night. Ugh. "That reminds me," I groaned. "I told Officer Pervert that I'd bring a fruit salad. I should get going."

***

My first thought was to make myself look hideously ugly to ward off the horny perverted cop, but on the other hand, there was no way that I was purposefully going to make myself look like a white trash trailer hag again. That look was special and there's no way I could ever try to duplicate it on purpose. I opted for a pair of black shorts and a denim shirt over a loose-fitting white tank top. The entire ensemble read "I just want to play volleyball and be friends." *That should do the trick.* I dabbled a smidge of mascara on my naturally long lashes and smeared some awful smelling Carmex on my lips as a repellant of sorts. I also had plans to eat an entire onion with dinner, followed by a couple of skunky imported beers.

The address that Tony gave me was in the Fisher's Landing district of Vancouver. Just a couple of miles east of my house in Cascade Park. When I turned onto his street, I could see the multitude of SUVs and could see the billow of smoke rising from the backyard. It already smelled like barbecue sauce and mesquite. I inhaled to both ingest some oxygen and calm my frayed nerves. It's not every day that I'm blackmailed into dating someone. Dating was scary enough, without the blackmail part.

The door was wide open, only a screen door was present to keep out the bugs. Kids were screaming and running around the front yard with Super Soakers. I managed to get to the front door before being sprayed. I knocked to be polite and a short brunette woman met me with a smile.

"Hey!" she screamed out over my shoulder. "Watch where you're spraying with that thing, or I'll throw it in the garbage."

The kid nodded and went back to squirting his friend.

"Hi," I said with a slight stutter. "I'm Angie."

"Well, you're just as Tony described." She smiled and opened the screen door for me; reaching out to take the bowl of fresh fruit I'd spent an hour preparing. "I'm Tina."

"Nice to meet you." I looked around and quickly decided that this couldn't be Tony's house. *It must be a friend's place.* "Is he here?"

"Out back," she said. "Would you like a beer, soda, iced tea?"

"Tea would be nice, thanks." I followed the music out into the backyard. Tony was sitting near the kiddy pool sipping beer with a gaggle of men, I presumed fellow officers. They all had that stance about them. Like they were trying to be relaxed, but really weren't because they were expecting tragedy. He saw me and smiled, rose onto his bare feet and hurried toward me.

I felt nauseous at best.

"Glad you could make it." His grin was devilish as he wrapped his arm around me and started looking frantically over my shoulder. He looked left, and right and then straight ahead again. "Did you have trouble finding it?"

I swallowed with great difficulty and shook my head in lieu of actual words.

A minute later, Tina came out, handed me an ice tea and told Tony to go have a word with his son.

Son?

"In a minute, babe," he said and leaned over, gave her a quick peck on the lips and returned his attention back to me. I felt like I was in some sort of perverse universe. "I want to make an introduction first."

She shrugged, smiled at me, and walked away.

The music was loud, the barbecue was still billowing smoke, and when I looked just past the hot tub, I saw a familiar face. I felt my lips tug into a smile and I had no idea where the hell that came from.

"Ah, ha," Tony said under his breath and I was suddenly being pulled toward the friendly face. "King, you remember Angie Shirpa, don't you?"

Scot's smile was even wider than mine. A multitude of bells went off in my head. *This was Tony's house, Tina was Tony's wife, his son was out front playing cops and robbers with water guns, and I was being set up...again.*

"Nice to see you again," I said to Scot, extending my hand to him in order to give Tony his big moment of pride.

"And you," Scot played along rather well and even brought my hand up to his lips. He kissed it softly, never taking his eyes off mine. I felt a tingle rush up my arm, but I squashed it rather quickly by remembering that *celibacy rocks.*

"Well, I have to attend to some business out front. Why don't you make her a brat, big guy?"

I watched Tony as he sauntered away, his head held high. Scot released my hand and sipped from his microbrew.

"So." I blinked a couple of times and applauded myself for doing my hair and applying makeup.

"So." His eyes lit up with mischief. "You must have gone back to class, I take it."

"Yep," I said. "Let me take a wild guess. Tony's that best friend of yours that wants to see you happily married."

"How'd you guess?" He laughed and motioned to the empty lawn chairs behind us. "You want a brat, or a burger?"

"Burger, please," I said as I eased back in the seat.

He opened the cooler, fished around for a meat patty, and tossed it on the grill before sitting down beside me and charming me with his smile. "What do you think the odds are of us being set up *twice* by two completely different people?"

"Slim to none," I said, but kept the smile from my face. "Don't go thinking there's some cosmic reason for it, because I don't date."

"Neither do I!" he groaned, probably put off that he didn't get to say it first.

I stared into space and felt compelled to go one further. "I've decided that I'll date again when I'm sixty and ready to have a man wait on me hand and foot. Until then, celibacy rocks." I actually snarled after I said it.

We sat in silence for a few minutes before he got up, flipped my burger and handed me a beer. "You need one of these."

"What's that supposed to mean?"

"Are you always so uptight? Or is it me?"

"It's you. I happen to be a very pleasant person." I said haughtily and twisted the top off my beer. It wasn't an import as I had hoped, but Portland Brewery knows how to make a great pale ale.

He stared at me, bit his lower lip, and shook his head a couple of times. The silence became unbearable, but the funny thing was, it was somewhat nice that he didn't get up and run away from me. He could have. He easily could have walked away and never looked back, but he didn't. He fixed me a burger, handed me a napkin and then sat back down beside me while I ate.

Tony's taste in music was something else, but my toe began tapping to the beat of the Bee Gees once I started feeling friendlier. It must have been the ambience of having so many happy, laughing people around. That and I finally had food in my stomach.

"Sorry," I said when I felt a little better. Sometimes low blood sugar adds to my foulness. "It's not you."

"I didn't think so," he said. "Although, I was beginning to wonder if you were ever going to forgive me for arresting you."

"Oh." I had completely forgotten that I was holding that grudge against him. Boy, he didn't stand a chance. "I *haven't* forgiven you." I sent him a small smile and I narrowed my eyes suspiciously. "So, why would your best friend set you up with a woman who you hauled in for..." I stopped to sip my beer and recollect exactly how Tony had put it that first night in class. Tony had the police report right there in his hand that night, so I know he knew Scot was the officer that I poked in the chest. I continued on. "...going after you with malicious intent?"

Scot laughed, which I appreciated. He also blushed slightly, which I hadn't expected. "I think I may have mentioned once or twice that I thought you were cute."

I gasped and almost choked on my beer. "I looked horrible!"

He laughed, I mean really laughed. In fact, it was sort of a turn on. I felt the tiny hairs on the back of my neck stand up and do a little dance. *Now, if I could just make a little love...*I swallowed fiercely and slapped my clammy palms together, wondering where the hell that random thought came from. *It must be the disco music.* I refocused on what he was saying and simultaneously brushed the errant hairs from my eyes.

"Yeah, you did. But I was talking about that night at dinner – after you showered and transformed into a human being again."

"Oh." It was I who blushed that time. I bit into my burger and chewed on it for a few long seconds to keep my mind from going places it had no right to go.

So, he thought I was cute.

I guess I thought he was sort of cute too. Why else would I suddenly be so nervous?

Thank goodness, Tony and Tina made it over to break the thick layer of ice that had formed between Scot and me.

"So, Tony tells me that you two know each other already." Tina sipped her iced tea and smiled at me. I should have complimented her very pretty sundress when I arrived, but I was a bit preoccupied with the thought of being Tony's mistress for the evening. Her eyes were very big and she was much shorter than Tony, but there was more of her. Tony was tall and thin and Tina looked like a mom. A busy mom, with hips to prove it.

I hate admitting it, but I was jealous. I wanted to be a mom. I wanted wider hips too, damn it!

"Yeah, he pulled me over, tossed me in the back of his cruiser and the rest is history," I joked and finished my beer just as Scot handed me another.

"That's very romantic," she said, wrapping her arm around Tony's lean waist. "It's a good story to tell your grandkids someday."

I felt the blood rush to my cheeks, so I excused myself to the little girls' room.

Their house was a one-level ranch style. The sliding glass doors led into the kitchen and beyond that was a long hallway that dissected a large great room. The walls were all painted a different color, mostly pastels. It sang of joy, happiness, and Martha Stewart. Duck décor plastered the bathroom, but it beat the heck out of the lilac bathroom at my house. I could see that she was a tidy housekeeper, probably a stay at home mother who took real pride in her home.

When I finished, I found Scot waiting for me in the kitchen. He was leaning back against the counter, with his hands folded across his chest.

"Sorry about that."

"Hey, it's okay. I have one too, remember," I said with a smile. It was much wider and brighter since I'd finished a beer. I was more relaxed and my defenses were down.

He scrunched up his nose at me and then he also smiled. There was a whole lot of smiling going on. It was unnerving.

"You have an amazing smile. You should do it more often."

I smiled again, appreciating the compliment.

"Can I tell you something?" I said and he motioned to the living room. The house was quiet because the partygoers were still milling around the barbecue and dancing on the patio.

We sat down beside each other on the long sectional couch. I got comfortable and tucked one leg up under my butt, turning slightly so I could see him better.

"I thought Tony was hitting on me."

He chuckled softly. "What gave you that idea?"

"When I first met him, he asked me if I was married and he was always looking at me and then last night when I came back, he asked me to do him a favor and said if I did he'd forgive my absences from class."

He just watched me with his big brown eyes that were much softer now. Less serious, I guess.

"I honestly thought he was blackmailing me into dating him."

"That would explain why you looked like you were in pain when you got here," he said with a chuckle.

"Don't tell him I said that, okay? I guess I'm a little embarrassed now."

"Don't be. Tony's a great guy and has a pretty wild sense of humor. He'll get a kick out of it and Tina's the best woman I know. They've been married almost twelve years. Toby is ten and she's pregnant with number two." He looked out the window at the partiers in the back yard. "They're hoping for a girl this time."

Every fiber of my being cried out in pain. Again, that familiar tension grew behind my eyes. I felt a wave of nausea, followed by a clenching sensation in my chest."Wow," I said. "That's amazing."

He looked at me as if I'd said something completely off-color. His eyes grew wary again.

"Why is that amazing? Twelve years is nothing. Marriage is forever." He shook his head at me in a way I did not appreciate.

I don't know why it made me so damn angry, but it did. I felt suddenly embarrassed and almost ashamed about my failure.

"You know what, screw you!" I stood up and planted my hands on my hips. At least I didn't poke him in the sternum that time. "I'm not to blame for my failed marriage. I believed that marriage was forever too, but guess what, pal? It's not. Four out of five marriages will end in divorce and it's not pretty. All I was saying was that I thought it was amazing that they've made it as far as they have, and perhaps their marriage will be the one out of the five that will last forever." My head pounded, my vision blurred, and boy I felt myself losing control and fast. "You have no right to judge me because I'm divorced..."

He leaned his elbows onto his knees and grinned.

"I wasn't judging you. I was simply stating my personal feelings. So your marriage didn't last. So what? It doesn't mean you have to jump down the throat of every person you meet. Shit happens. I know you're pissed off about your ex, but get the hell over it. Everyone's had their heart stomped on at one point or another. It's how we know we still have a heart...don't you think?"

I choked back a tear or two and then sat back down. *Damn it.*

"Sorry," I said, but made no move to go anywhere. "I should just go." I was fairly certain I hadn't scared him off, which was slightly unsettling. He sure could take a beating.

"No," he said. "I don't want you to go." He got up, opened the cupboard near the bookshelf at the end of the couch, and took out a deck of cards. He sat back down and started shuffling. "But let's not talk about divorce anymore. It's not good for your blood pressure."

"Deal," I said with a partial smile.

We played gin, crazy eights, then four or five others joined in, and soon we had the poker game of the century going on. The man who everyone referred to as Lieutenant Dan wanted to play strip poker, but Scot and I were the first to jump up and squash that idea. I know why I didn't want to play, but I couldn't see why Scot would be embarrassed to shed his clothes. My God, he had muscles that never ended. Not that I was looking. But after he had a few more beers, he shed his outer rugby and was just wearing a tight black shirt that showed off his muscles nicely.

"I haven't played this in years." I lied through my teeth and pretended not to know the difference between a flush and a straight. Bull and my dad taught me poker at an early age. I once lost my entire piggy bank to Bull, but after I cried, he let me win it all back and then some. "Hit me," I squealed like a girl and continually took pot after pot. Every so often, I would fold, but for the most part, I ruled the first seven hands. "Beginner's luck," I said with a shrug, but I think Scot was onto me. He hadn't stopped staring at me since I dealt the last hand. Perhaps I shouldn't have been so cocky, now that I had a contender.

"I raise you two bits," Scot said with narrowed eyes after everyone else folded. The room had gotten fairly silent. Toby had been tucked into bed with his best friend. Tina and Tony were saying goodbye to the rest of the guests and five of us remained around the kitchen table. The pot looked as if it had at least three dollars in it and Scot had just done the unthinkable and raised the maximum bet. "Chicken?" he challenged.

"No," I stuck out my tongue and giggled like a girl. For some unexplained reason, I let him win that hand. But when I was dealt two aces on the next hand, I vowed to take him for every cent he had.

"Two please," I said to Lieutenant Dan, who was dealing. He flicked me two cards as I discarded my lame two of spades and three of hearts. As I held my aces and king of spades, I kept my face completely stoical as I added my new cards. First came the king of diamonds and then a six of clubs. I had two pair. Two pair of the highest caliber I might add. Perhaps I don't have crappy luck after all.

The others took their turns raising the pot here and there, which I called. Then it was Scot's turn. I could see in his eyes that he wasn't about to let me off easy. I'd never met a fiercer competitor and it was exciting. I enjoyed the look in his deep brown eyes, just about as much as the smirk on his face. I do have to say that I have a better poker face than he does. Mine was flawless and completely unrevealing. Soon, his pile of change had diminished to a couple of pennies.

"Whatcha got, little lady?" Scot leaned back in his chair and grinned.

I cracked a wide smile and dropped my two pair on the table in front of him.

"Ahhh," he groaned and almost tipped over in his chair. If it hadn't been for Tony walking by and saving him, he would have fallen on his head. "She's good," he said to his friend. "Real good."

Tony yawned as did Tina and we all knew that universal sign.

I felt a bit loopy, so I wasn't about to drive. Since I was sitting among cops, I was somewhat encouraged to ask for help. A number of them hadn't been drinking, but Scot had been nursing beer all night, so I was sure he wouldn't be volunteering.

"I've had a few too many," I confessed.

"That's okay, you can come home with me," Scot said with a wink.

Tony and Tina's eyes widened and my jaw dropped.

"I don't think so." I looked around for help. No one came to my rescue. "But you're drunk too."

"I didn't drive," he winked again, stood up and grabbed a bag of sour cream and onion potato chips off the table. "You coming or what?" he asked on his way to the front door.

I stood up and looked around at the mess. Pop cans and leftover party platters cluttered the kitchen counter and the garbage was overflowing in the can. "Maybe I should stay and help clean up." I looked to Tina, who just smiled and waved her hand at me.

"We'll do it in the morning. It's late and we have an early baseball game. I appreciate the offer, but you go with Scot."

I gathered my purse and denim shirt and said goodbye and thanks.

Scot was already across the street by the time I made it outside. Frogs and crickets were making sweet songs in the cool breeze. My legs felt like Jell-O and I was in no shape to be hanging out at a strange man's house. I know my determination was strong, but alcohol had done stranger things to me in the past.

"Where are you going?" I yelled at Scot.

"Shhh," he replied and pointed to a two-story house on the other side of the driveway he was standing in. "Mr. Williams needs his beauty sleep." He waved me over and, to my surprise, took a key from his pocket and opened the front door to the house that was kitty corner from where I was still standing.

"Unbelievable," I said under my breath and headed across the street.

His house was also a one-level ranch style house. Large maple trees lined his front yard along with large rhododendrons that blocked the front windows. I walked steadily toward his house and felt my stomach flop around in my belly. I wouldn't have guessed that a single guy would live in a house like his. The yard was well kept, the blinds matched the carpet. He was very tidy for a man.

"Thanks," I said when he placed my purse and shirt on the couch.

"Coffee, water, bed?"

I think I squealed and I know my knees buckled. Then he laughed and tossed me the remote.

"Coffee would be fine," I said as I looked around. I didn't mean to snoop, but he had exquisite taste in photography. The one above the fireplace looked like the Oregon Coast. "Wow, who took this?"

"Me," he said as he dumped coffee grounds into the filter. I turned to watch him pour in the water and flip the switch.

"Impressive," I said. He kept adding to his likeability factor...*I hate that*! I needed to get out of there and fast. "I should just call a cab. I don't want to intrude."

"You're not intruding," he said as he met me by the fireplace. "And you don't have to worry about me making a move on you. I'm not interested in dating you, or anyone else for that matter. I love my life. I like my freedom. I'm just not ready."

"Okay, then." I smiled and sank down onto the couch. It was overstuffed, very comfortable and the color of faded denim. "That's good because I'm not interested in dating you either."

We sat in silence for a moment while I tried to find something decent to watch on TV. He got us both a cup of coffee and sat back down.

"So, why aren't you ready?" I had to ask. Blame it on the alcohol, or blame it on the fact that I'm meddlesome. I care not!

He chuckled slightly, didn't meet my gaze, and stared at the television. "I haven't quite gotten over *it* yet."

"*It?*"

I sipped my coffee and nearly burned my tongue.

He groaned, and rolled his head along the back of the couch to look at me. "Jill Berenger broke my heart. I asked her to marry me, she said yes and then she moved to Colorado to be with her high-school sweetheart when he got divorced. Okay. End of story."

"Okay," I said. We all have stories and now that I knew his, I swore to myself that I would shut up. "When?"

Oops, I did it again.

He smacked my thigh with his big hand and curled his fingers around my knee, tickling me until I nearly lost bladder control. "End of story. Now shut up and get sober before I throw you over my shoulder and carry you to my big bed." He bobbed his brows and released my knee.

Color burned my cheeks. *Embarrassing.*

***

I had no intention of falling asleep on his couch, but I did. When I woke up, the sun was burning into my forehead and I felt the horrible onslaught of a hangover. I remembered watching a movie, or part of a movie. I think it was a war movie starring Bruce Willis. Then I closed my eyes. This morning after I found myself in an incredibly awkward situation. I had cottonmouth and just wanted to escape without incident.

That wasn't going to happen.

"Mornin'," he said from the kitchen table. Of course, he was already showered, dressed in fresh jeans, a long-sleeved baby-blue oxford, and sipping coffee. "Coffee?"

"No thanks," I moaned. "You got any Diet Pepsi?"

"What do I look like, a girl? Of course, I don't have any *Diet* Pepsi. I got Pepsi!" He got up and grabbed one out of the fridge before I could answer. A smile lit up his face as he brought it over to me. His big green U.S. Marines blanket was still draped over my knees.

"Sorry. I didn't mean to fall asleep."

"You have a lot on your mind. I figured you needed a good night's sleep." He was staring down at me. Levi's will never again do any other man justice, now that I've seen them on Scot King. I licked my dry lips and averted my gaze to the kitchen table.

"I guess I did. What time is it?"

"Eleven."

I felt my skin shrivel. "Shit!"

"You have somewhere you have to be?"

I stuttered a bit and tossed his blanket onto the back of the couch as I stood up.

"I...uh...well, let's see...."

"I can help with that you know."

I dropped my jaw and stared at him, waiting for some further explanation.

"Come on, I can get inside information and they never let me play with the big boys anymore. It'll be fun."

"What are you talking about?" I said before downing half my Pepsi. It was way too sweet, but the bubbles were doing wonders for my sour stomach.

"Chad told me about your plan. I can help, if you'll let me."

My face reddened. "That little piece of dog-shit! I believe that would be considered treason on his part—talking to the damn-pig-cops."

"Hey," he shouted. "Damn-pig-cop standing right here." His hands were at his hips by then and he looked seriously *hot!*

"Why would you want to help me?"

"Because," he replied, stepping toward me. He brushed the crumpled mass of hair from my eyes and smiled. "I live for excitement and intrigue. And, I don't think you killed Walter Dobbs."

"So, you're willing to help me even though…"

"Yes, even though I don't know you and I don't want to date you… I want to help."

"That's pretty thin, Officer King."

Why would a practical stranger want to go out of their way to help little old me? Men are not that nice and selfless, are they?

He groaned again and lightly punched me in the arm. "What, you can't handle anymore friends in your life? Are you that popular, that you can't find it in your heart to make one new friend?"

A smile tugged at my lips. "That's a new one."

"Hey, it ain't easy for me either, but I think I'm beginning to like you."

He raised his coffee mug to meet my Pepsi can. "To friends."

"To friends."

Four

I'd been coerced into having breakfast at Denny's with my new friend – to go over the details and meet up with Chad and Lily to go over the plan. The plan wasn't even really a plan as of yet, it was more of an idea of a plan, but since I'm a schoolteacher and so is my partner; we had no idea where to start.

Lily was more concerned with why I was being so nice to Scot than she was about the plan. Every time the conversation lulled, she was searching for information about last night.

"So, how'd it go with Tony and why are you here with Scot? I thought…" she shut up when Scot came back to the table with a couple more napkins. She made googly eyes with me and grinned like we had a secret.

"Why did the police immediately come to me? Is that normal?" I stared at Scot and waited for his grand explanation. It didn't come. He shrugged and chewed his toast.

"I don't know anything about it, but I'll do some digging tomorrow." Scot said and I had a feeling he was holding something back because he wouldn't meet my gaze. Then again, I didn't know him well enough to make that call. But what I did know is that he has a terrible poker face. "How did you get this information about Dobbs?"

Scot seemed like a street cop through and through. A soldier, an army ant, one who follows orders and doesn't ask questions. He sure wasn't an intuitive investigator like I was.

"We asked his business partner over drinks," Chad said. "It was Angie's idea, so I pretended to be a reporter for the Oregonian, and the man sang like Aretha Franklin."

Scot looked over at me. "You're a schoolteacher, right?"

"Right," I said smugly. "Dobbs was in financial trouble and had numerous bouts of infidelity. I'd have to put my money on an angry client, or his wife."

"My money's on one of the neighbors," Lily said. "That whole street is a bit wacko. I bet if we started digging, we could unearth some fairly substantial skeletons in those people's closets."

"What about the kid?" Scot asked.

"No way!" I shouted. "Dale's an intellectual and probably the smartest kid I've ever met. He's a genius and has a full ride to Stanford. He's not a killer and even if he was, he'd do something more sinister like concoct a special poison that is untraceable."

"I was just asking. Sheesh!"

My fingers tapped relentlessly on the yellow Formica table. That is until Scot reached out and grabbed my hand. His hot flesh surrounded my delicate fingers and set them on fire.

He didn't look at me; he just gave it a squeeze. "You're making me nervous."

"Sorry," I rubbed my hand to make the tingles go away. Geez, it was only a small gesture, but it sent my skin ablaze with sensation. "Lily and Chad, why don't you work on the neighbors and see what you can get. Scot, you take the wife and I'll have a look into his clients."

"What about the kid?" Scot said again as he sipped more coffee.

"The kid is out, because even if he did do it, I wouldn't blame him. Walter treated him like shit and humiliated him every other minute. The asshole deserved what he got."

Everyone at the table sat in silence. I had said a mouthful and had just given everyone an idea of how much I hated Walter Dobbs.

"I didn't do it," I said for good measure and we all got a good laugh before everyone went his or her separate way.

***

My first order of business that day was to meet Dean Hopper at his office. I hated downtown Portland. It was sleazy, dirty, and just too crowded for my tastes. Of course, the bonds office was right in the center of sleazeville and I had to step over a couple of street bums before reaching the door. I pulled a tissue out of my pocket to place between my skin and the black door handle.

The door chimed a couple of times when I got it open.

"Hello," I sang out and waited patiently, careful not to touch anything. "Mr. Hopper?"

Dean Hopper rounded the corner and grinned a toothless smile at me. It wasn't completely toothless, but he had an incisor missing as well as one of the front ones. His black hair was matted down with a gallon of motor oil and the jacket he was wearing looked like something out of a Michael Jackson video; red leather with lots of zippers.

He extended his hand and although I had to hold back the urge to gag, I took it and gave it a friendly shake. "I'm Dana Hoffman. I believe you spoke to my boss a couple of days ago." I did a good job at lying. Kept my poker face on and pretended to be an assistant to Chad. Dean Hopper had met him previously. I was actually having fun.

"Sure," he said, hitching up his pinstripe trousers. "What else can I do for you?"

"I was wondering if I could have a look at Walter's current client list."

I should mention that I know nothing about bail, or bonds, or creepy little men who smell like anti-freeze.

"Well, that would be highly unethical, now wouldn't it? Unless you have a badge or a warrant, that just ain't possible, little lady."

Where the hell was Bull when I needed him? I was in way over my head and I'd only just begun.

"Don't you want to find out who killed Walter?"

"Walter had many enemies, but I'm sure the po-lice already have an idea or two."

"Well," I said as I backed up toward the door. "If you can think of anything else, give us a call and we'll be talking to you again, soon. Thanks." I practically ran out of the office. My heart was thumping in my chest. Maybe I'm not cut out for this crap. *What an icky, icky little man.*

My second stop was at my old house. I wanted to say hi to the nice elderly couple that bought the place and, of course, I wanted to see what kind of reaction I could get from the neighbors as they watched me walk down the street. I pulled up in front of my old house and got out, sliding my sunglasses into my hair.

Mr. Duncan was outside watering my old azalea bushes. I was sad to see that they had cut down my favorite elm tree out front, but I'd known it had to be done. It was diseased, but I was too sentimental to chop it down and put it out of its misery. Ray and I used to lie under that tree and sip martinis and watch the neighbor kids ride their bikes. That was a pre-heart attack memory. After the heart attack, we'd sit under that tree and he'd stare at Mrs. Wallace's butt across the street. Strange how near-death makes a man horny.

"Hello, Mr. Duncan," I waved and let him know I was about to cross the lawn to see him. I didn't want anyone getting the wrong idea and taking a potshot at me for trespassing. "How are things?"

I expected the usual from the older man. You know, the aches and pains and gassiness he feels after eating. I was surprised when he went one better.

"The roof leaks in the bathroom. The tile is moldy and just last night I heard a damn creak in the bottom step. The house is falling apart right underneath us." His wrinkled hand shook slightly when he took a long drag off his cigarette.

"It's almost eighty years old, Don. It's an old house."

"Yeah." He exhaled a cloud of gray smoke, "Well, I'm an old man and I can't be falling through the steps. That sort of thing could kill a man my age."

So could smoking, you old nag!

He flicked an ash at my foot and scowled. "I heard about you from Mrs. Wallace."

"Oh, and what did she say?"

"Said you killed Walter. Walked right into his bedroom and stabbed him with your shovel."

I couldn't resist the urge to give his kicker a jump-start.

"Maybe I did!" I said haughtily and just walked away. I mumbled a few choice obscenities and the street cleared out faster than Amity Bay did when Jaws was spotted. Citizens dropped their hoses, tossed their shears into the yard, and fled to the safety of their homes. *I'm a pariah!*

I didn't dare do any knocking. That would just perturb the fine neighbors on Cherry Blossom even more, so I exited the neighborhood and fled to the comfort of my own home.

***

After dropping my purse on the counter and thumbing through my mail, I called Bull on his cell phone.

"Baby girl," he crooned on hearing my voice.

"Hey, I need a favor." I knew I had to say this very delicately because both Bull and my father were hell-bent against the idea of me helping with my own problem.

"I know you and Dad have everything handled, but a friend of mine suggested getting the client list from Walter's office downtown and, to my knowledge, I don't think anybody could just waltz in and ask to see it. You probably have to be sneaky about it." I bit down on my lip and nervously tapped my shoe on the hardwood floor.

"And you know this because…"

"I don't…I mean…. Hell, Bull."

"I saw you in his office, doll. What did he say? Come back with a warrant?" His deep voice boomed with laughter.

"It's not funny!" I grumbled. "What were you doing watching his office, anyway?"

"Same as you, I suspect. I'll get what I need tonight. You want to meet me for breakfast tomorrow?"

"Sure, Waddles at nine?"

"I'll see you then. And, Angie…" he said, as I took the phone away from my ear. "Leave the hard stuff to the big boys."

"Sure thing, Uncle Bull." I disconnected and screamed…*a lot!* ***

After another restless night's sleep, the incessant ringing of the phone woke me at seven a.m. I don't have caller ID in my bedroom, so I took a chance and answered in on the fourth ring.

"What did you do?" Scot practically shouted at me. "Ang?"

After my brain caught up with my eardrums, I felt a familiar tension behind my right eye.

"One, don't call me Ang! Two, don't wake me up before nine, and three, don't yell at me!" I shouted right back, my eye twitching wildly.

I heard him inhale sharply, then clear his throat. It's a very good thing he's not a rager like me, because our friendship wouldn't have lasted two measly hours.

"What did you do last night and don't lie to me."

"I slept last night," I said. "Okay… I watched *Sleepless in Seattle*, ate an entire bowl of popcorn and then I slept. Why?" I sat straight up and leaned against my headboard for support. I somewhat knew what might be coming, so I did my best to act surprised. "What happened? Did the cops find *my* pickax in someone's chest?"

I heard him laugh and that made me smile. "No," he said through the chuckles. "Tell me you didn't have anything to do with the break-in at Walter's office."

"I knew this was a bad idea," I groaned.

"Jesus Christ!" he yelled.

"I shouldn't have let you get involved because you're a cop and every little thing that happens in Portland from here on out is going to be my fault. Isn't it?" I shouted to make a point. I was completely faking my anger, because I was trying to throw him off his game.

"So you didn't break into Walter's office last night?"

"Doesn't he have surveillance?"

"It was disabled by a real pro and all that was missing was Walter's personal files. The whole damn cabinet!" he shouted again. "How the hell did you do that?"

I laughed and thought it was cute that he thought that highly of my criminal abilities. "Any prints?"

"None of yours," he said and then I heard him whistle. "Jesus Christ."

"What?"

"You said you were going to talk to Hopper yesterday—what'd you do, wipe down your prints? Wear gloves?"

I laughed again and something about his voice changed. He was breathing heavier and he almost sounded... *Nah! I have a very wild imagination.*

"I can't believe I'm getting turned on by this," he said hoarsely.

Ha!

I clamped my hand over the receiver and did a little jig. I *so* know men!

He cleared his throat loudly and stuttered. I wondered how turned on he was, and then I started imagining what my new friend looks like naked and aroused. *Holy hell!*

"Geez, Officer King, I had nothing, and I repeat nothing, to do with it." I stopped when I heard him exhale loudly, as if he was relieved. "I went to see Hopper, he didn't want to cooperate, and so I left. My prints were nowhere to be found because I used a tissue when I opened the door," I said quickly. "I have a cootie phobia."

"So you have no idea who could have done such a thing?"

I didn't want to answer that, so I pretended to have another call.

"I have to go, my call waiting is beeping and I'm expecting a call from my mom." It was just a little white lie, so much better than the big lie I could have told to the policeman on the other end of the line.

***

Breakfast at Waddles was my next task for the day. I showered, curled my hair, pulled it into barrettes, and headed to meet Uncle Bull at my favorite breakfast joint. Eggs Benedict was calling my name and Waddles made the best around.

Bull was already seated in a corner booth, sipping lemon water and, from the looks of it, going over the stolen files. "Hey," he said with a smile. "Piece of cake."

I looked at the files on the table and got very excited. "Is this all of them?"

"Most of them. Many clients are back in the slammer, so I sorted them into viable and non-viable suspects. Looks like I have my work cut out for me."

"Let me help, please?" I begged and grabbed a cup, flipped it over and hurriedly waved to the waitress to fill it up. "I'll just check out a few, pretty please?"

He eyeballed me with serious brows. "Your father would skin me alive."

"So, he doesn't have to know."

He grinned and looked around as if he were being watched by my almighty father. "Don't you know by now that your father knows and sees everything? All that man has to do is make a few calls and both you and I would be under constant surveillance."

"Nah," I too flashed an unholy grin. "Dad's got nothing on you, Uncle Bull. You're the invisible man and he doesn't need to know a thing about this."

He laughed and gave me a quick peck on the cheek. "I'll let you do some preliminary work—paper shuffling, things like that, but under no circumstances are you going anywhere near these scumbags."

"Fine, I can do paper shuffling, I can make phone calls and spy like the best of them."

Bull eased back in his seat and gave me the once over with his big eyes. "What made you change your mind?"

I'd known that someday he was going to ask me about why I decided not to follow my dad's footsteps and work for the Feds. He was so proud of me when I got my Criminal Justice Administration degree. I was on course to get my masters when my father got injured on assignment in Miami. Bull was so proud that he even offered to write me a letter of recommendation to get me into any training program of my choice. After Dad got shot, I changed my major to political science and shortly after, I met Ray. My decision was based solely on love and fear.

"When Dad got hurt, I guess," I said with a tearful gaze. "I got scared, and besides, I'd just met Ray and, as you know, I was head over heels and would have done anything to stay with him." I don't think Ray would have liked the idea of me working for the FBI, or NSA, or even the police department. He wanted me by his side, cooking his meals and rubbing his feet. Of course, I was a lovesick ninny and didn't want to leave him. "I think if I wouldn't have met Ray, I might have changed my mind again and gone back to my dream, but I had him to think about."

"That's why your marriage failed. You gave up your dreams and much of yourself to be with him."

There was Bulldog again, surprising the crap out of me with his sensitive bull. Perhaps that is why his nickname is Bull. He sure can fling it!

"My marriage failed because my husband had an affair."

"That was just a symptom."

"Whatever, Bull." I slammed my hand down on the table and glared. "I'm not here for marriage counseling. It's over. I'm fine."

He conceded and handed me a confidential file that he must have stolen also. I read over the report on Walter Dobbs' death. Very interesting. He died somewhere in the morning hours, between nine and eleven. The body was found around noon, when his wife, Madeline came home for lunch. There was no forced entry, no broken windows anywhere, but the sliding glass door that led into his bedroom was left ajar. The only thing they had to go on was the red garden shovel that was jammed into his chest. The officers questioned the neighbors.

That's when Mrs. Wallace told the story of the "Walter Dobbs Must Die" incident. Thus putting me in this predicament.

"They're just now getting into a full scale investigation because the prosecuting attorney feels they lack proper motive. Your prints were the only ones on the shovel, but they didn't find any of your prints anywhere else in the house. He was killed coming out of the shower, and died on his bedroom floor. Not a nice way to die."

"So, I'm not being ruled out, they're just digging deeper for a motive."

"Correct," he said sternly. "I spoke to the prosecuting attorney as your counsel and as long as you don't leave the country, you're okay to move about. Go on vacation, do whatever… just don't be caught sneaking around where you don't belong. That's not going to do you any good. Got it?"

"Got it," I gulped and then ordered my breakfast from the perky waitress with extra large boobs.

Bull was kind enough to pay for breakfast and let me take home three files to check into. He wasn't sure which of the subjects were still in the area and what they would have to gain by killing Walter, but it was a start.

After I said goodbye and promised again not to tell my dad on him, I kissed him goodbye and went home.

                              ***

I was home for not more than four minutes when I heard a loud thud on my door.

"Ang, open the door!"

I whipped open the door and came face to face with Officer King, in full uniform. His Portland police cruiser was parked in my driveway. "Don't call me Ang!"

"Why not?" he asked as he moved past me and began pacing in the living room as if he owned the place. "Lily and Chad call you Ang."

"So, they've been my friends for years…you've been my friend, for what…twenty-four hours. It's too soon."

He looked at me with crazed eyes and a clenched jaw. "Who's the guy?"

"Guy?" I looked around my living room to see if I'd left a man behind the curtains or something. I was sure I hadn't. I'm sure I would have remembered harboring a man in my house. "What guy?"

"The guy," he said with his hands flailing in the air. "The man you had breakfast with – G.I. Joe."

I laughed and rolled my eyes at my new friend. He smelled so damn good I wanted to be closer. God help me. I moved a few steps toward him and inhaled before speaking. *Damn pheromones!*

"You mean Uncle Bull," I said with composure. "What, now you're following me?" I stepped back, giving him the once over with hands planted firmly on my hips.

He winced, probably feeling like a cad for following me...or for downright admitting it. "Oh," he said a bit quieter. "So, he's not the guy who you hired to break into Walter's office?"

"Geez, Scot. You're sounding an awful lot like a cop." I looked at his shiny gold badge and cringed.

He laughed.

"And I'm not supposed to sound like a cop because..."

"Because you're my new friend and you begged me to let you help."

"And by helping you, that means I have to be okay with a couple laws being broken. Is that it?"

"Oh for Christ's sake!" I shouted and headed toward the kitchen to pop a couple of antacids down my throat. I opened my oak cupboard, rummaged around past the cold medications, and found an old roll of tropical flavored Tums. "I know nothing."

"You liar," he groaned and pulled my arm so I was facing him again. He could have let go, but his hand remained on my shoulder as he spoke to me like a big brother. That's why I had to keep looking at him because the more I looked, the more I liked. "What do you think is going to happen if they find you've been stealing Walter's files? This isn't a simple road rage class you'd have to take; we're talking about murder, years spent in a penitentiary. You're cute and all, but I don't think you'll look all that good in orange."

I swallowed my pineapple-orange Tums with an exaggerated gulp.

"I personally don't want to admit to anyone that one of my *friends* is in the tank for murder."

"I appreciate the warning, but I'm fine."

"Fine." He released my arm and let his hand trickle down my bare arm.

I was wearing just a black tank top that was a bit tight for my tastes, but it was hot outside and I was out of laundry soap. The caress didn't feel just *friendly*…at all! It felt sexy. When his fingers made it down to my wrist, he felt his way down to my fingertips and entwined his hand with mine. Then, after I caught my breath, I looked up and found him staring at my mouth. Sweat formed between my breasts and I couldn't breathe all that well. He started to lean toward me; I think I leaned toward him too. Then he blinked a couple of times.

"Shit!" he shouted as if he'd just been bit in the ass by a rattlesnake. "I'm on duty." And he ran out the damn door.

Wow.

But nooooo!

Celibacy Rocks!

It took me a couple of minutes to regroup from that episode. Friends, my ass! The man was actually going to kiss me. I was positive of it and what if he had? Oh boy, we'd surely be in trouble then because friends don't kiss. They never kiss, because if friends kissed, then kissing would no longer be special. There would no longer be those intense moments in which you long to lock lips with someone of the opposite sex. Kissing would just be like shaking hands, only a lot sloppier. By golly, what incredible hell that would have been. Kissing Scot King. I could barely think about it without going into full-on convulsions.

I spent the entire rest of that day convulsing about every other minute.

***

The following couple of days were much better, except I had gotten nowhere with Walter's client list. Lily checked out the neighbors, but since no one was talking, she was hitting her head against a brick wall. Chad wasn't having much luck with the other side of the street and I think Lily must have been ovulating because they spent a lot of time in bed.

I made a few calls, got called a few dirty words and pretty much hit a dead end with the list that Bull had given me. I was certain that he'd only given me that list because it was a dead end. But what Bull didn't know was that I copied down a few tidbits of information off one of his files when he had used the restroom at Waddles. I too can be a sneaky bastard! I made a call inquiring about a Juan de la Hoya and, of course, my first question was, "Are you any relation to Oscar?"

The man actually laughed at me and told me what a snake Mr. Dobbs was. I was speaking to Juan senior, not the junior version that I was looking for, and I didn't catch on until he kept mentioning what Walter had done to his son. He called Walter some very bad names in Spanish and then told me that I could find Juan tending bar at O'Riley's in the Pearl District. "Thanks so much, Mr. de la Hoya," I said and disconnected just in time to throw on my sweats and rush off to road rage 101 with Officer Tony Little.

Only it wasn't Tony at the head of the class that night, it was Scot.

"So, what exactly do you do in here?" Scot swung his Nike clad feet onto the desk and flipped through a couple of road rage awareness brochures.

The biker dude was the first to pipe up. "He takes roll call and then he leaves to drink coffee and eat sprinkled donuts. We all go home."

Half the class laughed, half the class was asleep and I was still dumbfounded that Scot was the substitute teacher. *I think fantasies are made out of nights like this.*

I raised my hand, folded my feet under my chair like a good catholic schoolgirl. I would have given anything to be wearing anything but my old gray sweats. Not that it mattered;

I'm not trying to impress him or anything. I spoke after clearing the sudden tension from my larynx. "We left off on where road rage has become a huge problem in society. I believe its page forty-six in your manual."

I heard lots of snide remarks from the other deviants, but none as fun as the one from Scot.

"Teacher's pet, I presume," he said with a wink.

I chuckled and blushed like a catholic schoolgirl.

He tossed around a hacky sack that he confiscated from one of society's problem children, then made his way to the back of the room where I was sitting.

He turned to address the class when he got to the edge of my desk. My gaze dropped to his denim-covered buttocks. I couldn't help it, his ass was very nice.

"Write a paper about why you'll never drive like a lunatic again."

He plopped his fabulous butt down beside me and grinned. "I read your paper from last week."

"Oh," I said, trying to keep my smile from spreading. "What did you think?"

He shook his head and raked his fingers through his dark hair, letting his hand come to rest on the back of his neck. "Was I that big of a jerk?"

"Well, let's see," I said as I leaned back in my chair. My sweats really were unattractive; as was the big oversized tee shirt I was wearing. I'd been doing yard work all day and hadn't even taken a shower. *Oh well, what can ya do?* I cleared my throat and continued. "You didn't listen to me when I explained about the bimbos swiping my bumper and that just made me madder. Then you wouldn't listen to me explain about why I didn't have my license on me and then, when I poked you, you didn't even scowl. Do you know how infuriating it was to me that you all but ignored me?"

"I'm sorry," he said with a smile. "But you're not supposed to get out of the car. You're not supposed to approach a cop and you're for sure not supposed to poke a cop in the sternum. I didn't know you from Adam and I hate to say this to you, but you looked like a freaked out meth-head."

"Nice," I bellowed and then chuckled lightly. "I was thinking more along the lines of white trash trailer hag."

"Well that too, babe. But your eyes were dilated, your hands were flailing in the air and I could barely understand your ranting, besides your car was a piece of shit and you were wearing boots – in the summertime. I assessed the situation and acted accordingly. Can you blame me?"

"No, I guess not." My fingers were digging into my thighs because I was having another convulsion after staring at his lush lips for too long. "How long have you been a cop?"

Half the class was still busy writing and the other half was snoring. Scot handed me his coffee, which I sipped from and then handed back to him. We were friends after all.

"I joined right after I got out of the Marines. That was twelve years ago."

"How long were you in the Marines?"

"Are you trying to figure out how old I am?"

"No. Well...sort of... I guess." I fumbled my words like I usually do under duress. "I was just wondering if you went to college, that's all."

"Are you going to think less of me if I didn't?"

"No."

I think that may have been a little white lie. I guess I'm somewhat of an educational snob. I worked hard to get my master's. My father and Bulldog were highly educated and my ex, of course, had a Ph. D. I'd never really considered dating a man without a higher education, so it was sort of a good thing that Scot was just a normal man, because I don't date!

"Then, no, I didn't go to college. I joined the Marines right after graduation and stayed in for six years. When I got out, I joined the force in San Diego and then moved to Portland a year later."

"Marines, huh?" That was impressive. I had to give him extra points for that one. The military turns out a few good men.

"Semper Fi, baby!" he chortled with pride.

"What the hell does that mean, anyway?" I asked.

My father was a Marine, as was Bull and they had never told me. Actually, my father told me to go look it up in the dictionary, but I wasn't *that* interested. Besides, I think it's Latin and therefore wouldn't be in the standard Merriam-Webster.

"If I told you, I'd have to kill you."

"Like I've never heard that before," I scoffed.

He stared me straight in the eyes, and then looked down at my mouth. It took him a moment to speak again, and suddenly his eyes widened with recognition of something. "Uncle Bull's a Marine, isn't he?"

"Well, well, aren't you a smart one? What gave it away? The hair or the bad-ass scowl?"

"Hair and demeanor, I guess."

"My dad and Bull were Marines together in Vietnam."

"That's impressive. I take it he's not really your uncle then," he chuckled slightly. "That explains the lack of family resemblance."

I smiled and watched as he stood up and stretched.

"What do you say we send the delinquent kids home early and go get a big, juicy burger?"

"I'd love to, but it's getting late and I have an early day tomorrow," I said without a hint of emotion on my face. Then I quickly yawned for good measure.

"You're the world's worst liar. What are you up to?"

"What?" I said as I too stood up.

"Hey," he yelled over his shoulder at the lackadaisical deviants. "Everyone go home and drive carefully. See you on Thursday."

I turned to grab my purse and straightened up when I heard the news that he would be instructing us again on Thursday. I stared at him and he knew what I was thinking.

"I'm not spying on you. Tony has a Little League tournament all week and asked me to cover." He laughed, slung his arm around my shoulder, and coerced me into telling him the truth. It took him awhile but I finally caved.

"Why did you say I'm the world's worst liar? I've got a perfect poker face."

"Too perfect," he said. "I know when you're lying when I can't read your face. It's your tell."

"My tell?"

"Yeah, every poker player has a tell and if you pay close enough attention, you can usually find it." He opened the door of his truck for me and motioned me to get in. It was nearly dark, the parking lot was desolate, and there was a light breeze blowing from the east, chilling me ever so slightly. Of course, the chill may have been from Officer King's hand on the small of my back.

"I can drive myself, just meet me there."

"Yeah, right," he all but lifted me into the truck. "You'll ditch me, and then tomorrow they'll find this Juan guy's body in a dumpster."

I dropped my jaw in indignation. "You're sooo..."

"Cute?"

I groaned and crossed my arms in front of my chest.

"Sexy?" he sneered.

I felt my loins flush with warm blood. "Infuriating!"

He snorted with laughter. "Same damn thing."

***

O'Riley's was abuzz with jolly men, sipping beer and tossing darts at the bull's-eye on the wall. Few women were in the joint, which made me glad Scot was by my side. The air was smoky and difficult to see through. I actually held my breath. We made it up to the bar without incident and Scot ordered a burger for himself and ordered it with half an onion on top.

I think I stared at the side of his face for too long, because he turned to me with a frown. "What? I like onions."

"Nothing," I said and began playing with my cocktail napkin. I knew I shouldn't drink, but I needed something to take the edge off. Those damn convulsions were killing me!

"I'll take a…Merlot please," I said daintily and the Hispanic bartender all but laughed at me.

"I got burgundy in a box."

"Chardonnay?"

"Chablis in a box."

"Corona?" I replied in surrender.

"My kind of girl," he winked and popped open a bottle of Corona. He didn't do the fancy lime trick, but it was cold and I had better things to ask him…like if he killed Walter and was trying to pin it on me.

I think Scot noted my nervousness because he wrapped his arm around me and planted a kiss on my temple.

Full-on convulsion. I shivered and downed half my Corona.

He leaned into me, like he was going to kiss me again, but instead he whispered in my ear. "Be cool. Where's your poker face now?"

I grinned, inhaled deeply, and casually looked around. I did a double-take and looked back over my shoulder. My stomach knotted and I felt vomit surge in my throat when I spotted Bull in the corner booth. He gave me a little wave with a look of absolute disappointment on his face and I knew I was busted. *Double damn!*

He motioned toward the bathrooms and I groaned before getting up and straightening my oversized tee shirt.

"I have to pee," I said to Scot and then sheepishly headed for the john. The bar patrons were all too busy playing pool and darts to notice that I was trembling and walking like a puppy with its tail between its legs.

"What the hell … Angela Reese Harrington …do you think you are doing?" Bull grabbed me by the shoulder and pulled me around the corner near the men's room, just past the pinball tables.

"Outside," I groaned and motioned toward my date at the bar. "Please."

"Oh, if I weren't in a crowded bar, I'd give you a spanking you'd never forget," Bull said, as he grabbed my upper arm and pulled me out the back door.

Before he had time to lay into me again about my stupidity, I started crying. Just like the time he took all my money from my piggy bank. Only this time I wasn't twelve years old and I didn't have my daddy nearby. "I'm sorry," I sniffled. "Geez, Bull. I just wanted to help. All those files you gave me were bullshit, weren't they?"

"And for this exact reason," he said and pulled me against his chest. I could feel his heart pounding against my breasts. His adrenaline must have been surging at that point. Before I could break away from his embrace, Scot came barreling out the back door.

"Who the hell are you?" Bull bellowed and bowed his shoulders like a rooster getting ready for battle. Putting himself between Scot and me.

Scot looked from me to Bull and then back to me as I tearfully cowered behind a man who could very well be confused with Denzel Washington. Recognition flickered in his gaze.

"Jesus Christ, Angie." He shook his head at me. "Don't scare me like that. Some guy told me a big burly dude just kidnapped you."

"He did." I sniffled again. "Bull, this is my friend Scot. Scot, this is Uncle Bulldog."

They sized each other up, then extended hands, and shook fiercely. I think Bull was causing him a great deal of pain, but Scot kept the grimace to a minimum for the sake of his own dignity.

"I don't want to know." Scot retreated back and shook his head. "This is no coincidence, I take it."

There was nothing I could say because if I said anything about the files, then I would be implicating myself and Bull.

"Do me a favor and take her home," Bull said, staring me down.

"What about my burger?" Scot groaned.

Bull rammed his hand into his pocket and then handed Scot a ten-dollar bill. "Stop and get one. It's on me."

"I'm not a little girl, Bulldog Mathers!"

"And I'm not taking no for an answer. Go!" He pointed toward the street.

"Fine."

There was nothing left to do but moan and walk away.

* * *

When Scot caught up to me, I was in tears again. I couldn't catch my breath and all I wanted to do was curl up in a little ball and cry 'til I could cry no more. I know Bull loves me like I was his own daughter, but I have a dad and sometimes I wish he were more of a friend than my second father. I wept against my hands until Scot twirled me around and comforted me in his arms. I then wept on his shoulder and left a puddle of drool on his red and yellow rugby.

"Sorry," I sniffled and wiped the excess bodily fluid from my lips. It could have been snot, it could have been tears. I don't think it mattered much. "I'm sorry you didn't get your burger."

"It's okay," he confessed with a chuckle. "I really don't like onions."

I laughed, almost too hard, then sniffled again, and wiped the tears from my eyes. We'd only made it half a block down the street. His truck was parked another block or two away.

"Want to tell me about it."

"It's a long story." I kicked a rock with my tennis shoe and stared at the ground. I don't know why I felt compelled to pour my heart out, but I did. "Reese—Uncle Bull, was my dad's superior in Vietnam. They were in the Marines together for two years, in the same platoon and then were sent overseas. Reese was single, carefree and after his mom died, Dad became his only family while they were stationed overseas. They did some wild shit, covert ops, stuff the government really didn't want anyone to know about and then during one op in Hanoi, Dad came back without Bull. He thought he was dead."

I sniffled again and our walking slowed to a crawl. The streets were fairly quiet by that time of night, but in downtown Portland, you can't hear the crickets and frogs. All that I could hear were faint sirens in the distance and the roar of the city buses. Scot pulled my hand into his and tangled his fingers with mine. It was nice. I looked up at him and felt the sting of tears again.

"Anyway," I said as I diverted my gaze from his intense darkened eyes. "Dad got sent home and I was born a year later. They named me Angela *Reese* Harrington in his memory."

I really began crying then because I love Bull like a father and I hated disappointing him, just as much as I hate disobeying him. "They found him in a POW camp not more than two weeks after I was born. He came home, spent twelve weeks in the hospital, and then moved in with us. He lived with us until I was nearly four years old. Then he married Priscilla, who had his son Eddie a year later. Eddie is the closest thing I have to a brother and Bull is more like a second father to me than a good friend of the family. He was there when I took my first step—when I lost my first tooth and when my marriage went to shit and everything in between." I sucked back my tears.

By that time, we were almost to Scot's truck.

"I could see how much he loves you." He brushed the hair from my eyes and planted a lingering kiss on my forehead. "He's worried about you."

He opened the door to his truck and held my hand as I got in.

My eyes burned from my tears and my stomach was growling. "You know who makes the best burgers this time of night?" I said once Scot eased himself behind the steering wheel. "McFadden's near the college."

"You're the boss." He pulled out and on the way to McFadden's I told him all about the great things that Uncle Bull and I used to do together. It was fun to reminisce about the past. The years prior to my failed marriage and my more recent foul mood.

The parking lot wasn't full, but the lights were still on. McFadden's stayed open late for the college students who pulled all-nighters and needed nourishment. Their burgers really were second to none and I hadn't had one since I graduated from Portland State. Being there again in that college atmosphere made me feel young and invincible, like I had no fear.

"Do you want onions?" Scot asked as he recited the order at the mahogany counter. By the way I was feeling toward my new friend, I should have ordered onion rings too. My lips were craving just a simple kiss. One smooch to tie me over until I'm done obsessing over my ex-husband and his Latino ho.

"Yes, please. Lots of onions." I smiled at the girl behind the counter and couldn't look at Scot. Vulnerable and emotionally unstable are not a good combination when faced with a sensitive man with perky lips.

Down, girl.

We took our seats at the far end of the restaurant, far away from the other patrons who were sipping beer and talking obnoxiously loud.

"Thanks for stopping," I said as I sipped my Diet Pepsi. "I'm sorry if I ruined your night."

"Ruined?" he scoffed. "You just made it that much better. It's not every day that I get to meet a real American hero. I'd love to sit down with him and hear his stories."

"I'm sure that can be arranged, just don't expect too much from his present life. I'm not sure exactly what he does, but I call him the invisible man."

"Oh."

I'm sure he got my meaning loud and clear.

"Now I'd love to hear your story. Did you always want to be a teacher?" he asked.

I shuffled in my seat and got comfortable. "Not really," I began, leaning back against the leather booth. "I love it, don't get me wrong, but it's not what I started out to do."

"Really?" He sipped his root beer. "I thought women were born knowing what they wanted out of life."

"What's that supposed to mean?" I said, clearly confused. Having a male friend was turning out to be such an unexpected learning experience.

He shrugged. I liked looking at his shoulders. They were broad but lean and he seemed humble about how magnificent his body was. I liked that too.

"It seems like every woman I meet already knows exactly what she wants from life – career, a house with a picket fence, two point five kids, a minivan with automatic sliding doors, and a padded bank account."

"Where do you meet your women? Mars?" I shook my head. "When I was young, I wanted to be a police woman, a doctor, an artist, a writer, a mom, a cowgirl, a quarterback and a beauty queen." I stopped for air and began again. "I grew up and grew out of most of it, but my senior year of high school I decided I wanted to be just like my dad, to have an awesome job, travel to interesting places and kick some serious ass."

"I thought your dad made wine."

"He does now, but for thirty years, he worked for the federal government in one capacity or another. FBI, DEA and about two or three other government agencies that no one knows about. My father was a consultant, an agent and the director of operations for the west coast."

"Holy shit!" Scot whispered. "And you wanted to be just like him. What happened?"

I smiled and felt more relaxed with Scot than I felt with most of my other friends. Lily and Chad excluded. They were the kind of friends I could be flatulent in front of or ask if I had things hanging from my nose when we were swimming. I talk openly with both Lily and Chad about sex, woman problems, and why I can't have an orgasm after I drink wine. Friends like them are rare.

"I got my bachelor's degree in Criminal Justice Administration and then went on to get my masters. After a couple of months at Portland State, my father was shot during a routine drug raid in Florida. I got scared, changed my major to political science, and shortly thereafter was swept off my feet by my ex. Ray was fairly controlling about what I did and I loved him so much that I became a teacher and gave up my dream of becoming an agent or an administrator like my father."

"Jesus," he said as he began pulling at his neck muscles. He wrenched them a couple of times before exhaling loudly and leaning back in his seat. "Brains and beauty. I don't stand a chance," he mumbled under his breath, but I heard it due to the lull between songs. "Wow. So, what now? It's not too late you know. You're only...what, twenty-nine, thirty?"

I chuckled lightly, enjoying the sincere compliment. "Try thirty-three." I shook my head. "I like teaching and, yeah, I think about changing careers often, but it's scary. I mean, what kind of a life could I give my children if I was always running off on missions to save the country?" I said it playfully, but it's the truth. Motherhood was my most pressing assignment, one that I was eager to try very, very soon.

"Children?" His brow lifted suddenly.

"Yeah," I said. "It's fine for a woman to have it all these days. I don't need to be married to have kids."

"Sure, you'd make a wonderful mom," he said and I felt my vagina contract slightly as I noted the seriousness in his eyes. "But alone?"

"Why not?" I said triumphantly. "They have a wonderful daycare at the high school and so what if I'm not married? Lots of women do it every day. Why not me?"

"They have a daycare at the high school. What the hell for?"

"For the young mothers who need daycare."

"Oh boy. That's really stupid," he said. "It's the same as telling these girls it's okay to have a baby without being married. Sure, go ahead, 'cause the government will pay for your daycare while you get your diploma.' How insane is that?"

The waitress dropped our burgers on the table and handed me a bottle of ketchup.

"Thanks," we both said together and then began digging in. I sank my teeth into the steamy burger because I was seething, but once I finished my first bite, I sipped some cola and let him have it.

"You just completely contradicted yourself, pal." I glowered and quickly took another bite. He couldn't respond because he had a mouthful. "You just said it was fine for me – that I'd be a good mom – and in the very next breath, you told me how you feel about unwed mothers. Geez, Scot, tell me how you really feel." I ferociously inhaled another bite and winced when I bit into the thick onion. *Ick!*

"Fine," he wiped his lips with his napkin. "Call me old-fashioned, but I think you're out of your mind. Bringing a child into this world should be something a husband and wife do *together*. They should be married, in love and completely devoted to each other and ready to give their kids the best life possible. I think single mothers are selfish people, to be totally honest. And unless you have vast wealth, it's financially impossible to provide a child with enough love, attention and comfort." He actually slammed his fist into the table. "What's your big ass hurry, anyway?"

I turned to hide the sudden onslaught of tears. "That's so unfair." I sniffled loudly. Unfair that I was not ready for a man like Scot King and even more unfair that he wasn't ready for me.

"What?" he said softly. "I was just being honest."

"I know," I moaned and then I convulsed again. *I think I adore you for it.*

***

There was no hand holding after dinner. He took me back to my SUV, said goodnight that sounded more like, "g'night." And I went home and cried. But I wasn't crying over Ray anymore, I was crying because no matter how hard I was trying to keep Scot at arm's length, "Celibacy Rocks" was becoming harder and harder to believe. That scared me more than prison did.

Five

Wednesday morning, I got up before the sunrise, did some calisthenics in front of the TV, and called Uncle Bulldog.

"Sorry about last night," I said as I sipped coffee in the early morning sun. I loved dawn, although I usually hated waking up early to see it. "What did you find out?"

"Nothing," he said with a twinge of frustration in his voice. "Juan's not our man. He was in San Diego at a Santana concert during that entire week. I know when someone's lying to me and he was straight up."

"Any other leads?"

"I got his bookie's name."

I knew better than to ask for more details. "Anything else?"

"No, except I did learn last night that the cops have your old street under surveillance and you were seen walking around the other day."

"Is that a crime?"

"No, but I'm sure they're still looking to nail you, so don't make waves. I think you need to take a step back and let me handle this. By the way, you ever heard of a guy named Isaac Moncrief?"

"No, who is he?"

"Don't know yet, but something odd is going on. Most of Dobbs' clients are bonded with some sort of collateral or at least a couple of contact people—you know, next of kin, someone with money or a house that he could go after if they skip town. Anyway, this Moncrief guy has none of it. His file is blank except for a copy of a company check for fifteen grand made out to the guy from Walter."

"Is there a picture?"

"None. Not even a current address," Bull said

I let it sink in but since I'm new at this stuff, all I could think to say was, "Weird."

Bull laughed and then got serious again. "Would you like to find out who he is?"

"Really," I shouted and planted my bare feet on the cold patio. "You'd let me do that?"

"Make some calls. I don't have a social on the guy, but the internet is a wonderful thing. I'll drop the file by this afternoon. Promise me you'll be careful and discreet."

Oh boy! I was so excited I felt like throwing up. "I will be! Thanks Bull. I love you!"

"Love you too."

"Uh, Bulldog," I said before he hung up. "Do you think I'd be a good mom? Even if I was single?"

"I think you're going to make a great mom and, down deep in my heart, I wish you'd wait before making any rash decisions. A lot could happen in a short time. You never know when you'll be standing next to someone and suddenly...wham -- it hits you like a bolt of lightning."

"You're the weirdest man I've ever met."

"And you're the most stubborn little girl I've ever met. Do me a favor and stay out of trouble. By the way, who's the cop?"

"Cop?" I said. "Oh, you mean Scot? How'd you know he was a cop?"

"Baby girl, I know more than you think," he chuckled. "Remember...wham. Like lightning."

And then he hung up without another word, leaving me to ponder his last remark.

***

I got right on the computer and the first thing I did was check for arrests on this guy Moncrief. I hit the jackpot and discovered that he was arrested for assault and battery on April eleventh just this past year. He was probably in the pokey, but he was worth looking into if it meant I could shine some light on another viable suspect other than myself. Personally, I felt the police were being a bit hasty with their snap judgment that me, a high school teacher with no criminal past, would actually sneak into my late neighbor's bedroom, and give him a few whacks to the chest with my own shovel. For one, I wouldn't be caught dead in that man's bedroom—let alone right after he showered because that would mean I would have possibly seen him naked and that, I'm sure, would have killed *me!*

I understand they were just doing their jobs, but come on!

Then again, the simplest answers are usually the right ones and the shortest distance between two places is a straight line. Still, makes me wonder what kind of brain-food these Detectives are eating, if any.

I showered quickly, just in case I had a visitor like I did yesterday.

Okay, here's the truth. How pathetic am I? I actually showered, put on makeup, dried and curled my hair and then paraded around wrapped in just my yellow bath towel for an entire hour just in case I had a visitor. I am so full of crap. I guess going an entire year without sex is pushing it because I felt completely out of sorts. And yes, it had been officially over a year since Ray left. Come to think of it, we hadn't really made love for the four or five months before he left. He always said he was too tired or hadn't taken a shower. Ah hell. I'm riper than I thought!

I fiddled on the computer some more and then the phone rang when I finally disconnected from the internet.

"Hey, I've been trying for an hour. Where you been?" Lily sounded distraught and abnormally bitchy this morning.

"I was surfing the net. What's up?"

"Dale was beaten to a pulp last night outside the Lloyd Center mall. He's up at the hospital with thirteen stitches in his face. The cops are all over Cherry Blossom and I just thought you should know." Her voice cracked slightly. "I know he was one of your favorite students."

That he was. Dale was like no other high school kid I had ever taught and my heart broke for him. My pulse also raced from anger and, of course, I was going to go see him.

"I don't think that's wise," Lily said after I told her I was on the way. "What if the cops... I don't know. Just don't go. Besides, you might upset him even more if he really thinks you killed Walter."

"Are you kidding? If he thinks I did it, then he'll probably want to thank me." I hung up on her and grabbed my black shorts. I threw on my old Joe Montana 'Niners jersey and ran to my car. Tears were streaming down my cheeks and my stomach was burning from all the acid mixing with my coffee. The entire situation was getting way out of hand.

***

When I entered the hospital, I noticed the gaggle of police officers between the elevator and the gift shop. All of them were in uniform but those weren't the scary ones. The scary ones were the ones I saw when I stepped off the elevator on the floor where Dale was being cared for. All eyes converged on me as I stepped off. Detective Smalls was the first to approach me.

"Miss Harrington," he said with a nod. "What brings you by?"

"Dale," I said and quickly tried to move around him. He was quick and cut me off before I could take three steps.

"Dale Green? As in Walter Dobbs' stepson?"

"Yep, same Dale Green. Can you please get out of my way now?" I said sternly and actually put my hand on his shoulder to push my way past him. Of course, that was a no-no and three more officers congregated on me and shuffled me to the waiting area, where I was practically shoved onto a very bright red couch. "Is he okay?" I growled to Detective Litchfield, who was my least favorite.

"He's going to be fine," he said warily. "What's your connection to the boy?"

"Do I need my lawyer?" I hissed and stood up. "Look, if you'd done your homework, you would know that I taught Dale at David Douglas. He was in my Law and Political Science class as well as my teacher aide for fifth period." I huffed snottily and hiked my black purse strap onto my shoulder. "Now if you don't mind, I'd like to see how he's doing." I shoved through the throng of plainclothesmen and headed straight for the nurse's station. My heart was beating wildly and I had to clench my fists a couple of times to relieve my anger toward the nice officers.

The blue-haired nurse kindly offered to take me to Dale's room. I glared over my shoulder at the detectives and followed the nurse into the room. The blinds were pulled and Madeline Dobbs was curled up beside her son in his hospital bed. I closed the door behind me and stepped toward the bed. That's when Madeline's eyes opened and she sat up. Her short brassy hair was sticking up on one side and her hideous makeup was smeared under her eyes. Not to sound snobby or anything, but Madeline Dobbs was a classless woman. She wore nice clothes, probably designer, but not the right style for her short stocky frame. Basically, she dresses as if she were a twenty-year-old model, when in fact she was forty-nine and very out of shape.

Madeline and I barely knew one another. She was a real estate broker and worked long hours. I think we had said hi to each other a couple dozen times in the past, but that was about it—well, except when she thanked me at graduation for being such an inspiration for Dale. She also thanked me for the nice letter of recommendation I wrote for him when he applied at Stanford. Not that he needed it. The boy was valedictorian and the brightest student I knew.

She sat up abruptly and wiped the sleep from her eyes. "Angie?"

"How is he doing?" I whispered and she got up and came to me.

"He's got a few broken ribs and some major bruising, but he's a strong kid. He'll bounce back." She looked weary-eyed at me, but didn't attempt to scratch my eyeballs out for killing her husband. She must have believed in my innocence. She sent me a weak smile and looked down at her bare feet. "This floor is freezing," she said and then looked back up at me. We stood in awkward silence for a heartbeat or two before she spoke again. "I know you didn't do it."

"I know I didn't do it too." I smiled back. "I know this is uncomfortable, but do you think we could talk for a minute?"

She nodded and then the door swung open, flooding the dark room with bright light. Detective Litchfield was seething and ordered a uniformed officer to extricate me from the room.

"What the hell was that for?" I shouted after I was clear out in the waiting room. I didn't want to disturb the entire floor with my ranting, but I was fairly angry.

"Do you really think you should be here?"

"I think I have every right to be here. More than you do in fact!" I shouted. Saliva actually flew from my mouth. "You don't know him. You didn't watch him grow up every day for five years! You didn't help him with his college application, or help him study for the SATs, did you?" I shouted again. "No! That was me, you stupid…"

I didn't get the rest of the words out because someone had covered my mouth with his huge hand. I whipped around, ready to give whoever was holding me a good slug to the mouth, but he quickly pinned my arms to my sides and hauled me to the nurse's station. "What the hell are you doing?"

"I was going to tell Dick-face over there," I glared over at Detective Litchfield, who was already on the phone. "That he's a stupid putz. Is that all right with you?"

"I think you need anger management classes, sweetheart. Isn't this what got you into this mess in the first place?" Bull said, and to my surprise, he looked like my lawyer, not the invisible man. I rarely see him in anything other than jeans and tight black tee shirts, but today he was wearing a very nice double-breasted pinstriped suit. The dark suit brought out the color of his chestnut eyes. Right now, those eyes were burrowing into my soul.

I inhaled deeply and then let it out slowly, methodically. "I'm just worried about Dale. There's no crime in that...and what the hell are you doing here? How'd you know I was here?"

"Instinct." He pulled me by the arm and took me into a private conference room. He shut the door behind him and turned back around to look at me. "You can't be in the same room as the widow. She's a suspect, you're a suspect, hell at this point, even the kid is a damn suspect. Don't you pay attention to what you teach in class?"

"You know what..." I growled, ready to explode again. The blood pounded behind my corneas. Then I remembered the night before and how distraught I felt after letting Uncle Bull down. I didn't want to put myself through that emotional anguish again, so I hugged him tightly and smiled. "You're right. Now, what are you really doing here?"

"I heard about the kid and when I came over to tell you, you were gone and your coffee pot was still on, along with your garden hose... by the way, you just about drowned your carrots and beets. I deduced you were already here."

"You're a scary guy," I said.

We shared a cup of coffee and a bagel with fruit schmear. I would have preferred a fat-laden Danish, but Bull wouldn't go for it. He really needed to learn to throw caution to the wind once in awhile. He filled me in on the meeting he had with Walter's partner, Dean Hopper. I got the distinct feeling that he didn't care for Dean Hopper, so it wouldn't surprise me if that guy ended up in the Willamette river fully clad in cement shoes. Although, I don't think Bull has as big a rage problem as I do. It's a good thing, because he could do serious damage with his size and well-defined muscles.

An hour passed, in which the detective pool thinned and I was allowed to visit with Dale, as long as Detective Jessup was in the room. Bull also remained in the room, so I didn't get to ask Dale all the questions I wanted to ask, but it was still fine.

"How's Ella?" I changed the subject from his injuries to his girlfriend. "Is she still going to San Jose State in the fall?"

He nodded, pain was clear in his eyes. I noticed a tear drip from the side, so I wiped it away with the corner of his sheet and sent him a small smile.

"Did you see who did this?"

Dale shook his head slowly. Again, I'm sure there was pain. "He hit me from behind."

The detective was fidgety, but he remained staring out the window. I leaned in closer. "There was just one? Did he say anything?"

Dale nodded again and then opened his eyes wide and made a conflicted face, straining his eyes toward Detective Jessup. I leaned even closer, so he could whisper in my ear.

"He thinks I killed Walter and he's coming back to get me and Mom."

I choked on my own saliva. Bull patted me between the shoulder blades until I could breathe again. Detective Jessup hurried to the bathroom to get me a drink of water and Dale took the chance to talk freely.

"I know you didn't do it," Dale said quickly once I sat back down. "This guy was serious, Mrs. Shirpa. I didn't tell the cops because he told me not to, but I'm worried about Mom."

Bull was looming over my shoulder and heard every word. He immediately grabbed hold of the bathroom doorknob and held it tightly, so Detective Jessup couldn't get out. "Hurry, he's gonna be pissed." He yelled to Dale.

Dale stuttered and hurried with his statement. "The guy said he knows it was either me or Mom, and he'd be back to get what was his. That's all he said and then he called me a bastard pussy and kicked me in the ribs. All I saw were his shoes because I was face down. They were tall leather boots, like a biker would wear and he was wearing frayed jeans. He smelled like cloves and skunk."

I could barely hear Dale's voice over the screaming and pounding from Detective Jessup inside the bathroom. The pounding got louder and then it just got quiet, like he was trying to listen in.

"That's all I remember. Please don't tell the police." Dale winced as he tried to sit up. "Please."

Dale had just shut up when two more detectives burst into the room. Bull let go of the bathroom door handle and stepped back from the door with his hands at his sides. Detective Jessup burst from the bathroom with his cell phone in his hand and began screaming obscenities in Bull's face. Big mistake. The guy had balls, but wasn't very bright.

Bull stared into his eyes and shrugged his massive shoulders in a menacing fashion. "Whatcha gonna do?"

Hell, I almost peed my pants and Bull wasn't even talking to *me*!

I was shuffled out of the room, along with Bull. But Bull wasn't shuffled, he was just asked to leave. Apparently, I didn't deserve that kind of respect. Perhaps they didn't fear me the way they feared my beefcake uncle.

Detective Jessup made a call on his cell phone, while Bull and I sipped coffee and waited to see what kind of crime he was going to attempt to charge us with. Probably interfering with a police investigation, or some bull-crap like that. Whatever it was, it wasn't going to be pretty and when he got off the phone he looked smug.

Bull's cell phone immediately blipped on his hip and he excused himself to hear what kind of trouble we were in.

Detective Jessup approached me from behind. "I don't know what you're up to, but you better stop before you dig yourself in deeper."

I turned to have a look into his smug brown eyes. He must be Italian because his hair was ebony and his skin was dark olive-toned. "I just wanted to make sure he was okay."

"I know you didn't do it," he said quietly, glancing over his shoulder. "Why don't you help me out and I'll see how I can help you out."

"No thanks," I replied confidently. "I have Bull."

"That's what you call him?"

"Actually it's Uncle Bull, but you can call him Mr. Mathers."

"This is a one time offer, Angie." He handed me his card, with a couple of numbers jotted down on it. "Call me when you want to cut a deal."

"I don't cut deals."

I know I sounded like a complete nimrod, but I was trying to stay snotty and standoffish, so I wouldn't start crying and beg for mercy.

Bull came back with a sullen expression. "The D.A. wants to see me. You need to leave and don't come back without me."

"Fine," I took his arm and walked down the hall with him. "What does he want?"

"He thinks they may have found their motive."

"Dale?" I said as I felt the color drain from my cheeks. We stepped onto the elevator and I pushed the button to take us down to the parking garage. "I just keep doing it to myself, don't I?"

"Don't worry. He just wants to chat." He kissed my forehead and took off through the parking lot.

***

For the rest of the afternoon, my mind was on what Dale had said. The beating was clearly connected to whatever happened to Walter and this thug had now poisoned my mind with the possibility that Madeline or Dale had actually done it. My heart couldn't bear the thought that Dale could do something like that, so that left me with Madeline. Clearly, it had to have been a crime of passion.

I called Lily to see if she'd made headway with any neighbors yet.

She answered completely out of breath.

"Are you doing it…again?" I asked.

She laughed and took a deep breath. "No, we're done now." She giggled a couple of times. "How about dinner tonight? It's supposed to be over ninety, so we could barbecue and dip our toes in the pool."

I loved how Lily referred to her three-ring blow-up kid's toy as a *pool*. Her sister's kids pretty much lived at her house during the summers, so Lily had bought it to keep them occupied while she tried to save me from going to prison.

"Can I bring anything?"

"Just Scot." She chuckled and I rolled my eyes at the photo I had of her in my room. It's actually a picture of the two of us at her wedding. She looked amazingly happy on her wedding day. Thinking back, I wondered if I was amazingly happy on my wedding day, or if perhaps I'd just been brainwashed by my infatuation with a tall black man with a perfect smile. Did Ray and I have anything in common? Did we share the same morals and values? Apparently not, because he cheated on me. *Hello.*

"How's is going with him, anyway? Is he a good kisser?" She made smoochy sounds through the phone. How obnoxious is that?

"Again, we're just friends," I said for the third time in three days. "Do you really want me to invite him?"

"Chad already did. I was just hoping you'd save gas and come together."

"Always thinking about the environment. How earth conscious of you," I sneered. "There's no use, Lily. He isn't into dating and neither am I. He's not ready and that's just fine with me."

"He's not ready?" She balked with a snort of laughter. "Is that the line he gave you? Jill left more than four years ago. He's ready. He just hadn't met his one true love yet...well, now he has, so you better just get over yourself and snatch him up before it's too late."

I listened, but couldn't believe what I was hearing. "He told me he wasn't into dating. I mean, that's exactly what he said.... even that first night at dinner. He was adamant about not wanting to get involved. I don't know where you get your information, but he's not interested."

"Oh, he's interested all right. Geez, Angie. I saw the way he was looking at you the other morning at breakfast. When he touched your hand, his face flushed and he couldn't stop staring at you. Wake up, and smell the chemistry. He's nuts about you!"

I sank down on my sofa and tried to catch my breath. "But I... I, you know... Ray and ... *Shit!*"

"*Ray?*" she said in her teacher voice, condescending and patronizing as hell. Unlike Lily, I usually only use that voice on my students; not my best friends.

"Ray's gone and, personally, I'm glad. Ray was a controlling jerk who kept you in his little bubble. I know you don't want to hear this, but I'm going to tell you anyway." She paused and I heard her suck in a deep breath. "Ray was not a nice man, Angela Reese, and I think you are beginning to see that now that the lust and obsession is wearing off. I know you don't want to admit it, but I think you liked him because he reminded you of..."

"Don't!" I yelled. "Don't you fucking say that to me ever again! I don't have some sick, latent passion for my father's best friend and Ray is nothing like Bulldog. Bulldog is nice and Ray was a complete jackass most of the time. Ray treated me like an object not a human being and I resent the implication that you think I was trying to marry... Oh you make me so damn mad!" I slammed down the phone and wept hard.

Half an hour later, after decimating about an entire box of Kleenex, I found my way out of the fog and began to realize that Lily might be partially right. I think I've always had a small crush on Bulldog. How could I not? Everyone probably has crushes on someone they look up to and Bulldog's been in my life... since forever. How could I have not seen this before now? They even look similar. He's tall like Ray, has very short hair like Ray. They are both of the same heritage. Damn, even their jaws are both hard-set and they both have amazing bodies and perfect smiles. They both have dominant personalities and tend to take the room by storm when they enter one and they are both the kind of men that women shamelessly swoon over.

I hate it when she's right! *Double damn.*

I was always my own person before I met Ray and fell in love. I had goals and a plan for my life and I did what I wanted, but in those nine years that I was with Ray, I gave up everything to be with him and that's not good. Not good at all. So, I have two choices now. I can wallow over my failed marriage, or realize that Ray did me a huge favor by poking a Spanish harlot.

I choose the latter.

When I tried to call Lily back, she wasn't answering, but I would just apologize at dinner. I'd decided to take the plunge and ask Scot if he'd like to pick me up before dinner. I called him on his cell and got him on the second ring.

"Like a date?" he asked after I explained that we'd be saving gas, which really made no sense because he lived closer to Chad and Lily than I did.

"I don't date," I said quickly. "Remember? Neither do you."

"Then if it's not a date, why would I pick you up?"

"Never mind. Did you find out anything about Madeline Dobbs yet?" I changed the subject rather smoothly, don't you think?

"She wasn't hurting for money. In fact she has more than he did and his life insurance policy goes to his son."

"Son?" I felt a knot form in my stomach. "What son?"

"I don't know. You didn't know he had a son?" Scot said and I clearly heard a siren in the background.

"Are you pulling someone over right now?"

"Just a trailer trash meth-head, I'm sure," he chuckled lightly. "No, not that. We just nabbed a guy for pulling a gun at a mini-mart cashier."

"Do you need to go?" I asked.

"No," he said through what sounded like clenched teeth. "I'm still being triaged. So, should I bring anything to dinner?"

I swallowed hard and paced around the living room in my bare feet. "Triaged?"

"How about chips and salsa. I make a *mean* salsa."

"What happened?"

"It was nothing. Just a flesh wound. I'll bring beer too, it sounds like you may need a few." He chuckled and then disconnected.

I felt my knees buckle. That's what my dad had said to me when he called from the hospital in Florida all those years ago.

"It's just a flesh wound, baby. Dad's just fine, Pumpkin." He had hung up and within hours was rushed in for emergency surgery because the bullet had dislodged and was en route to his lungs, or heart, or hell if I remember, it was all a big horrendous nightmare. Mom and I flew to Miami and spent two days in the hospital, taking shifts sleeping and waiting for him to wake up.

I managed to find my car keys under a couple of overripe avocados in my fruit bowl and the next thing I remember I was walking through the door of St. Peters hospital just a block or two from the Parkrose police station. I'd called every hospital in town and hit the jackpot as I learned that two officers had been brought in just minutes before.

When I found Scot, he was sitting on the edge of a gurney without a shirt on and a large white bandage was strapped to his upper ribcage.

He looked shocked to see me. "Angie?"

"My God. Flesh wound my ass!" I yelled and stayed right where I was, just outside the curtained area. I'd lied to the nice nurse and told her that Scot was my brother so she'd let me into the back room.

I felt as if my shoes had somehow congealed to the linoleum.

"Calm down." He put his hands up and stood up to walk toward me. I tried not to look at the blood, but that just meant that I was *forced* to look at his amazing pectoral muscles. They were less hairy than I had imagined, which was just fine. *Oh my!*

"Are you going to be sick?" he asked when he finally reached me.

"No!" I shouted and looked up at his face. "What happened?"

"It barely grazed me, really. It looks worse than it is."

My God, his arms curled around me and I not only convulsed, I think I felt a slight tremor of pleasure. I remained in his arms, curled up tightly against his naked chest and after a minute or two, I too wrapped my arms around his lean waist and inhaled his scent. He mostly smelled like sweat and antiseptic, but it was fine with me because he also just smelled intrinsically like my new friend. *Snap out of it, woman! Friend. He's your friend?*

I think we stayed wrapped together for a little over an hour because that's how long it felt and by the time he let go of me, my muscles were fatigued.

He leaned back and looked into my eyes with compassion and sensitivity. I think I looked at him with wanton lust and sex on the brain.

He smirked and playfully clipped my chin with his fist. "I'm fine."

"That's good." I stepped back and shuffled my feet. "I just came to tell you that chips and salsa would be fine. I'll see you at six." I turned and practically ran out of the emergency room.

***

Bull met me at my house around three, just as he promised.

"So, how did it go? Should I flee the country yet?" I stammered and opened the sliding glass door that led to the patio. We stepped into the backyard and flipped our sunglasses over our eyes. Just a couple of secret agents on a bright sunny afternoon, discussing whether or not I was being charged with aggravated murder.

"Not yet," he joked and then got serious. "A lot of what I'm about to tell you is classified." He cocked a brow and gave my hand a squeeze. "I want you to understand this is serious shit, Angela Reese."

"I know, I got this lecture from Officer King already. I'll be more careful."

"I can tell he cares about you," Bulldog said, watching my every move, I'm sure. My poker face was on!

"He said the same thing about you last night."

"He's a smart guy." He tweaked the end of my nose and bobbed his eyebrows. "Wham! Like lightning."

"Ohhh!" I grinned and then took the file he was handing me. "This Isaac guy was arrested for assault in April, that's all I found out so far."

"Keep digging. I have to go to Virginia for a couple of days, but I'll be in touch. If you hit a brick wall, just call me and I'll have some pros look it over. Whatever you do, don't give this information to your cop friend. I know he means well, but if he starts poking around on your behalf, we'll be creating quite the scandal. This needs to be clean and professional."

I swallowed hard and tightened my jaw.

"I didn't mean to make it sound like that. Geez, Ang. I'm not as bad as you think."

"I don't know," I teased. "Colombia, 1986?"

He has a better poker face than I do. "You did your homework?"

"Yep."

"Did you know your father was shot because of Colombia 1986?"

"No!" I said as my hands began to shake.

He took my hands and gave them each a little squeeze. "Do your homework!" He grinned and gave me a quick salute. "I'll be in touch."

Six

"Do my damn homework?" I mumbled under my breath while trying to apply mascara. It was difficult because my hands hadn't stopped shaking since Bulldog Mathers abruptly turned my stomach. I could never get a straight answer from either my father or Uncle Bull about anything in the past. They hemmed-and-hah'd and constantly had me running for encyclopedias or old newspaper clippings. I spent the majority of my high school life shacked up at the library going over old microfiche, learning more about the Vietnam war, Colombia, Guantanamo Bay, Cuba and anything else that happened regarding the United States security and other world news events. They were probably just playing with me so I wouldn't have time to date and therefore would stay a virgin until I was twenty. Well, it worked, damn them.

I tucked my blonde ringlets behind my ears and then shook my head at my reflection. "You big dope," I muttered and then wiped the blush off my cheeks. I had a great tan and I don't know why I was suddenly trying so hard. We were still just friends and that was actually good for me.

I changed out of my linen khaki trousers and into my faded denim shorts, threw on a black tank top and pulled my hair into a ponytail. *Best to be casual at a barbecue.*

I couldn't help the urge to go to the computer one more time and finish looking up all the gambling establishments in the area. If Walter had a bookie, then I would find that bookie

and then... Well, I don't know what I would do then, but
Bulldog was on his way across the country and I had three days
to play super spy. I jotted down the addresses to the local
casinos, racetracks, and even the laundromats just in case that's
really where bookies do their business. I saw that in a movie
once.

At nearly six p.m. I grabbed the bean dip I had made and
headed for Parkrose. Lily and Chad had a monster two-story
house fairly close to the fire station he worked at. He worked
four days on, four days off. His four days on were spent
entirely at the station. When he got an hour off here and there
to do grocery runs or get supplies, he would run home and see
Lily. Lily's mother had helped them buy the extra large family
home the year they were married. They work hard to make the
payment and are slowly furnishing it, room by room. They've
been married for three years and are by far the cutest damn
couple in the universe. Chad's not much bigger than Lily. I
think he might be five foot seven. His hair is almost the same
shade of red as hers, but he has more freckles.

"Hey," I said to Chad as I sheepishly walked up the steps
to their front porch. Hanging baskets of flowers lined the front
of their house and one of those old-fashioned swings was
hanging by a sturdy chain. Chad had recently re-stained the
deck to its former glory-, a deep chestnut color.

"Hey."

"Is she mad?" I asked as I handed him my bean dip and
bag of Fritos.

He bobbed his brows and held the door open for me. Lily
was on the couch, flipping through her giant cookbook.

"I need a good marinade for tri-tip," she said as she flipped
the pages. "Chad, will you please make our troubled friend a
margarita." She still hadn't looked up at me.

I dropped my black purse onto her wicker couch and
sighed. "Make it a double please," I said to Chad and then I
turned to Lily. "Are you mad?"

"Are you still in denial?" She flipped the book closed and
gave me a look of warning. "I'm not trying to bust your chops,

Ang. But you have got to get over this anger. I can't take it anymore. You're like a time bomb and I never know when you're gonna go off."

Chad makes a fast margarita. He interrupted us just as I started to cry.

"What is it?" Lily grabbed the frozen drink from Chad and shooed him away. "Is it that you're really scared to like this guy, or is it that you enjoyed the way Ray treated you? Because frankly, I think he did you a favor by divorcing you. Now I've got my friend back and, you know what, you've been smiling a lot lately. Despite being wanted for murder... you've been smiling."

That made me smile, even through my tears. "What if I'm angry because I messed up my life by marrying Ray. What if I'm so internally pissed off at myself for giving up my lifelong dream that I can't get past it? What if..."

There was a knock at the door and we all knew who it was. Scot peeked his head in the door and must have noticed my tears right away. "Oh, am I interrupting?"

"No," I brushed my eyes dry and stood up. "How's your flesh wound?"

He chuckled, then grabbed his side, and cringed. "Sore. Don't make me laugh!"

"Flesh wound?" Chad came back into the room with a grin. "You get shot again?"

"Again?" I felt the color rush from my cheeks. "What are you, some sort of pain junky?"

"No, I just have rotten luck."

We all moved from the front room into the kitchen. Chad helped Scot pour his salsa into a dish and then Scot did something that literally took my breath away. He dipped a chip into his homemade salsa and leaned over the counter, bringing the chip up to my lips.

I opened my mouth and closed my eyes as he fed the chip to me. It was spicy, yet sweet and had just the right amount of cilantro. It truly was amazing. I licked my lips and smiled at him and it was as if we were the only two people on the planet.

Lily, Chad and even the bright yellow kitchen were just blurs floating around me. I was in heaven for that brief moment.

"Good, huh?" Scot's deep voice brought me back to reality. "Too hot?"

I felt my cheeks flush as if someone turned on the heat full blast, but it wasn't the peppery salsa. "No, it's perfect. Very good." I brushed my sweaty palms on my shorts, grabbed my margarita, and followed Lily out to the pool. I flipped my sandals off and dipped my toes in while sipping from my drink. "I'm in big trouble."

"That good, huh?" Lily smirked and moved her chair closer to mine. "Now where were we? You don't think you're angry with Ray after all. You're pissed off at yourself for being such a spineless twit the past nine years."

"Something along those lines. Yeah."

"So what are going to do about it?"

"I'm going to cool my jets, get myself out of this murder wrap, find out who killed Walter and go from there. I have too much on my plate right now. One thing at a time." And I meant that. I wasn't sure what I wanted from my career anymore. I knew I wanted a family and I had a sneaking suspicion that I wanted to kiss Officer King… a lot! But, one thing at a time.

"So what's first?" she asked. "I think the neighbors are a dead end and besides the cops are all over that street. It gives me the creeps." She sipped from my margarita and handed it back to me. "How's Dale? Did he tell you anything?"

"Yeah, but this can't go past you and me. Mr. Bigmouth can't tell Scot anything about this. I promised Dale."

She nodded and widened her already big blue eyes. She nervously listened as I told her all about what Dale had said. "Weird," she said breathlessly and I had to agree.

"You can lay off the neighbors. In fact, there's nothing else you can do for me unless you want to help me find out who Isaac Moncrief is?"

"Sure," Lily said wearily, as we both turned to see the men hauling out the briquettes. "Who is he?"

"Some guy that Walter gave fifteen grand to a couple of weeks ago. That's all I know." I kept my voice quiet as I watched the fine hindquarters of Officer King bend over as he retrieved his beer off the patio. I bit my lip, tilted my head to the side, and actually moaned aloud.

Lily laughed like any best friend would do. "I saw that."

"You didn't see anything." I giggled and kicked my feet wildly to give her a little splash. "Attraction only goes skin deep. I was too attracted to Ray, so when and if I do ever start dating again, I'll be more careful about falling for good looks and debonair charm. I'm smarter now."

"But Scot's the one," Lily smirked. "I have a special feeling. You just keep on being his friend and one day when you're ready, it will just happen. You'll get struck with this overwhelming desire to jump into his arms... almost like being struck by lightning."

I choked on my margarita and narrowed my eyes on Lily. Lily doesn't run in the same circles as Uncle Bulldog and I doubt that they are in cahoots together to get me married off. Lily doesn't need anyone to cavort with in that department; she's doing just fine on her own.

But in all honesty, Lily's a very smart woman.

"Ladies," Chad yelled from the other side of the yard. "Talk a little louder, we can't hear you."

And that set us all into a fit of laughter. Scot came and sat down next to me when Lily jumped up to make marinade. He kicked off his Teva sandals and flicked the cool water with his toes. Attraction is a strange thing. Sitting there beside Scot made me realize that I was attracted to him on a multitude of levels. It's not skin deep with him. Sure, I wanted to kiss him and see him naked, but I was also attracted to the smell of him and the way I felt completely comfortable with him. I was attracted to the way he crinkled up his nose every other minute and that his left cheek dimpled slightly when he laughed at me. And speaking of laughing, I was awfully attracted to the fact that he laughed a lot. In fact, I loved having a new friend like

Scot because he made me smile, despite my messed-up trouble with the law.

"Did you happen to find out anything about Walter's son?" I shaded my eyes with my hand and gazed at his jovial smile.

"I got shot," he chuckled. "I haven't really had time to find out who he is and run him through the system, but I will." He sipped from his cola and eyed my margarita like it was "crack" in the eyes of a junkie.

"Do you want me to make you one?"

"Can't," he said, "pain killers. But it looks good." He dipped his chip into the salsa and took a bite. I watched his jaw clench as he chewed and then realized that I'd been staring at his mouth for way too long. "You want some of this?"

"Umm," I stuttered. What exactly was he talking about? His lips, or more chips and salsa. I licked my dry lips and smiled. "Sure."

He bent toward me and lifted another chip to my lips. I leaned forward to take the chip in my mouth and again the world around us disappeared. I was floating. Perhaps I'm allergic to cilantro because I felt high.

"What's in this?" I asked after swallowing my bite. *LSD perhaps?*

"The usual and then something extra special." He winked and I sighed.

"Do you want to tell me what happened now?"

He shrugged and gingerly rubbed his side. "I got shot!" He bobbed his eyes at me and grinned. I can't believe that I didn't jump into his arms the first time I ever saw him. That little waitress at the Crab Shack was right. Scot was adorable.

I rolled my eyes at him and he sighed in resignation.

"The guy wasn't cooperating and I think I may have pissed him off because he shot me." He chuckled again and downed more cola.

"Do you ever plan on getting off the streets so bad guys won't be inclined to shoot you?" I had to ask because he's a friend and if he becomes more than a friend, I don't want to have to kill him for getting shot at.

"I already did that for a year. I hated it and now I'm back on the street."

"You hated what?" I was intrigued beyond a doubt now. I knew Scot was a good cop, but I just figured that every cop had the ambition to become detective someday. To get to wear street clothes and give up pulling over trailer trash meth-heads.

"I hated being Detective King and working side by side with that asshole Detective Smalls."

"Oh. Homicide huh?"

He shrugged again. "Litchfield isn't too bad once you get to know him and Jessup is a hell of a guy, but Smalls just pissed me off every other minute and I was bored out of my mind. People think there's a lot of murder cases, but honestly, there aren't. Not in Portland anyway. Most of the time, it's drug related and we catch the guy within a day. No mystery there. I like the street. Everyday is different and I feel like I'm making a difference." He looked at me with those big brown eyes again and I couldn't help but smile even wider. "And yeah, I get shot at every once in a while."

I had nothing to say to that, other than, "Wow." I was surprised and rather turned on just thinking of how sexy he looks in his uniform.

A minute passed before he reached out and grabbed my hand. I liked the way he entwined his fingers with mine and held it tightly, but I wasn't expecting to be pulled into the pool. Not that it's really a pool, but it was filled with about a foot of water, so I did get completely drenched. As did Scot because he was practically laying on me after he slipped and fell in with me. I sputtered some water from my lips and grinned.

"Serves you right," I quipped.

"I thought you looked hot!" He leaned his head down and for a moment… one alarming moment, I thought he was going to kiss me. He didn't. He just rubbed his forehead on my chest to get the water out of his eyes. His arms were straight, holding his chest above mine and he didn't look all that eager to get up. "Am I squishing you?" he asked playfully and lowered his face again. His lips were a mere inch from mine when he stopped and looked from my lips into my eyes. I felt as if they were as wide as saucers. *Oh my God*! My nipples were puckered under my tank top from either the cool water or the sensation of having a man's body against mine after all this time. Whatever the cause, it was fine by me. Celibacy or no celibacy, being squished by Scot King was wonderful.

"No," I whimpered and tried to inhale. I failed miserably and then fear kicked in as his lips parted slightly and they got even closer to mine. "Please don't," I gasped.

"Really?" he said, easing back a couple of inches. "Wow." He rolled over onto his back beside me in the water. His head rested on the edge of the inflated rim and he rubbed his ribs. "I probably shouldn't get this wet." He started to get up and then extended his hand to me. I took it and then nervously pulled my tank top away from my breasts.

"Sorry," I said.

"No, it's okay." He stared at his feet. Head down. "I just think I know how to read people pretty good, and well..." He looked up and right into my eyes with a serious expression. "I was sure you wanted me to kiss you."

Poker face!

He chuckled. "So you *did* want me to kiss you?"

"I didn't say that," I said as I turned to grab another chip. I dipped it in the salsa and chomped on it so I wouldn't have to talk anymore.

He stared at me, fixed his damp hair with his fingers, and then moved closer. My toes were being stepped on, but it was bearable because he smelled delightful.

I prayed that Chad and Lily would magically appear and save me, but that didn't happen.

I finished swallowing and narrowed my eyes on his. "You wanted to kiss me?"

"I think we've already established that I just tried." His fingers were now tickling down my bare arm. I had goose bumps from the cold water and when he touched me, they enlarged ever so slightly and began to pound under the surface of my skin. Like a little army of sensations pleading for more.

"Why?" I asked, trying to keep my heart from leaping out of my chest. "I thought we were friends."

"We are friends, but you wanted me to kiss you." He said, his voice deeper than normal. His breathing was also slightly altered.

"But you must have wanted to kiss me too, or you wouldn't have tried."

"We could do this all night." He groaned and rubbed his fingers along the back of my neck. A jolt of tiny prickles raced up my spine. I hadn't had a man's hand on my neck in *sooo* long. My neck was alive with sensation. One big erogenous zone informing my other erogenous zones that celibacy sucks!

"We could," I said slowly. "Or you could just admit that you wanted to kiss me. That perhaps you wanted to kiss me yesterday too."

"I don't date. I told you that, so why would I want to kiss you?" His hand was still hot on my neck and his breathing grew intensely labored as he leaned forward and teased me… tormented me with his salsa breath. "You're so…"

"Cute?" I chuckled to break the moment of sexually frustrating hell I was in. "Sexy?"

"I was thinking more along the lines of stubborn." He grinned and finally moved away from my lips once we heard Lily and Chad's voices growing nearer. "But yeah, that too."

"I found the perfect marinade recipe," Lily said with pride, but my God, they could not be more obvious if they tried. Her sundress was buttoned incorrectly and he still had a bit of a leftover chubby.

Both Scot and I laughed and turned to hide our amusement. We didn't need to embarrass our friends. They were attempting to make a baby and nothing is more beautiful than that. Besides, Scot and I had our own little episode to keep quiet.

I made my way over to Lily, and Scot watched me the entire time. I felt his eyes hot on the side of my face as I helped Lily set the patio table with plates, flatware, and condiments.

Dinner conversation consisted of anything and everything to do with how I was still in trouble with the law. Scot was fairly quiet and was practically nodding off at the dinner table. I blamed that on painkillers and after Lily and Chad cleared the table, I moved over one chair to sit beside Scot and quickly learned there was something else to be blamed on Vicodin.

"Are you okay," I asked, but he clearly wasn't.

"I'm sorry," he said, looking at me and trying to focus on my face. He was either just coming down, or had just popped a couple more. I'm not an expert on narcotics, so I didn't have a clue. I just knew that he was loopy. "I shouldn't have tried to kiss you. It's the drugs. They make me all funky and loose. I hope I didn't offend you." He sipped some water, but kept his eyes locked with mine.

"It's fine," I said and turned to escape his gaze. I was lying of course, so I was sure my poker face was once again going to give me away. The truth of the matter was that it wasn't fine. It blew me out of the water and... *wait a dag-darn second!* Vicodin ingestion can't be to blame for yesterday's attempt, although it wasn't a very good attempt. I mean, I think he was going to kiss me, but perhaps I was imagining things. "You're not thinking straight, because if you were thinking straight, it would never have happened because we both know that neither of us want any sort of romantic involvement, so it was just the drugs. I understand. It's fine." I blabbered endlessly, and before I could finish, his eyes had closed again.

"Scot," I said with a little nudge to his arm. "Hey."

"Bed!" he yawned. "Take me to bed, please."

I felt my vagina twitch and it felt like someone had a death-grip on my throat. The lawn chair tipped over and smacked the patio as I stood up abruptly. Scot's eyes widened and Lily and Chad came running to see what the ruckus was about.

"Geez, Ang." Lily picked up the chair and stared at me. "Help me with dessert, will ya?"

"I think someone should take Scot home. He's in need of his bed." I looked at Chad, and he quickly volunteered.

***

I couldn't sleep that night after ingesting some of Lily's homemade strawberry shortcake. It wasn't the indulgence of dessert that was keeping me up, it was the fantasies I was having about driving over to Scot's house and molesting him while he was comatose. Okay, so that fantasy is wrong on so many different levels.

The next morning, I actually got out my running shoes and took a two-mile run around my quiet neighborhood. I loved having the majority of the summer off. Most other folks had to get up and hurry to their jobs, which meant the neighborhood was quiet most of the day. Kids went to daycare, so the screaming was at a minimum, and for the second day in a row, I had woken with the sun. Wow, I felt as if I'd climbed out of a depression and was actually excited to get out of bed everyday. Tonight, I knew I got to go to Road Rage class and see Scot. Yippee! And I also got to do some super spy investigating to find out who this Moncrief guy is and why Walter gave him money on the sly. I knew Dean Hopper wasn't going to help me, well, unless he didn't know he was helping me! They were partners and I knew Walter frequented the Dancing Beaver. My money would be on the probability that Dean also visits the skanky establishment.

Wow, I'm a genius when I'm out of breath!
***
To my utter surprise, the Dancing Beaver was open at nine a.m. I guess just in case men need a quick lap dance on their way to the office. *Oh my God. I have never seen such big boobs.* I diverted my gaze away from the naked girl on stage and headed straight to the bar.

"Hey," I yelled over the horrendously bad music. It was dark, so I couldn't even tell if the bartender was a man or a very butch woman. "Do you know a man named Dean Hopper? Or Walter Dobbs perhaps?"

The person behind the bar stood up from their hunched over person and surprisingly that didn't help me much in my quest to designate a gender.

"No." *It* pointed toward the back area where the lap dancing probably took place. "Ask the girls. I'm new."

"Okay, thanks." I knocked on the bar with my knuckles, acting like I knew what I was doing. Inside, my stomach was knotted and I was berating myself for leaving home without my latex gloves. I swallowed hard and entered the back room. Tall velvet curtains cordoned off a section of the back area, tied up with thick gold tassels. That's where I found six or seven young girls sipping coffee. Surprisingly, they were all dressed. Some in ripped jeans and camisoles, some in sundresses and one was wearing a fuzzy pink bathrobe.

"Hi," I said as I approached. "I was wondering…"

"Hey, he said he wasn't married." One of the girls stood up and backed up a few paces. *Okay!*

"No," I actually chuckled lightly. "I was wondering if any of you know a man named Dean Hopper."

They exchanged glances and since I'd taken my hands out of my jacket pocket, they looked more relaxed.

"Sure," a small brunette said quietly. "I know Dean. Is he dead now too?"

"No, I just need some information."

Okay, so I'd only seen things like this go down in movies, but I thought it couldn't hurt for me to flash a couple of twenty dollar bills.

It seemed to work!

"Dean comes in on Friday nights usually. Sometimes he brings a couple buddies. Big guys, lots of hair and leather."

That's not quite what I was looking for, but I sat down beside the brunette and coaxed her along by asking specifics. "Have you ever heard of a guy named Isaac Moncrief? Maybe he came in with Walter a few times?"

A tall redhead, the one wearing the bathrobe leaned across the table. "Sheila used to dance for Walter, but we haven't see her in weeks."

"No!" I gasped. "What's Sheila's last name?"

No one responded and even the brunette got suddenly tightlipped and I figured these women to be pretty loose... if you catch my drift.

"Please. This is important and I'm not a cop. I just need to find this Isaac guy and if your friend is missing, maybe she needs help."

Three of the girls got up and huffed off. Two more sipped their coffee while narrowing their eyes at me and the brunette squirmed in her seat before speaking.

"Sheila's not her real name. Her name is Laura Moncrief and she lives... or used to live in the apartment building behind Wal-Mart. Number ten I think it was, I think Isaac is her son."

Wow, holy hell, and oh my God. I am good!

I handed the girl the three twenty-dollar bills. "I can't thank you enough." And then I wanted to give her more advice, like stop dancing for a living and get a real job or finish school. When she smiled, I wanted to tell her to brush her teeth and stop using meth. But, I didn't.

I was so high on my success and proud of myself that I stopped for a mocha at my favorite coffee bistro and trembled when I realized that I still knew nothing. I needed Bulldog, or at least a cute cop who once wanted to kiss me... probably twice.

When I got home, I called Scot's cell phone, only to get a message. Three hours passed in which I watered my garden, weeded my flowerbed and stared at the dirty screens on my windows and contemplated cleaning them. Three hours and I hadn't heard a word from Officer King, so I called again, got his voice mail again and called the station.

"Can I please speak to Officer King?"

The nice receptionist put me on hold and then I was connected to another officer.

"Can I help you, ma'am?"

Let's see, you can help me by actually connecting me to the officer whom I was calling. I wanted to shout, but I didn't. My father told me to play nice with the police, so I behaved.

"Actually, I was wondering if I could speak to Officer Scot King."

"Is this an emergency?" he asked.

"No, but he gave me his card and said if I was serious about kicking my meth habit, he'd point me in the right direction."

When nothing else works, lie!

"Well, Officer King is on leave for a week or so. I can certainly get you in touch with the right people."

"No thanks." I groaned and hung up, hoping the cop-shop didn't have caller I.D.

"Double damn." I growled out loud and tried his cell phone one more time. Voice mail again, so I hung up and sulked for an hour.

Sitting around feeling sorry for myself was not helping my legal woes, or my mood, so after another hour of not hearing from Scot, I got worried and began pacing and then I just got mad and grabbed my car keys, ready to let him have it at my biweekly road rage awareness class.

To my utter surprise, Scot was not our instructor this evening. It was a middle-aged officer with a really bad toupee. You would not believe what we did in class.

Seven

I was really starting to get freaked out after class, so I took the liberty of calling Scot one more time and then again when I got to the freeway exit that led to his neighborhood and then I just gave up and decided it was best to see for myself that he was still alive and kicking.

By the time I pulled up into his driveway, I was so angry and emotionally freaked out that I had to sit there in my SUV and get a handle on my emotions. I'd been so used to flying off the handle about the littlest things this past year, that I really needed to find a new way to handle my anxiety. Only, I was completely unsure of why I was so angry, and my angst had me worried that perhaps I liked Scot a little too much. "He got shot, so what?" I shrugged and relaxed my white-knuckle grasp on the steering wheel. "It was just a flesh wound and the bullet wasn't lodged in his spine like in my father's instance. Why am I so freaked out?" I looked up and saw a shadow move behind his front curtain. "And why am I talking to myself in my car? What a dufus I must look like." I shook my head and got out just as Scot opened his front door and peered out at me.

"You coming in, or are you going to sit out there talking to yourself all night?" He gestured me in and I felt my lips tug upward.

I got out and entered the house. I shut the door behind me and wandered into the living room where he was sprawled on the couch, munching on Doritos and drinking hot tea.

"You okay?" I kicked past the empty pop cans and sat down in the recliner across from him. He looked completely disheveled and was still in the same clothes from last night. A pair of denim shorts and a button down blue cotton shirt with a Hawaiian print around the middle. His feet were bare and I was sure he was in pain because he winced about every other second. He turned off the television and finally looked at me.

"What's up?"

"I was... I mean... you... hell," I said while he tried desperately not to laugh at me. He failed miserably and clutched his side. A bottle of Vicodin was directly in front of him, but it still looked full. "What? You're not taking them anymore?"

He groaned and rolled onto his good side. "They make me sick and I can't drive."

"I heard you're off for awhile."

"Yeah," he said. "Doctor's orders."

"But you just had to overdo it last night, didn't you?" I was acting like my mother, God forgive me. I got up, carried his empty pop cans into the kitchen, and surveyed the mess. "You want some dinner?"

"You cook?" he asked, cuddling under the blanket I'd thrown over him. "Sure."

I got to work, busying myself in the kitchen, which brought back all sorts of horrific memories of being married. Don't get me wrong, not all my memories were horrific. But as the fog of depression began to lift around me, I started remembering that life with Ray was no picnic.

I managed to rummage up sort of a pasta primavera dish with lots of peppers and plenty of onions.

I handed him a plate and after half an hour of silence, I finally spoke. "I was worried."

"I could tell." He grinned and forked some pasta after saying thanks in a very sincere tone. "You called, what... eleven times, but only left one message. Geez, Ang, you're worse than my mother." He paused between mouthfuls. "This is awesome," he murmured with a smile. "I told you, it's just a flesh wound."

"I know, but I can't help it." I sat down and fumbled with my words before telling him exactly how my father had been shot. Since he also thought highly of my father and uncle Bulldog, I told him what Bulldog had said about the Colombia incident being connected.

"Your entire family is full of intrigue. Maybe I'll have to marry you after all."

He said it with a quick smirk, but then almost choked on his red pepper and immediately looked at me with a startled expression, as if he couldn't believe that he actually said that aloud.

I chose to laugh it off, and the thought of jumping into his lap did cross my mind. But hold on there for one damn minute. We were friends. Friends who desperately wanted to kiss each other, but we were friends just the same. I am not ready! I am undeniably not ready to start a relationship with a man who could very well possibly be *the one*.

Silence ensued for a few short minutes before he placed his fork on his empty plate and leaned back onto the couch. "Thanks, I owe you one."

"How long are you off?"

"A week, maybe two. The bullet shredded some muscle so I'm not supposed to strain too much."

"That sucks," I said as I carried his dish to the kitchen. While I was there, I decided to do his dishes and wipe down the countertops so as to not attract any more flies.

"I missed you in class. The new guy is a bozo and we actually had to do a couple role-playing scenarios. What a joke." I continued telling him all about the skits we performed as a class and even laughed at myself a couple of times. He was fairly silent, but I was inclined to keep talking because I was pretty nervous. Nervous about many things, but mostly nervous because I felt completely at ease in his kitchen. I even knew where everything was. Which is odd, because even in my mother's kitchen I have to open the drawers and cupboards a number of times to find what I'm looking for. Scot's kitchen was set up just like mine at home. We even kept our dish soap in the same spot. Ahhh. Just imagining Scot doing dishes sent me into a fit of dizzying lust.

His eyes were closed when I finished the dishes. The stereo was tuned to a light-rock station, but I could still hear his heaving breathing over the crooning of Phil Collins. I sank down in the recliner and just watched the rise and fall of his chest. It was mesmerizing, but after a couple of minutes, I just felt ridiculous staring at his unconscious body with a sappy grin on my face. So, I left him a cute-friendly note on the coffee table, pulled the blanket up around his chin, and eased down to kiss his forehead. I kid you not, he has the smoothest, silkiest forehead I have ever kissed—like a baby's bottom. I had to forcefully extract my lips from his skin because it felt so good.

The entire way home, I tried reciting my mantra a number of times to delude myself into thinking that I wasn't interested in Scot King. CELIBACY ROCKS! turned into *celibacy rocks?* Which turned into celibacy rocks... and so forth. It was becoming harder and harder for me to stay strong. But, alas, I just wasn't ready.

***

Friday morning I was again up with the sun. I had coffee, some Kashi cereal and soymilk and then I went for a long walk. I knew that Bulldog would be back in a day or two, and I had lots to do. Yet I was still in need of some pertinent information. I had a connection between Isaac Moncrief and Walter Dobbs, but I still had no idea why they were connected, unless of course, he was being blackmailed. Yes, that was entirely possible because he was probably boffing this dancer named Sheila, and her son found out that he was married and decided to take him to the bank... literally. Okay, so it's thin, but it's all I have to go on.

Blackmail could work, so I did the unthinkable and called Dean Hopper at his office.

Except I forgot what name I had previously used, so I botched my introduction.

"This is…um, you know, that reporter's secretary from the Oregonian."

He chuckled wildly and then got stone cold serious. I heard his heavy breathing and I almost lost bladder control. "Funny thing about that. The Oregonian ain't never heard of a reporter by the name of Ron Trump."

I snapped my fingers. That was it. Chad had pretended to be Mr. Trump.

"Oh, well. I think we both know that I'm just trying to find out who killed your partner. I'm a detective." I lied through my teeth and I don't really know if he bought it or not, I just heard him exhale loudly. "I've been hired by Madeline Dobbs."

"Oh," he said slowly. "What is it that I can do for you then?"

I was leery, but continued anyway. "Isaac Moncrief."

"What about him?"

"Do you know him?"

"Course I do."

"Well?"

I wasn't expecting this to be so easy. *Wow, I'm good.*

"And, what can you tell me about him."

"Nothing," he said impatiently. "What kind of detective are you?"

Or not!

"The one who asks questions." *You moron.* "When was the last time you saw Mr. Moncrief?"

"You can't be insinuating that Isaac killed his dad?"

I almost dropped the gosh-darn phone. *Crap!*

"No sir," I stammered. "I just need to have a word with him."

"He hangs out at Tino's, if he's not on the road already."

I hung up and sat down hard on my bed. My towel was still tightly wrapped around my head, but it fell to the floor when I put my head between my legs. I needed oxygen and blood to return to my brain and quick, or I was going to pass out!

***

I wasn't stupid enough to travel to Tino's bar without an escort, so I took Lily.

"This place gives me the creeps," she said snottily as we pulled into the lot. Twenty big hogs were lined up out front, but we could only see two or three bikers milling around outside.

"We haven't even gone in yet. How can you say that?" I turned off the ignition and had second thoughts when I noticed the tall boots that the bikers were wearing. "Shit. Biker boots." I gasped and grabbed Lily by the elbow when she attempted to get out.

She looked at me funny, which she does often because I'm an idiot. "What?"

"Dale said the guy who beat him was wearing biker boots, tall leather boots like a biker would wear." I sat in silence and listened to the pinging of the car. Lily shut her door and the pinging stopped. "It makes sense, don't you think? If Isaac thought Madeline or Dale killed his dad, then of course he'd be angry and he'd want revenge. But what would he be coming for that he thought was his?"

"The family photo album?" Lily giggled. "The good china? His grandfather's urn?"

I snorted with laughter. We had a good laugh about it and got over our case of the nerves really quick by doing so.

"Do you have a camera phone?" I asked. I'd never understood the need to own a cell phone that takes pictures, but suddenly it sounded like an ingenious idea.

"What?" Lily laughed. "You're going to take pictures of boots and see if Dale can identify them."

"Bad idea?" I opened my door with a smirk.

"Ridiculous."

We stood side by side, watching the front door of Tino's open and close as bikers came in and went back out. There was no way in hell we were going to fit in with this crowd. We'd be eaten alive, so we went to get Mochas.

We spent the rest of the day sitting by the "pool" and discussing our theories.

Lily's theory was the best. She said that Walter probably had some money stashed away in the house. Going after that sounded like something a sleazy guy would do, so we talked about how we could approach Madeline—the woman whom I could think most likely killed the man. *How the hell do we do that?*

"Carefully," I said. "I think we should wait for Dale to get out of the hospital and then you should go over with flowers. She knows we're friends and he was in your English class, so she'll just think you're being kind," I told Lily as I dabbled my legs with cold water.

"And then what? I just ask her if she has a wad of cash lying around. Or should I ask her why her husband was still messing around with the mother of his kid?"

"Good one," I said. "Ask her that."

"I was kidding."

"Yeah, well so was I. Sort of."

We laughed and laughed, then my cell phone rang, and we stopped.

"It's Scot," I said as I held it up to show Lily. I didn't know if I should answer it.

"Answer it."

"Okay." *I am such an immature goober.* "Hey," I smiled at Lily and she grinned back and rolled her eyes. "How are you?"

"Back on drugs, so I'm actually functioning. You want to have dinner?"

"Umm," I made a face at Lily and mouthed "dinner?"

She nodded vigorously and retreated from my side.

"Sure," I said. "I have some things to check into so how about seven? Pizza?"

"I was thinking of making you a steak. Do you like steak?"

"I do," I replied. "Can I bring anything?" *Oh lord, I am so not ready.* My palms were sweating, as were my temples, but then again it was almost ninety-degrees out.

"Just a smile," he said and then he hung up.

I didn't need any extra encouragement in that department.

***

Lily agreed to take flowers to Dale, but since she didn't want to go to the house where Walter was murdered, she agreed to take them to the hospital and see what kind of information she could get out of him or his mother. I trusted that she wouldn't fail on her mission and I took off toward Scot's house, after jotting down some notes in the little black notebook that I'd bought for a very special occasion. The occasion was that I was single-handedly going to find out who killed Walter Dobbs.

I know I was being delusional, but even if my name was suddenly cleared, I was already in too deep. I knew too much and now had a sick urge to go all the way.

***

My only thought as I pulled into Scot's driveway was whether or not I was going to survive the night without being kissed.

"Hi," I said as I handed him a bottle of Harrington Merlot. "I know you can't drink yet, but I had to bring something." I stepped inside and watched his eyes light up with a sincere smile. I inhaled a couple of times and moved around the counter. "It smells delicious." He already had salads on the table, along with a couple glasses of iced tea complete with lemon slices floating on top. "What changed your mind about the drugs?"

"I just got some prescription strength Ibuprofen instead."

"I guess I don't ever have to worry about you having a drug problem." I snickered and when his hand caressed the small of my back, I stopped, turned, and looked up at his lazy-eyed expression. His eyes seemed to be narrowed in on my lips again and as he leaned forward, I felt another rush of tingles flood my veins. He stopped just millimeters from my lips and smiled.

"Are you hungry?"

I swallowed hard and blinked. "Yeah." But I didn't move. I should have moved away, far away, but I didn't. I grasped the countertop and held on for dear life. I remember closing my eyes, parting my lips, but then nothing happened.

"You're not ready," he said, like the wind against my lips. I could almost feel him when he spoke.

He was torturing me. "I'm going to do this, but I know you're not ready."

I blinked and begged to differ with my narrowed eyes.

He kissed me then. Oh my God! I thought his forehead was magnificent, but his lips were even more glorious than I could have imagined. It was like coming home. And he hadn't even touched me with his tongue yet. His hand moved up to cradle my face. I think I may have moaned and then he stopped.

He backed away, looked right into my eyes, and said, "Yep, just like I thought. You're not ready."

"What's that?" I dizzily blinked a couple of times.

"You're still pissed at me for arresting you, aren't you?"

I didn't know how to respond. Honestly, I thought he was talking about why I didn't think I was ready and he was completely off on another tangent. One that I had completely forgotten about. "No," I said clamping my mouth shut. "I guess I haven't."

Ohhh. I was seething, but I remained in control. Kudos for me!

"You will be," he said rather smugly.

I wondered.

"And then what?" I moved my hands to my hips and it felt good that I could actually feel my hipbones again. It really hadn't dawned on me until then that my exercise had been paying off. Wow, I can feel my bones. Yippee. But then I scowled. *What kind of a game is he playing?*

"And then…" He looked at my mouth again, licked his lips, and shrugged. "We'll do that again sometime." He turned and tended to something on the stove.

"So, this whole friendship thing is just a ruse?"

"No, this whole friendship thing is for us to get to know each other better until you forgive me and we can get on with it." He sipped something from the spoon and then brought it over to me to try. I opened my mouth, licked the spoon, and then returned to argument mode, which is exactly where I needed to be. "Well, too salty?" he asked.

"No, it's fine. What is it?"

"Béarnaise."

"Oh," I said. "Get on with what exactly?"

He threw his hands in the air and growled with pain as he did so. He muttered an obscenity or two and then relaxed his jaw. "Life. Angie. Get on with life. Have fun, make out, go to movies together. Cuddle under the stars and make love until we can't see straight. Life, Ang."

I didn't mean to stare at his butt, but he had a nice one and I was incredibly flattered that he was attracted to me and wanted to make love to me. Angered, but flattered. "What exactly was your plan here, Scot? Fool me into thinking you were just as emotionally unstable as I was and then seduce me into bed once I trusted you...because you were my friend. That's so..."

"Low?"

I groaned.

"Romantic?" he said as he grabbed for my hand.

"I don't know exactly, but it's..."

He entwined his fingers with mine and gazed deep into my eyes. He had Béarnaise sauce on the corner of his mouth, so I wiped it off with my thumb. He stilled as I wiped it along the edge of his lips and then he moaned deeply and nibbled my skin, setting my thumb on fire. I let it sink farther into the depths of his mouth and then we just came together in a mind-numbing kiss that sent every erogenous zone over the edge. I clawed at his back, opened my lips for his tongue and *my God* that Béarnaise tasted so good in his mouth. I sucked a deep breath through my nose, and raked my hand down his back, accidentally ripping the corner of his bandage off in the process.

He howled in pain, and then breathlessly clutched the back of my neck with his big hand when I tried to escape.

"I'm not ready," I gasped with as much control as I could muster. Okay, so I was ready. My body ached to do this, but I wasn't twenty-two years old anymore. I'm more mature now and I know that jumping into bed would just blow up in my face and I wanted Scot in my life. So, I eased away from him and bit down on my lip.

He once told me that he knew when I was lying to him, so he did what I expected and carefully watched my expression. Fear was most likely apparent, as was lust and a bit of apprehension, because he just smiled and said, "I know, but if it helps speed up the process... I am sorry that I didn't listen to you and I do have a surprise for you to make up for it.'"

I felt much calmer. My pulse returned to normal and I helped him with the rest of the dinner prep. I sliced the bread, put the butter on the table, and opened the bottle of wine that I brought. "I'll bring you another one," I said as I poured myself a hefty glass. "So, what's my surprise?"

While placing the plates on the table, he gave me a little hip bump and said, "Be patient!"

I don't know exactly how it happened, but I'd gone from this amazingly angry woman to this incredibly relaxed person and the funny thing is that my life is even more messed up now than it has ever been. I mean, I'm actually being investigated for killing a man and I can't keep the damn smile off my face. It's kind of annoying because sometimes I watch movies and suddenly the characters come together in this heated rush of passion while aliens are trying to disembowel them and I sit there in the theater and think, "How can these stupid people be thinking about sex at a time like this?" And then I chalk it up to Hollywood having to throw in a sexual scenario to keep our attention. But now I think differently. Perhaps adrenaline and fear are a huge aphrodisiac. I've never been so horny in all my life and I have a murder wrap hanging over my head.

"What's on your mind?" his voice once again interrupted my pleasurable thoughts.

"Not you," I snickered and gave him a coy wink. I was actually flirting.

"Are you having any luck clearing your name? Because I've got some bad news and some bad news."

"Bad news first please." I set down my fork and swallowed my bite of steak so I wouldn't choke to death on the *bad* news.

"The detectives on the case think that you may have killed Walter because of the kid. You didn't do yourself any favors by that little stunt at the hospital."

"And the bad news?" I asked matter-of-factly.

"They're putting you under surveillance."

"Oh, fantastic," I grumbled and bit my lip to stop the tears. "How am I supposed to find out who killed Walter if the cops are on my ass?"

"Well for one, it's not your job to find out who killed Walter. I thought it was a good idea at first and I know I sort of nudged you into taking initiative, but I had no idea you knew what the hell you were doing. I thought you were just a schoolteacher and you'd give up after you hit your first dead end."

"Thanks a lot." I crossed my arms and couldn't help feeling small.

"I didn't mean it like that, I just thought you'd have your fun and give up." His voice began to rise at that point. "What the hell were you doing at Tino's anyway? Heinous crimes are committed there about every thirty-seven minutes."

I narrowed my eyes over the table at him and grabbed another piece of bread. "You're following me again?"

"Well, someone has to. You're a maniac and you're stepping on some very important toes. I've been told to ask you to back off and kindly stay out of the way."

"Yeah," I chuckled. "I'm sure that jerk said it that nicely."

"Actually," he said as he leaned over the table and planted his elbows. He handed me the butter. "He told me to tell you to stay the fuck away from Dean Hopper and stop messing up the fucking investigation or he'll bring you in for..."

"I know," I said sternly. "I went to school."

"Then why are you doing this?"

"To save my ass!" I buttered my roll and shook my knife at him, but not maliciously. He was fast and grabbed the knife before I had time to reapply more butter.

"Saving your ass would be sitting at home gardening or making lesson plans for September. Saving your ass would not entail interrogating strippers and ending up at biker joints with your best friend. Geez, do you not think about how this looks to the cops?" He slammed the knife down beside his plate and watched me with wary, tired eyes. "I'm supposed to be on leave, but *noooo*. I'm forced to follow around the lunatic girl that I'm hopelessly crazy about. Christ, Ang, give me a break. I'm recovering from a gunshot wound here."

"It's a flesh wound!" I shouted and stood up. "No one asked you to follow me around. In fact, knock it off. You're probably making it worse. Just let me do this and don't worry about me. I'm a big girl!"

"You're a schoolteacher, Ang!"

I cringed when he said that to me. I couldn't help my abrupt departure. I was mad, hurt, and angry. Angry again with myself for my ridiculous choice of giving up a fulfilling career of fighting crime so that I could be the trophy wife of Dr. Raymond Shirpa.

The door slammed behind me and I had almost made it safely to my SUV when Scot grabbed my arm and twirled me around to face him.

"We aren't done."

Tears were already streaming down my cheeks at that point. I was sure that if he didn't have a "flesh wound," he would have thrown me over his shoulder and taken me back into his house.

"I can't do this right now. Please, just let me go."

"Will you think about what I said?" he asked as he let go of my arm. He dropped his hands to his side and rocked back on his heels. "Did you even hear what I said?"

I nodded and stared out over his shoulder, afraid to meet his gaze.

He stepped back a few paces and I slid in behind the steering wheel and turned the key. It wasn't until I was out in the street, driving away that he actually turned and walked back inside.

Had I blown it?

I sure hope not. I may not be ready, but I still have a heart.

***

It had been three days since I'd heard a peep from Scot. I did see him in my rear view mirror this morning as I headed to the courthouse in downtown Portland to see what kind of information I could get about Isaac Moncrief's next court appearance.

I dialed his cell phone when I got to the restaurant where I was meeting Bulldog for lunch.

"Hey," he said. "What did you find out?"

"Besides the fact that I know you're still following me… not much." I climbed out from behind the steering wheel and grunted when I saw him waving at me. "I thought you said I was being put under surveillance soon. I have yet to spot a pig… except you."

"That's not a nice thing to say to your future husband."

I couldn't help the sudden snort of laughter. The guy always took me by surprise. "Are you trying to make me lose bladder control, or are you that delusional?" I felt my muscles relax slightly, but I was still perturbed. I was not just a schoolteacher and I had more to offer a man than my ability to grow fresh vegetables and keep a spotless house. I would never fall into that trap again. I now had more to prove than ever.

"Delusional," he said. I could sense there was a smile behind his reply. "Can I join you, or do I have to eat in my car?"

"I'm not eating alone." I turned to watch Bulldog's badass Hummer pull in beside me. I quickly stuck my tongue out at my future husband and flipped my phone shut.

"Hey," I said to Bull and pulled him by the arm before he could spot the chuckling officer in the big blue pickup.

"I have some good news and some bad news."

He held the door open for me, ignored the young hostess and took a seat at the first table. "Good news first. I had a helluva trip." He sat down and removed his sunglasses. He was wearing new jeans and a tight blue and orange Orioles tee-shirt. "What happened while I was gone? You look happy."

"Lightning did not strike, if that's what you're thinking." I rolled my eyes and browsed the menu as I spoke. "Isaac Moncrief is Walter's son. His mother is a dancer at the Dancing Beaver, she uses the name Sheila, but it's really Laura Moncrief. Isaac can be found at Tino's biker bar and I'm pretty sure that he was the one who beat up and threatened Dale Green."

He didn't look stunned by anything I said. "Interesting. Why's your cop friend following you?"

I looked stunned.

"Umm," I stammered. "He's being a pain in the ass. Ignore him."

"Have you spotted the other guy yet?"

I turned my head sharply and began perusing the parking lot for anyone of importance.

"Dark sedan, ten o'clock. Cheap sunglasses, reading the paper," he said. "That's your tail. From now on you're out, baby girl."

I wasn't out. I just had to be more ingenious. "Do you want Laura's address?"

"You got an address?"

I jotted it down for him, but kept my original. He glared, gave me a long look of warning and I pocketed the address.

"Once we find out who did it, how do we get the cops to figure it out?"

"We leave a trail of breadcrumbs. You're the loaf of bread, so you go where I tell you to, when I tell you to. If these guys have half a brain between them, they should be able to make an arrest. So, you think the son beat up the stepbrother. Why?"

"Lily said when she went to talk to Madeline and Dale, they didn't seem to know anything about Isaac. Madeline said that Walter once mentioned he had a son, but he didn't ever see him and she didn't even know his name. Said Walter never talked about him and, to her knowledge, he never saw him in the five years that they were married."

"But he's coming back for something that he believes belongs to him?" He eased back in the booth and scratched his chin that was at least a week overdo in the shave department. "Must be money then."

"That's what we guessed, but Madeline and Dale know nothing about any stash. Lily said Madeline actually got angry and started cussing about that fact, because she said she'd been giving him money every month just to keep his business up and running."

"You did good." He smiled and when our food finally arrived he winked at me and threw me a bone. "I owe your dad my life. You know that, right?"

I felt my breath catch in my throat. I didn't know that and that made me want instant answers. "Colombia 1986?"

He winked and finished his bite of wheat toast. "I gotta run. Stay out of sight until I call you. And, baby girl," he turned before tossing a couple twenties on the table. "Keep doing whatever it is you're doing. I love to see you smile."

I blushed. When he left, Officer King entered the establishment and sat down at the counter across from where I was sitting.

"Dark sedan, cheap sunglasses," I said without looking up. "I probably can't be seen with you right now, huh?"

"I could hide you under my covers."

I liked the sound of that, but no!

"Hey, you never told me my surprise," I said as I finished my bowl of fruit. "Do I still get it?"

"I found the girl who hit your car."

"Really?" I turned and quickly looked back down. It mattered not anymore that my Volkswagen was in car heaven, but it was still thoughtful and a bit endearing. "Why would you do that?"

"Because I'm your friend and I didn't listen to you."

"How... I mean, how did you find them after all this time?"

"Hey, I was a detective once! I have my ways," he said with a smile, but kept his eyes diverted. "By the way, someone ransacked the Dobbs' place last night. Took everything that wasn't nailed down."

"What?" I practically shouted. "I thought their place was under surveillance. How could that happen?"

"Salvation Army truck pulled into the driveway and they just thought the Mrs. was donating some of Walter's things." He kept his eyes on the menu. "I just thought you should know. I know you're worried about him."

"Where is Dale now?" I stood up, grabbed my purse, and stopped to grab a toothpick from the basket near his elbow. He remained silent until I clocked him in the butt with my purse. "Huh, where is he?"

"At the station with his mom." A second passed before he grabbed my arm and yanked with purpose. "Don't even think about it."

And then I smacked him again and stuck out my tongue.

***

I called Lily from my car, asked her to call Madeline and beg her to meet up with Lily again. Lily was more than eager to help me out, as long as we didn't have to return to Tino's Biker Bar. After I told her the plan, I drove to her house, grabbed the key from under the frog on the back porch and I let myself in to pace and gnaw on my fingernails. I did tidy up a bit and threw her clothes in the dryer. It was the least I could do to thank her for running to my rescue, again.

Forty-five minutes passed and when I had finished folding the last of Chad's boxer-briefs. I heard the garage door open, so I ran to meet Lily.

"So?" I waved my arms frantically after flinging open the door. "What happened? What'd she say? Was it this Moncrief creep, or what?"

She took a moment to gather her small bag of groceries and shut the door of her car. "You want the Reader's Digest version, or do you have time for the extended version, because this is getting good. Who knew I'd be this excited about interviewing a woman who most likely mutilated her husband? She's as cool as a cucumber, but the kid…Geez, he's wound up tighter than you."

"I'll make some tea." I held the door open for her and hustled into the kitchen. I found a couple of bags of herbal cinnamon apple tea and turned on the burner to heat the water.

Lily dropped her bags on the counter and sat down. I think she liked me waiting on her. "So, Madeline takes Dale in to get his stitches out yesterday morning and they're only gone for about two hours tops. When they got home, the entire house is wiped out. Electronics, kitchen gadgets, you name it. Every earring, necklace, bracelet. Every DVD, even some of her more expensive designer shoes."

"So, that's it. That's all? They just got robbed?" Pulling two mugs off the shelf, I turned to her and dropped a tea bag in each flowered mug. "I think this guy came back to find what he was after, don't you?"

"Dale seems to think so too," Lily began again. "There was a note that said, 'I'll be back and you'll pay for what you did.'" She reached over the counter and pulled out a couple of spoons.

"And, of course, they gave that note to the cops, right?"

"No, Dale pocketed it and intends on burning it. He's scared out of his mind, and rightfully so. The kid looks like someone used him as a punching bag. He can't fight back."

"Did you happen to get him alone to talk?"

Her head nodded slightly. "She got a phone call and stepped aside for just a minute and that's when he told me that he's worried about her." She bobbed her eyebrows at me and grinned. "I think he knows she killed Walter. Why else would he be so worried about her?"

"But why would Madeline kill Walter? She's a bit trashy looking, but I don't see her flipping out and stabbing him with my shovel."

"Like you said before, she probably found out about him and his ex and went berserk. Crimes of passion are fairly common among the married. Hell, I've wanted to knock Chad upside the head a number of times." She sighed. "Especially when I see girls staring at his butt. He's like a rock star or something and all he does is investigate arson. It's not like he's one of the hunky hose men."

"You're so cute." I leaned over and kissed her cheek. "You have nothing to worry about. Chad's a good man."

Sighing heavily, she smiled and got up to pour the hot water because I had gone into space-out mode. I just couldn't see Madeline doing something like that, but then again, how well can you really know your neighbors?

"Well," I sipped my scalding hot tea and burned my lips due to my impatience. "I thank you again for getting involved. It will all be over soon and then I won't ever ask you for another favor as long as we both shall live."

"Yeah right," she giggled. "So, what's going on with Scot? Are you ready to cave and jump into his arms?"

"No." I couldn't help the smile. "I'm waiting for the lightning."

***

Tuesday, I spent the entire day at my house. I hated having a cop following me, so I gave them no ammunition that day. Instead, I drew up every scenario I could think of for why Walter was dead. I made one of those circles on a big piece of paper and then drew lines that connected to every single person I thought might want him dead. I even drew a line to my name because I hated the way he put Dale down and I hated his dog. Pretty lame motives, but I was on there just the same. The circle was soon surrounded with me, Madeline, Dale, Walter's son Isaac, and his partner Dean Hopper (just because I don't like the guy and what if Walter was embezzling to pay off his debts?) I wrote the word "Bookie", although I was still at a dead end there, and I wrote a number of neighbors just because I was enjoying myself.

The only place I went was to Road Rage awareness class at seven that night. Tony was still absent, and, thankfully, Scot was at the head of the class and not the guy from last week.

"Light duty?" I said as I passed by his desk.

He dropped his Nikes to the floor, stood up and followed me to the back of the room to my desk. The class size had dwindled even further. Now we were down to seven. Biker dude was still seated to my right and I couldn't help but admire his boots.

Scot sat down behind me and introduced a special guest speaker.

"This is Martha Switzer from SW Medical Center. She deals with stress management and will be our guest this evening." Scot turned the floor over to Martha and then pulled his desk closer to mine. The lights went off and I felt as if I was back in high school and the cutest boy in class had just chosen me to sit by. His hand rested on the back of my chair, he leaned toward me, and every other second, he was knocking his knee against mine in a mischievous fashion.

"Pay attention," I said, trying to keep my lips from quivering with delight as I got close to his ear. "And stop doing that." I grabbed his knee and dug my nails in. I think he liked it, because he growled and squirmed in his seat.

Martha went on and on about the importance of dealing with anger and frustration in a positive, constructive way. She had a high definition diagram of the heart and cardiovascular system and what happens when a body has to deal with constant stress. She spoke of different ways to relax the body and mind. I could only think of one thing that would totally relax me and that involved Scot and a couple hours of hot, steamy ...

"Sex," he said as he leaned closer. His gaze dropped to my chest. I'm sure my breasts were heaving from the near mention of the physical act of love. "Sex is relaxing, don't you think?"

"Uh huh," I stammered with a high-pitched squeal. I was wound so tight I could almost feel my vagina contract in my throat. "Shhh."

"How about it?" He nudged my knee again. "After you help me put on a new bandage, we could relax..." he bobbed his brow at me when I turned to scowl at him... "together."

"Friends don't do that."

"Why not? Who says we have to follow the rules?"

His tone was light and fun, but I was taking it way too seriously. I had to pinch my thighs together to stop the onslaught of pre-arousal contractions. "Shhh," I said again.

His hand dipped down and tangled in the back of my hair.

"I'm not ready, remember?" I whispered again.

"You don't have to forgive me to have sex with me. We could have angry sex, I bet you like angry sex."

I snapped my head around and narrowed my eyes, but I had no comeback for that one. I could very easily have angry sex with him. Right now! Bring it on!

"Sheesh. Will you at least come over and change my bandage?"

He gives up way too easily. Another moment of heated exchange and I would have taken him on that little desk in front of the entire class and Mrs. Switzer too.

"Sure, but that's all. There will definitely be no *relaxing* going on," I whispered and then returned my attention to the front of the class. The lights flickered on and Mrs. Switzer thanked us all for our time. I wrote my paper on how I'd learned how to relax and relieve my stress and then I followed Scot home.

Lord, give me strength.

Eight

He let me in the front door before shutting and locking it.
He even locked the deadbolt as if he was retiring for the night.
I watched him carefully as he struggled out of his tee shirt. He
winked at me as I stared in wonderment, and then he walked
toward the back of the house half naked.

There are two kinds of people in the world. Those who see
someone as half dressed, and those who see someone as half
naked. I'm a half naked type of person, especially when the
naked half looks better than the dressed half.

I'd gone to the bathroom in his house a few days prior, the
one near the front door, but I hadn't dared to venture past the
hall, because I knew there was a bed back there. A bed that had
pillows on it that smelled like him.

I felt a sudden flush when I heard him yelling my name. If
he thought I was voluntarily walking into his bedroom, he had
another think coming. Besides, I was afraid to look in his
master bathroom, because it might be disgusting and, therefore,
my image of him would be shot to hell. Soap scum can do that
to me.

"What?" I yelled and set my purse on the kitchen counter.
His kitchen was spotless, as was the living room, front room
and, "wow," I peaked my head into his garage. It too was
spotless. He must be bored out of his mind being on sick leave.
I continued walking around his house, looking at his

knickknacks and attempting to keep my mind from mentally wandering into his bedroom. "What?" I yelled again.

He sauntered into the living room, where I was staring at his trophies. "I won't bite you. Are you going to help me, or what?"

"Sure," I said. "Bring it out here."

"It's already in there." He pointed down the hall and sent me a devilish, completely sexy smile. "Chicken?"

"No," I said and followed him into the back of his house, warding off my fears by reminding myself that celibacy rocks. The hall was long and every step I took seemed to cause my knees to wobble even more. I sucked in my breath when I entered his bedroom. It was spotless also. No clothes on the floor, just a pile of gauze and medical tape thrown on the bed. The comforter was dark green—very manly, as were the cellular blinds and two plants hanging in the corners. It was a man's room through and through, and I felt a sudden urge to run. Instead, I steadied myself against the bed and grabbed the piece of gauze.

"Be careful," he grouched as I tore at the tape. He was lightly hairy, but not at all like an ape-man or anything. I'm sure it still hurt though, because I know what it feels like to be waxed.

"It's better this way," I said as I held tightly with one hand and ripped the tape with the other.

"Motherfu—" he groaned and clenched his jaw. "Ouch!"

"You're the biggest baby I've ever met." I teased and then kissed just above his boo-boo, right where it had reddened from the tape being removed. I moved my hand around his waist. My palm tight against his naked skin. The muscles of his back tightened under my hand and I kissed him again, slower.

Huge mistake. No, I take that back, it was a phenomenally stupid mistake. I felt the change in his breathing and heard the little moan of pleasure he made when my lips touched his bare chest. I hadn't meant for the kiss to be sensual or erotic, but my lips must have told a different story. *Oops.*

I looked up at him with wide eyes.

His eyes were soft and filled with unrestrained desire. His chest rippled slightly as I moved my hand off the small of his back. "Oh boy, Ang."

"Oh boy, what?" I gulped loudly.

With a fairly swift motion; he had me smashed against his chest, my chin knocking against his collarbone. It took me a minute to realize that he was really going to kiss me and from the look in his eyes, I was sure it wasn't going to stop at kissing. We were butted up against his large king size bed, my ass was covered by his hand and he either had a hell of an erection or he had a nightstick in his pocket. The moaning started, followed by my futile attempt to get away. That just backfired because I was rubbing against the said erection, causing him to whimper even more. He planted a mesmerizing kiss on my lips. Boy, he can kiss. I felt the pull everywhere, from my pinky toe to the tip of my ponytail. I went with the reckless desire I was feeling and wrapped my arms around his waist, coddling his boo-boo, but keeping him tightly pressed against me as I kissed him back. Tongues tangled together in a heated battle for who was going to delve deeper into the warm depths of our mouths. I felt a sudden moisture down south that I'd been without for over a year and realized that my body was going ape shit over a kiss. One damn kiss and I was ready to straddle him.

I came up for air and moaned against his lips. "Why are you doing this?"

"Do you have to ask?" he said before kissing me again. He held my jaw with the hand that wasn't caressing my butt and he held me tightly against his lips as he kissed and suckled the soft flesh of my neck. I moaned. I tried not to, but I did and then I lifted my thigh and rubbed it against him, frantically. Like a dog in heat, I rubbed against him and then did the unthinkable and grabbed *his butt*! Magnificent glutes, by the way. Tight, yet tender and begging to be spanked.

"No, but you said I wasn't ready," I gasped. "Why are you pushing it? It's too soon." Hearing my mouth utter those words caused the rest of my flailing body to cease and desist. "It's only been...what... a week? Are you really afraid that I'm going to go to prison, so you're trying to get laid before I'm hauled away in shackles. Is that it?"

He laughed at me, and then kissed me again.

"Why are you suddenly rushing it?" I leaned far from his lips and demanded an explanation. He kissed my lips softly and wrapped his arms around me in a tender embrace. I felt him sigh heavily, before he pushed back and engaged me with his eyes.

"Because," he said with another exaggerated sigh. "When you finally realize that you want to kiss someone, then every damn day – every minute, hell, every second seems like an eternity. Sorry, I can't help it." He tilted his face forward and kissed me again, slowly taking his time and easing away from my swollen lips even slower. "Do you forgive me yet?"

I groaned and scooted away from him so I could think clearly. I needed air and a dozen condoms...*but no!*

"Yes, I forgive you. I don't hold that against you. You were just doing your job and I was a raving lunatic," I said as I adjusted my tank top.

He all but tried to pounce on me, but I put my hands up to halt the attack. Both hands splayed across his muscular chest. "But that's not why I'm not ready."

He crinkled his nose and lifted me up, tossing me into the middle of his bed. I bounced and then was squashed by his entire luscious body.

"Tell me about it," he said as he conceded against my wiggling and rolled onto his side. "What's Angie so afraid of?"

"I'm not afraid."

Poker face.

He tweaked my nose with his fingers. "You lie."

"Yes, damn it." I struggled to sit up and escape his gaze. "I'm afraid."

"Why?"

"Why aren't you?"

He tickled his fingers up and down my back and laid back, resting his head into his pillow. "I never said I *wasn't* afraid."

"That's right," I replied haughtily. "You just kept telling me that you weren't interested in dating. That you weren't ready because Jill broke your heart and you were annoyed with your best friend trying to marry you off."

I inched further away from him and noticed his wound was oozing. "Oh, God." I helped him sit up. "You're so full of shit, King!" I ran for the bathroom and held a washcloth under the hot water for a minute. His bathroom was as clean as mine and it smelled like vanilla.

I clutched my heart and sighed heavily before returning to the patient. "Here, hold this on there." I handed him the washcloth.

"Thanks." He did what I said and held it tightly while I got the gauze ready. "Why am I full of shit?"

"Because you were playing me the entire time." I unrolled the gauze and cut a piece about as big as the former piece that I was about to rip off him. I ripped without warning.

"Shit!" he glared. "You did that on purpose."

"Baby." I stuck my tongue out at him and continued with my speech. "So, what's your explanation?" I wrapped the new piece over his wound and ripped a piece of tape off the roll.

He fidgeted for a minute, and then grabbed my hand after I had one side taped on.

I felt his fingers massage my palm and he inched down to the edge of the bed, entrapping me with his thighs. I could have escaped if I wanted to, but I wanted that explanation and... let's not kid ourselves anymore – I am crazy about him too.

"Well let's see, Sweetheart." He started off with a playful smirk. "I had just arrested you. You were the cutest thing I'd ever seen, but I had to do my job. I had no other choice than to pretend to not be interested because everything about you that night said, 'Back off, Jack-ass.' I knew I didn't stand a chance and yeah, Tony's been trying to marry me off for years. That wasn't a lie, I just chose to use it as a way to make you empathize with me."

He rubbed my back with one hand and kept massaging my hand with his other. "Do you think it was easy for me to sit there watching you be so mad and pissy all night and then, my God – you cried when the crab finally arrived. What could I do? Make a move on you when I knew you'd just tell me to go to hell?"

"Well..." I started, but he cut me off with a sweet kiss. "I guess not."

"That's why I wanted to be your friend. It wasn't a scam to lure you into bed, I knew once you got to know me, you'd jump right in on your own."

I couldn't resist the urge to give him a quick slap to the head. "You're so... cute."

"Not sexy?" He stood up and gave me a swift smack on the butt in retaliation for the head slap. "So, friends again?"

"Really?" I asked, clearly confused now. I mean I know I had just admitted to not being ready, but come on. Life wouldn't be the same from here on out if I couldn't kiss him anymore. "But..."

He handed me a piece of tape and I got him all taped up and good as new. He tossed the roll of tape onto the bathroom counter and pulled on a new white tee shirt.

"That's it?"

"You said you didn't want to *relax* tonight." He flipped off the light and sauntered into the living room. I shook my head with a smirk, standing there in the dark before finally giving in to the urge to chase him down. I was hot on his heels, like a lovesick puppy needing a good belly rub. He just kept walking, right past the kitchen and into the living room. "I'm not a forceful guy. When you're ready, you'll make your move and until then, I'm cool. Really."

I wasn't cool. I was flushed; even my toes seemed to be feeling the heat. I stopped and stared at him for a good few minutes, my breath captured in my throat. I couldn't think of one damn thing to say. "Well, goodnight then."

"Goodnight?" He sank down on the couch. "Don't you want to watch a movie? Come on. Let's give Detective Jessup something to think about."

I felt my skin crawl. "He's out there?"

"Probably not, but you should have seen the look on your face." He chuckled loudly and patted the couch. "I'll make popcorn."

"Can we have butter?" I asked before sitting beside him.

"I think that can be arranged."

***

Wednesday, I did the unthinkable and tortured the poor detective who was following me by driving to my parents' house for lunch. Truth is, I wanted to discuss Colombia 1986 with my father and ask him what he thought about me bringing a friend to his big celebration wine-tasting the following Sunday.

"Why not?" he asked, helping me slice the Brie and place crackers on a tray. "Why don't you bring Lily and Chad too?"

"Oh yeah, they're coming, but I just wanted to make sure you'd be okay with me bringing another friend, a guy friend."

"Oh." He stopped with his chore and looked at me. "Someone special?"

"A friend," I said with a wide smile. "Can we talk about Colombia now?"

"I told you once that you have to do your homework. Information doesn't come easily."

"Reese told me you saved his life."

My father didn't flinch, or change expressions. He was such a super cool guy. "Did he now?"

"Oh, come on!" I groaned. "You know I'm never going to be able to get that kind of information on my own. Not without cheating and asking Penelope."

Penelope Musgrave is the equivalent of Miss Moneypenny from the James Bond movies. She was my father's personal executive assistant for the past thirty years and had recently retired in Seattle. She was just a short three-hour drive away from me and probably knows my father better than my own mother does. "Can I call her?"

"She won't tell you," my dad said confidently. "She knows the rules."

I followed him to the patio where my mother and Aunt Rita were waiting, soaking in the sun and trying to make nice.

"Who's the stiff following you, anyway?" my father whispered as I set down the cheese.

"I think today it's Detective Jessup. He might actually be on my side."

The phone rang when I finally sat down. Dad got up to answer it and I smiled at Aunt Rita. She's here visiting for my dad's annual wine-tasting shebang. It's highly advertised and my father really does it up. Hires a jazz band, surrounds the vineyard with twinkling lights and makes a crap-load of money in one weekend. Buyers from all over the United States arrive in full force and place orders for the entire year.

Aunt Rita is my dad's only sister and, truth be told; she has hated my mother for years. I was surprised they hadn't engaged in a catfight yet.

See, my father's family is a clan of warriors, versus my mother's family who believes in turning the other cheek and praying instead of kicking ass. Grandfather Jeff was a minister at a Southern Baptist church in Springfield where my mom grew up. There was speculation that he was heard rolling over in his grave when mom married a Marine who was also Catholic. Boy, that didn't go over well.

Aunt Rita was an analyst for the DEA and lives in Florida. I guess I could always ask her about Colombia 1986. She probably knows more about it than she's letting on. Although, in 1986 she was a field agent for the Omega Sector, which is one of the agencies that I'm not supposed to know about. Guess what Grandpa Daniel Harrington did? You guessed it, he was the assistant to the director of the FBI and then started his own internal agency within the agency that consulted with other government agencies, thus making it very easy for my dad to find a good job after he graduated from college.

My dad's voice interrupted my mental climb up the family tree. "Ang, can I see you in the kitchen?"

I felt very uncomfortable because my father never calls me Ang. Not unless I was truly in trouble. I slid the sliding door closed behind us and turned to see his sullen expression. "What is it?"

"Bulldog said they've arrested Dale Green for the murder of Walter Dobbs. It's over, Pumpkin."

My chest tightened and not in a good way. I was not excited that I was off the hook. I was mortified that the brilliant, young, talented Dale Green was being charged for killing that horrible, horrible little man. "No." I physically felt as if someone punched me in the gut. I curled into a ball, shuffled myself into the bathroom, and then emptied the contents of my stomach. "No!" I slammed the toilet lid and began to weep. "No, no, no!"

"Pumpkin." My father rapped lightly on the door. "Are you okay?"

"No," I groaned and didn't leave the comfort of my parents' home for nearly two days.

***

Thursday around four p.m., I finally took a shower and blew the excess excretions from my nose. I'd gone over and over it in my mind and it just didn't make sense. Surely Dale didn't suddenly confess. And why were the cops so eager to toss him to the sharks? Were they that anxious to slap a case closed sticker on this case? I just didn't see how the pieces came together. I had ignored my home, ignored my friends, but now I had a class to attend and I knew if I blew it off, I'd hate myself in the morning, so I kissed my dad goodbye.

"I'll come as early as I can Saturday. I love you."

I turned to Aunt Rita, who I look amazingly similar to. She's my height, has my shade of blonde, but without the up-turned nose. Her nose is straight and narrow like Dad's. "I'll see you in a couple days. Don't forget what I said. I mean it this time." I winked as if I was pulling one over on my dad. We had a discussion to finish about why my dad had to run to Florida that crucial day over a decade ago. "Tell Mom I said bye," I blew them both a kiss and drove home without my escort. From now on, I was without a Portland Detective on my ass. *So, why was I still so glum?*

Traffic was horrendous, so I pulled into the college just about the time that Officer Tony Little was climbing from his minivan. It was still nearly eighty-five degrees and my shorts were stuck to my butt because of the heat.

"Well, well. Congratulations are in order. Nice to know my future best friend-in-law won't be going to prison after all."

"Very funny," I said with a sour smirk, "On so many levels."

He wrapped his arm around me and escorted me into the classroom. I was saddened that Scot wasn't there. I hadn't talked to him in days and I missed him.

I took my seat with the other five people in the room. Surprisingly, biker dude was still in class. He actually said hello to me when I sat down.

"Hi," I said back. "Have you learned your lesson yet?"

"Almost." He grinned a toothless grin. "I'm Andy."

"Angie," I said as I extended my hand.

"I know. You're the teacher's pet. You some sort of cop?"

"No," I chuckled. "I'm a teacher at David Douglas."

"No shit. I went to Douglas."

"Yeah," I motioned to Tony. "So did Tony. I think he said class of eighty-five?"

"Yeah, I remember him. Looks exactly the same if you ask me," Andy said, then snuffed his cigarette out on his massive boot.

"Nice boots," I grinned and then looked from Tony to Andy. "You remember Tony from high school?"

"Yeah, he was a nerd. I think I used to cram him in my locker." He bumped elbows with me. "Don't remind him, though. I can't believe he's a pig."

"I won't tell him if you do me a huge favor." I'm so dang brilliant sometimes I even amaze myself. "Ever heard of a bar called Tino's?"

"Sure," he said. "What about it?"

"Do you ever go in there? Maybe you might know a guy named Isaac Moncrief?"

"Sure, everyone knows Creefer. He gets the good stuff." He pressed his thumb and forefinger together and made like he was dragging on a fatty. "Get it, Creefer, like reef..."

Tony interrupted us with his scowl. "I think you both have papers to write."

He winked playfully at me, but continued scowling at the giant biker. I wrote my paper in ten minutes flat and then wrote a note to Andy and passed it to him when Tony was busy rummaging through his briefcase.

He looked at me and nodded.

I rubbed my hands together and sang hallelujah in my head. If Dale was guilty, I was Mother Teresa.

***

After class, I met Andy near my car on the south end of the parking lot. I wasn't going to be stupid and outright ask him for Creefer's phone number and address. I had to be cunning. Like a common criminal or moronic dope-head.

Before I could even ask, Andy handed me a piece of paper. "He's usually there on Mondays and Wednesdays, but he's supposed to be doing some time here pretty soon for A and B. Here's his pager number and make sure you bring cash. He doesn't take credit." Andy actually giggled. I was thinking he must have smoked a joint on his way out the door. "See you next week?"

"Sure thing," I yelled and then read the piece of paper on the way to my car. The sun was almost down and I wasn't paying attention to where I was walking, let alone who was around me.

I felt someone clutch my hips right before I felt a hot breath on the back of my neck. "Jesus Christ on a Popsicle stick!" I yelled as I jumped out of my skin. Scot released my waist from his grasp and kissed the back of my ear. "Don't ever do that again!" I shouted, but he wasn't listening, he was trying to read the note I had gotten from Andy. *Jealous, perhaps?*

"Where you been?"

"Hiding from you," I said as I wiggled away from his lips. "What are you doing, besides giving me angina?"

"Looking for you." He bobbed his brows playfully and then leaned against the car door so I couldn't open it. "Congratulations."

"On what?" I snapped. "The kid didn't do it."

He balked at me, and then grabbed the piece of paper from my hand. "Why do I get the feeling that you're up to something?"

"What?" I tried to grab it back and then flicked the bangs from my eyes. "I just wanted some good dope."

He laughed hard and leaned closer. "It's over. I'm sorry that you're upset about the kid, but he confessed. Case closed. You should be celebrating, or getting naked with me. Come on, Ang. This is good news." He tried to lean forward to kiss me, but I dodged his full lips. He groaned and I crossed my arms in front of my clearly aroused nipples in a stance that said, "don't fuck with me."

"Are you serious about this?" he asked, shaking the piece of paper in front of my face. "You really think the kid confessed to murdering his stepfather just for fun. Come on, you said it yourself, the kid's a genius and that makes no sense."

"Can I talk to him?" I asked. "Will he get out on bail?"

"Sure." He shrugged. "Dean Hopper will probably take care of it, but he's at the county courthouse right now."

I started to unlock my door, but he caught my hand and grabbed my keys. "It's late. Why don't you do it in the morning? You look exhausted. You need to *relax*."

His sexy smile gets me every time.

"I'll *relax* when I find out who killed Walter Dobbs."

We played grapple for my keys for a couple of minutes before I conceded and was pinned against my door by the rogue cop. I didn't mind. He was right. I needed to relax and relax and relax until I had trouble focusing my eyes. But I had a murder to solve, a garden to salvage and legs to shave. I couldn't *relax* right now if I tried.

His head bent forward, but again he stopped short and purposefully brushed his lips lightly across mine as he spoke. "I'm waiting, but if you don't hurry up, I'll be forced to relax without you."

"Really?" I couldn't help the impish grin. I licked my lips and whimpered sensually. "That's a very sexy image, Officer King. Can I watch?"

I've never seen a man blush so hard in my life. I think he was just joking with me and I had turned it around on him and gotten him good.

"Since you don't date and I don't date, how about going to my parents' house this weekend for a bit of wine and rest?" I was fully aware that this probably wasn't the smartest idea, taking the man I'm crazy about to my parents' house for a romantic weekend of wine, brie and fresh air, but who said I was smart?

"Will we be relaxing too?"

"Not unless you help me figure out who killed Walter Dobbs." I sent him a smile and then slid in behind the steering wheel.

He caught the door before it closed.

"Are you serious?"

"Sure." I shrugged. "If we find Walter's killer before Saturday morning, I'll let you relax my brains out."

"Ahhh," he whined. "You're killing me!"

***

I blinked a couple of times, not really sure if I was imagining things, or if I had really just heard my door creak. I sat straight up in bed and looked at the clock. It was nearly seven a.m. and at that point, I wished I had taken my father's advice and either bought a gun or a big dog like Cujo. Fear rippled up my spine, but as I sniffed the air and smelled hazelnut coffee, I just got pissed.

The door of my bedroom swung open just as I planted my bare feet on the floor.

"You're a dead man!" I shouted between hysterical breaths. "You big jerk!"

He winced slightly and then smiled and moved toward me.

"I could have shot you in the head, you moron." I inhaled deeply and stood up, because being in bed with Scot in the room is not a good idea, Not when I have morning breath, stubbly legs, and bed head. I actually said a small thank you prayer to Zeus for keeping his lightning bolts to himself this morning.

"You don't have a gun," he chided and handed me a cup of coffee as my jaw dropped. "Let's get cracking. Times a wastin'. We have a killer to find and a couple boxes of Trojans to buy. Get moving." He actually winked playfully at me while sipping coffee.

"What's up your butt, besides the obvious?" I wondered why the big change of heart. Just a mere couple of days ago he was begging me to give up and let the big boys handle it. Did he know something that I was unaware of, or did he just want sex? "I thought you were hell-bent against me playing detective. Did you find something?"

"Hey, I want what you want. The kid's at the courthouse and he won't be arraigned until this afternoon, so tell me what you got." He dropped his fine behind onto my bed and clearly had already indulged in a fair amount of caffeine this morning. I needed a cold shower and a pot of coffee just to catch up.

"There's no way we're going to find the killer in one day. I was sort of being facetious last night You know that, right?" I would never try to renege on a deal made by my own volition, but come on. One day to find out who killed Walter Dobbs? Scot's quest for sex was going to fail miserably.

"A deal's a deal." He tossed me a pair of sweats. I was already in my favorite oversized tee shirt, so I slipped them on and grabbed my tennis shoes. "After you." He motioned to the door and that was that. I pulled my hair back and secured it in a ponytail and he fed me breakfast, which he had made himself—in my kitchen. Ah, I nearly climaxed just watching him flip eggs.

"So what makes you think the kid is innocent? Have you thought this through, or do you just not want to see the truth?" He slid my plate under my nose and took a seat beside me.

"Are you still on leave? Or am I talking to the cops right now?"

I had to ask. I know it probably makes no difference, but I wanted him to understand that I didn't particularly want his cop-attitude.

"Still on leave," he said despairingly and engaged me with his glaring eyes. "But that doesn't mean I'm going to help you break any laws, or go off half-cocked. I want solid facts here, Ang. No bullshitting me. If you seriously think you have something concrete, then let me have it."

"Okay," I took a bite of eggs. They were cooked to perfection and had just the right amount of salt sprinkled on top. I had a hard time swallowing. "Thank you." I looked over at him and smiled.

"For what?" he asked between bites. "I haven't done anything yet."

"For breakfast." I actually had to choke back a tear. "No man has ever made me breakfast before."

His expression bordered on adoring, mixed with pride I guess. "Well, then, I guess you've been with the wrong men."

Silence between Scot and me had become something almost comfortable. It was no longer awkward to sit and eat and just be. It was nice.

When I finished, I pushed my plate away and planted my elbows. "Oh!" Then I jumped up and grabbed my wonderful diagram of potential killers.

He chuckled, but I didn't blame him. I'm a complete amateur. "I see you didn't like the guy all that well." He smoothed the line between the circle and my name with his index finger. "Who's this Isaac Moncrief guy?"

"Oh!" I said excitedly. I hadn't told Scot because Bulldog had warned me not to and I don't think Scot ever got around to finding out who Walter's son was. "He's Walter's son!" I sat down beside him at the oak table and scooted my chair closer before beginning my ramble. "His mother is a dancer at the Dancing Beaver and she was Walter's favorite. Isaac was arrested in April for assault and, apparently, Walter paid his bail. The funny thing is that the paperwork was sketchy and then Bulldog found out that the bail amount didn't even match Walter's check. Something fishy is going on, don't you think?"

He looked astonished at best. "So you think this Isaac killed his own dad?"

"No!" I said quickly, pulling out the rest of my information on Isaac, his boots, what Biker Andy had told me in class. "I think Isaac beat the hell out of Dale because he thinks either he or Madeline killed Walter. Dale said the guy was wearing biker boots and said he'd be back for what was his. Then bam... their house gets trashed and everything gets taken. The note said he'd..."

Scot grabbed my hand and gave it a squeeze. "What note and how do you know all this?"

"The note that the burglar left. It said that he'd be back to make them pay for what they did. Dale didn't tell the cops because he's worried about his mom." I took in Scot's quizzical expression and explained further. "He'd told me everything else at the hospital when Bull locked Jessup in the bathroom. Then Lily talked with Madeline and Dale and got the rest of the facts. I would have done it myself, but I was told I couldn't talk to either of them, so I sent Lily. We think it was Madeline Dobbs... or rather Lily thinks that. I personally think something else is going on. I'm thinking Dean Hopper." I pointed to Dean's name and Scot inhaled and exhaled a couple of times before getting up and carrying plates to the sink. My heart flip-flopped around for a bit and then I bit my lip to stop myself from jumping his bones right on the kitchen floor.

"What?" he asked as he turned around. "You look flushed."

"Nothing." Horny, horny, horny! Damn hormones! "So what do you think?"

Returning to the table, he looked over the diagram again and shook his head with a scowl. "I'm not going to be relaxing this weekend. Damn it!" He wiped his hands on his khaki shorts and groaned.

"Sorry," I winced. "You think I'm crazy, don't you?"

"No, I think you're very intelligent. But you yourself have no motive. And we've nothing solid to go on."

"No, but listen," I started to say, but he was shaking his head at me, much like Ray used to do. *Damn!* "Okay, so don't listen." I felt my anger race through my spine as I straightened out.

"I'm listening. Sheesh."

"Don't do me any favors." I grabbed up the remnants of my murder investigation and hauled it into the living room, pounding my shoes into the hardwood as I walked past him. He followed me and pulled me from behind, his hands locking together around my waist. He was solid and secure, holding me tightly. The heat of his breath was hot on my neck. "Don't." I shrugged from his grasp. "I haven't taken a shower and I'm mad."

Wow. That was very nice of me. I handled my anger in a positive way. Perhaps road rage awareness is helping me after all.

He let go and rammed his hands in his pockets. "I'll find out what I can about Isaac Moncrief. Is there anything else you want me to check?"

"I guess you can find out why Laura Moncrief, aka Sheila, hasn't been to work in a few weeks. Her dancing partners are worried about her."

"Can I still come meet your parents?"

I smiled and relaxed my clenched jaw. "You don't think it's too soon?"

"Hey," he chuckled. "I'm just going to meet them, it's not like I'm asking for your hand in marriage." He sent me a sexy wink, strolled toward the door and right before it shut behind him, I'm positive that I heard him say "…yet!"

Nine

My shower was probably the fastest one I had ever taken. Suddenly, I was on a quest of epic proportions to find Walter's killer and I had less than twenty-four hours to do it. Really, there wasn't that big of a rush. But I had decided the minute Scot walked out my door that finding Walter's killer by the time we leave tomorrow would be cool. That would mean I could potentially feign my very real excitement over getting to be naked with Scot and therefore, I could still assure him that I'm still not ready for a romantic relationship. That way I could have sex and then turn back into friends without embarrassing myself too badly. Because it would be just a deal, it's not going to mean anything. It would just be two friends following through on a wager of sorts.

I thought it sounded pretty lame too, but how am I supposed to hold a man like that at arm's length when every cell in my body is screaming *take me, I'm yours*?

I have to admit that every once in a while, I get struck by little static shocks. Like this morning when he made breakfast and then again when he cleared the table. But nothing massive yet. Nothing like a godly bolt of lightning that will suddenly make me okay with letting myself love another man. Because I think that's what it would take. Love is scary, I've been in love before. Once, and it was enough to destroy not only my life, but also my trust in mankind and the sacrament of marriage. Lust or no lust, lightning it will have to be.

I stepped into tan Capri pants, pulled on a pink tank top and slipped on my sandals. I wanted to talk to Dale, but I knew I'd have to wait a couple more hours, so all I could do was call Bulldog and beg him to meet me.

***

"Why are you doing this? You're done. It's over." Bull sat across from me at the coffee bistro near my old house, consequently near Walter's place too.

"Because Dale didn't do this. I'm sure of it."

"And your cop friend? What does he have to say about all this?"

"He's making some unofficial inquiries about Moncrief," I said, keeping my eyes from watering. Just thinking about Dale being locked up made my heart break for him. The more and more I thought about what Lily had said; the more and more I had to consider Madeline as the killer. It was all suddenly making sense. "*You* can talk to him! Tell him I sent you, and you find out why he confessed. Tell him that you know it was his mom. Get him to trust you and find out why, for me. Please, Bull."

"You think that might work?"

"I think you have a better chance at getting the truth from him than I do. Just tell him that I hired you because I believe he's innocent. I know him. I've watched him grow up, and then lie if you have to... tell him that Moncrief won't hurt him or his mother anymore. That we know where he is. Tell him he'll be safe soon." I bit my lip and cringed. "He doesn't know it was Walter's son who did that to him. YES!" I shouted with a great idea. "Go tell him that Moncrief beat him up. That I hired you to find out who beat him up and tell him that we got the creep."

"I'll try," Bulldog said quietly. "But don't get your hopes up, baby girl. This kid might be guilty as sin."

"Then I'm Mother Teresa!"

***

Bulldog left me alone and headed to the courthouse, so I sipped coffee, called Lily to tell her what time the shindig would be on Sunday afternoon and that I'd invited Scot to go with me tomorrow. And that we were spending the night. She actually gasped.

"So, does this mean you're ready?" I had to hold the phone away from my ear because she was squealing so loudly.

"It means that I like him enough for him to meet my dad. That in no way entails that I'm ready. I still have to figure out a good balance so I don't lose myself again. I can't be that person again, Lily. I loathed myself when I was with Ray, and I see that now. I can't be a trophy wife and stay home and cook and clean after a long day of teaching, and I don't know if I want to go back to teaching. All I know right now is that he makes me smile and I think I'd enjoy going to bed with him. That's all it is. I'm not in love, I can't foresee the future, and I don't want any pressure."

I sipped my coffee and took a well-needed breath. I guess I've wanted to say this to her for a long time, but I never could because I was so angry and confused and blew off steam every other minute. This is not steam. This is my – Angela Reese Harrington's – moment of emotional clarity. I've waited a year to feel this good and finally realize how I really felt. "He knows I'm not ready, and he says he's fine with it, so let's just have a wonderful time at my parents' house and leave it at that."

"Wow," Lily began to weep quietly. She sniffled loudly and whimpered. "You're back. You're back from outer space!"

"Just like the song says, babe, I will survive!"

I, too, wept and then we giggled and talked about how cute Scot's butt was and how good of a kisser he was. It was like being in high school again, without the pressure of whether or not I was going to lose my virginity. It was fun and I missed out on so much the last ten years. I am back from outer space and by golly… I will survive.

After the tear fest ended, I hung up and my phone immediately rang again.

"Hey." I was still sniffling, but his voice put a smile on my face. "What's up?"

"Isaac Moncrief is in jail. He got picked up yesterday because he failed to show up for his sentencing on the assault charge. My guess is the judge will just hold him until he gets sent down to the state pen."

"Oh, all-righty then!" I sure was happy to hear that bit of good news. Incarcerated and off the streets. In a roundabout way, justice has been served. "Can you go interrogate him in the slammer or is that taboo?"

"I've got an appointment in an hour. His court-appointed attorney has to be present and I had to bribe Tony into coming with me. I'm on leave and I needed a detective's help. I hope that's okay."

"Tony's just fine. Did you tell him everything?"

"Not yet, but I promised him I would. What did you learn? Anything?"

"Well, not much, except I just sent Bulldog to get into Dale's head. Are you still downtown?"

"Yeah," he answered and I could hear sirens and buses in the background, so I knew he wasn't lying. "What else do you need?"

"Dean Hopper. I never could get a straight answer from the guy. Can you pay him a visit?"

"Sure thing, over and out, babe."

I so wanted to be the one who was doing all the talking. I hated that I was not involved and couldn't just go down to Dobbs and Hopper Bail bonds, thrust a badge in that little worm's face and demand answers. I really don't have the stomach to do that anyway, but it's a fun fantasy. I had time to kill while I waited for my hopefully good news, so I went shopping for a new sundress or two for this weekend. I think Scot has seen me in just about everything I own and I think I've lost a few pounds, so I deserved something pretty.

It took me a minute to pry myself away from the window at Victoria's Secret, but I'd have to save that shopping trip for another time. Well, that is unless I get some super good news in the next eighteen hours, which I doubted.

I bought a pretty lavender sundress, then went back in and grabbed the spaghetti strapped blue one with white polka dots as well. It was tasteful and casual, but it also showed off some cleavage. The Cinnabon store was calling my name. After I inhaled a minibon, I waltzed back up to Victoria's Secret and did the unthinkable and went inside.

"Can I help you?" the size two gal behind the counter asked sweetly. I sucked in my stomach and berated myself for indulging in a fattening cinnamon roll.

"No, just looking." I smiled and continued to browse. I found three wonderful nighties and was headed for the dressing room when my phone blipped from inside my black purse. It was Scot.

"Where are you?" he asked, rather hurriedly.

"At the mall, why?" I said as I shut the door to the dressing room. All the outfits I had chosen were tasteful, yet slightly sexy. I pulled my shorts off and sat down. "What happened with Dean?"

"He wasn't in. What's the address of the missing stripper? I thought I'd pay her a visit."

I rattled off her address and then slid my bra off my shoulder, dropping the phone in the process. "Sorry," I said when I got it back under my chin.

"What are you doing, running a marathon?"

"I'm undressing actually and I just dropped the phone, I'm sorry," I said, and then felt my cheeks flush when he whistled.

"Maybe this stripper can wait. Where exactly are you?"

I laughed and sat back down on the tiny chair in the corner of my miniscule dressing room. "I'm at Victoria's Secret, but you'll never make it in time." My cheek muscles were actually becoming sore from smiling so hard. It was silent for a beat or two. I could hear nothing but heavy breathing. "Are you still there?"

"I'm on the way."

He hung up on me! The silly man hung up on me, inciting me to go into yet another bout of giggles. My stomach was still sore from my conversation with Lily. A minute passed, in which I tried on one negligee, and then the phone rang again.

"What damn mall?"

I chuckled again, then slid the nightie down, so I was bare naked, staring at myself in the mirror clenching my buttocks to see just how bad my cellulite actually was. *Not too bad.* "You're kidding, right?"

"Of course," his deep voice boomed. "But I got you all hot and bothered, didn't I?"

"Maybe," I said quietly. "I told my dad we'd be there by eleven, so we need to leave by nine. Traffic is horrendous in Dundee on the weekends."

"I'll be ready. You want me to drive?"

"No, I'll drive. I just want you to relax and have fun." I slid on the next negligee, which I liked better than the previous white one. Black really is slimming.

There was an eerie silence, and then I realized my mistake. "I just meant… I'm not ready."

"Then why are you in Victoria's Secret?"

"Because," I stuttered nervously. "Because."

He laughed and I hung up.

***

I ended up buying the black negligee that has a see-through lace front. It accentuated my breasts and covered my less than perfect stomach so it was the best choice. I don't intend on packing it for my trip, but it's nice to have on standby.

When I got home, I watered my garden, plucked a couple of dandelions from my lawn, and waited to hear from Bulldog. It was after three when he pulled his Hummer into my driveway.

I met him with a meek smile. "Well, was I right, or am I terribly naïve?"

"You were right… somewhat." He wrapped his arm around me and brushed his knuckles across my scalp. "I think we should talk about your future in crime fighting when all this is over."

"Maybe," I smiled. *If I'm not married and impregnated by then.* "Come on, tell me how magnificent I am."

He pulled his Ray--Ban's off his eyes and followed me through the house and into the backyard. "He wasn't willing to say much, but I know people and the kid is lying through his teeth. My gut tells me he's protecting mommy dearest."

"No." I felt the color drain from my face, once again making me feel lightheaded. "That's why he confessed, because he thinks she did it? Oh my God. How sweet is that…but no! We can't let him do this, can we?"

"He said there was a huge fight the night before Walter died. His mom screamed at the jerk and wondered where all the money was going and that she was sick and tired and wouldn't give him another red cent. Dale said he ran off that night, stayed at his girlfriend's house and came back in the morning and whacked the guy because he thought his mom would just give in and continue to give Walter money. Pretty lame motive if you ask me. A crime like that took passion. Anger and heated rage in the moment. You don't just get pissed off at someone and think, 'Sure, I'll just come back in the morning and stab him with a shovel.'"

"Yeah, I get that," I said, having once had anger and rage in the moment. Bull's right. Despite the fact that I felt a little better about Dale's innocence, my stomach was still tied in knots. "You couldn't get anymore out of him than that? Come on, what happened to brute force, that killer stare-down of yours. I'm a bit disappointed, Bulldog Mathers!"

"He was behind a Plexiglas partition. I did the best I could. I did note that he seemed rather relieved about Moncrief being fingered, though."

"After you left, I found out it's actually true. He's in the slammer and Scot's interrogating him in an hour." I bit my lip and began pacing again. "I hate this. What the hell is Dale thinking?" With a slow headshake, I gazed at Bulldog, who was leaned against my wall, staring at me. "I'm going to talk to him. Monday! Will you come with me?"

"Try and relax this weekend, okay." He pressed a kiss against my forehead. "This isn't your problem anymore. I understand you want to help, but you should take a minute to celebrate that you're no longer in serious shit."

"Thanks," I said as he waved goodbye. "See you at the vineyard."

***

It was nearly four p.m. by the time Scot called with his news on Isaac Moncrief.

"Can I come over?" he asked before giving out any information other than that he was fine and it went rather well. Oh, and that I have a knack for this stuff.

"It's late and I haven't packed yet, so no," I said with a slightly wavering tone. I don't know if I was trying to convince him or me. "What'd you get?"

He sighed, and then began his spiel, just as my doorbell rang. I clutched the phone under my chin and looked through my peephole to see Scot grinning at me. "Moncrief spilled his guts as soon as I mentioned that I was looking for his mom, that some of her friends were worried about her..."

I had to cut him off for a moment and opened the door. "Did you find her?" I said into the phone, but was looking right into his chocolate brown eyes.

"She wasn't home." He gave me a look of warning and walked past me, disconnecting and tossing his phone on the kitchen table. He turned to me with a smug grin and leaned back against my counter, waiting for me to fix my unhinged jaw. I was speechless.

"Anyway, he said he was sure that Madeline probably killed his father because she probably found out about his affair with Laura. Says they've been shacking up for the past three or four months and all his money has been paying her rent, her car payment and about eighteen years of past due child support." He paused for a minute to help himself to a glass of water. Again, I loved just watching him meander through my kitchen like he belonged there. Perhaps there's something to that. After a couple of sips, he sat back down beside me at the kitchen table and leaned back in his chair, tipping it onto the back two legs. I couldn't help but look at his bare knees. I love his knees, they're very cute. "So, Moncrief says Walter was planning on leaving Madeline after milking her for a couple more months because he's in such financial trouble with his bookie and his business partner. Apparently, Walt liked to doctor the books and Hopper was catching on. Now this is just a lot of probability and speculation. You know that, right?" His dark brow cocked upward as he glared at me with narrowed eyes. "He also got pretty carried away and admitted breaking into the house because he felt it was all his. Walt had been a deadbeat dad and he felt he had dibs on everything of value; that's why he came back."

I sat in awe and didn't know how to respond. I brushed the bangs from my eyes and reminded myself to breathe.

"I get the feeling he harbors some deep down envy for Dale, and of course we already know he has a problem with anger. You'd probably get along well with him."

"Very funny," I groaned as he continued chuckling. It wasn't the best time to try to make me laugh. I was having a semi-serious panic attack because I couldn't stop staring at his lips. "Is that all?"

"What...you were expecting a confession?" His brown eyes softened to a downright sultry expression. "Or were you just hoping for a confession so we'd be on our way to a relaxing weekend?"

My fingers tingled when he pulled my hand to his and began massaging the palm and licking his lower lip.

I snapped out of it and got up to busy myself with the dishes. It was a measly escape because my dirty dishes consisted of one spoon and two glasses.

Thank God, he remained where he was, sitting at my kitchen table, fidgeting with the purple placemats that my mother had knitted for me last year. "I should get going. I still have to pack too."

I turned just as he stood up and stretched. "See you in the morning."

"Hey," I said as he headed through the rounded archway toward the foyer. "Thanks for doing that for me. I know you didn't get what you were looking for, but I think some good progress was made. Don't you?"

"Progress would be having you half naked by now." He winked and was gone.

***

I was emotionally and mentally drained by eight p.m. My bag was packed and then repacked and then at the last minute I pulled my new negligee from the middle of my casual attire and hung it back up in the closet. Lust or no lust, I had to play it cool. Dale was still being charged with murder, my legs were still unshaved and it was too soon. What constitutes enough time to get over a life-altering divorce, bad marriage and blow to one's ego, I'll never know. But I was trusting my gut, and cute knees or not, I wasn't going to be that fool anymore. I'm thirty-three years old, for Christ's sake. I can control my hormones while spending a romantic weekend at my parents' vineyard with my new friend. Come on. How hard can it be?

***

I pulled into Scot's driveway at ten minutes before nine. He was already at the door clutching his black duffle bag with a grin on his face, looking just like a dog that got to go bye-bye. His choice in clothes was almost identical to mine. Except we were opposite colors. His button down Hawaiian shirt was mellow yellow and my sleeveless blouse was tan. His shorts were khaki and I was wearing a yellow pair of shorts that I thought made my butt look divine.

I smiled and he sauntered over to me, tossed his bag in the back seat, and took a seat beside me. No attempts at kissing were made, which was disappointing, but I couldn't have my cake and eat it too. Although, I wanted my cake and to eat him too. He looked rather yummy and smelled like Brut and spearmint Tic Tacs.

When we finished our talk about the weather, I flipped on the radio, slid open the sunroof and got down to business.

"So, I was thinking. What if Dale..."

His big hand cut me off as he leaned over and placed it over my mouth. My eyes popped open with surprise, and then he slowly peeled it off my lips and nuzzled against my neck. I swear to God, I almost drove off the road.

"Let's not talk about Moncrief or Dale or who killed Walter Dobbs. Please." He kissed me just below the ear.

I whimpered.

"Two days. That's all I'm asking."

His departure from my neck, albeit disappointing, left my skin crawling with sensational tingles.

"Okay," I said in a dazed trance and then I was silent. I had no idea what else to talk about and realized I knew nothing about this man other than he was a cop and got shot at from time to time.

"So, who's going to be at this big shindig?" he asked.

"A bunch of wine buyers, some restaurant owners and a horde of tourists who like to drink." I turned onto the freeway headed south and checked my mirrors to make sure I hadn't cut anyone off and that my hair wasn't too mussed from the sunroof being open.

"No, I meant like family I should know about… friends of your father's I should schmooze." He chuckled. "Come on, I'm going in blind. Help me out."

I found his attitude endearing. He wasn't coming to meet my family as a potential suitor, or my fiancé that I was dying to show off, but he was interested enough to have a head's up anyway. I liked that.

"Aunt Rita's an odd bird. She's an analyst for the DEA. She'll stand back and watch you for the first hour or so, and then she'll try to get in your head. It's a game she likes to play with my father. Secret agent crap and they're pretty competitive, so don't get cornered by either of them. You won't be able to miss her, she looks just like me, but without the ski-slope nose." I wiggled my nose, inciting him to send me a sexy smile. "And my mother and Rita don't get along, so try to stay far away from the flying daggers that they toss at each other with their glares."

"And what about Bulldog? What should I call him?"

"That's a touchy one. If my father introduces him to you as Reese Mathers, then clearly you've gotten off on the wrong foot, but if he calls him Bull, or Bulldog, then continue to smile and thank your lucky stars," I said. "And don't ask him any questions. He doesn't like that unless you're part of the family."

Scot gulped loudly and raked his palms down his thighs. "You're making me nervous. Is there anyone in your family who hasn't, at one time, been a super agent?"

"That would be my mother, but I have to warn you, she's a servant of God and sometimes that can be more intimidating than the James Bond boys. She can see through anyone's bullshit and if she likes you, she'll hold your hand all day. It's quite annoying, but she's just trying to spread God's love."

By that time, we had turned on the highway headed toward the Oregon coast, on our way down the long corridor of Hell that leads to Dundee, Oregon. Cars were already clogging the highway. People were camped off to the side of the road, waiting to get back into the long line of traffic. Wine country is what most local yokels call it, but I call it Hell. Harrington Vineyards was still twelve miles south. We had lots of time to discuss the crowd that Scot was about to meet.

"Oh, and don't say Jesus Christ or Goddamit it anywhere on the property. It's over eighty acres, but the church lady will hear you and you'll be damned the entire weekend for blasphemy." I couldn't help the chuckles. Scot must love to hear me laugh, because he reached over and grabbed my hand. Again, I felt tingly all over as he tangled our fingers together. It was nice and my hand remained stretched over into his lap for the next fifteen minutes or so. He asked more questions about my father's past.

"I never get straight answers from him, so don't expect too much. When the questions start getting personal, he'll start trying to pour more wine down your throat. Don't let him. He'll use it like truth serum and then take you for a long walk and ask you what your intentions are with his Pumpkin." I sighed heavily and stared out at the moronic tourists. "And then he'll come back and brief me on all the reasons why you're not the man for me and I'll get angry and tell him to mind his own business and then ten years later...I'll..." I bit down on my lip, but the tears dripped out anyway. "Sorry," I attempted a smile and then briskly wiped them away. "Anyway. That's my family. No brothers, no sisters, just a couple of dogs and a cat we haven't seen since they bought the vineyard."

"What happened?"

"We don't know, but my mother keeps putting food out and every once in awhile during a full moon you can still hear old Inky meowing out by the pond." I bobbed my brows playfully at him and gave his hand a squeeze. "I think she's haunting the place, but my dad just thinks she ran off and became wild." I shrugged. "Who knows?"

I knew I was forgetting so many other people to warn Scot about, but I was enjoying listening to Carly Simon and pretending that I was ready. The wild thoughts that were running through my imagination would make most people blush, but I was indulging anyway. The sun was starting to beat down on top of my head, so I shut the sunroof, then returned my hand to Scot's thigh and playfully rubbed my fingers up and down and around in little circles as I skirted around the traffic at the turnoff to our final destination. We were allowed to use the private gate, whereas the rest of the tourists had to wait in a long line to see if they were on the guest list or not. Tall pillars were set just outside the parking area, tied off with long lines of giant purple and gold balloons. Those were the colors of my father's wine labels.

Without moving my hand from Scot's thigh, I punched the secret code into the panel and smiled as the gate opened. Scot scooted around in his seat like a nervous ninny. But I thought it was cute. I gave his thigh a squeeze and winked.

"Oh, and there's Penelope Musgrave. Very serious woman. Used to be my father's personal assistant. She's very nice, but hard to get to know. And then Father Ashley had a stroke recently and has temporary short-term memory loss, so he'll introduce himself and then ten minutes later, he'll do it all over again. Just play along, or avoid him all day. Whatever you feel more comfortable with." I took a long-needed breath and continued with my last minute scramble. "Oh and I know there's tons more. You do like wine, I hope."

He nodded and now I felt just as nervous as he looked. "Okay, so if you meet anyone and they say they are financial analysts... they're agents, so don't be telling any off-color FBI or DEA jokes."

Scot's sensual kiss cut me off at that point just as I pulled up behind the house. Tingles, shivers and some fairly intense pangs of sexual interest jolted my senses into overdrive. "Oh," I said when we broke from the best kiss I'd had in days. Hell, the only kiss I'd had in days. Boy, I missed his kisses.

I, in turn, leaned toward him and kissed him, planting my hand on the back of the neck so he couldn't get away before I had time to part his lips with my tongue and give him something to dream about all weekend.

"Wow!" His eyes slowly blinked open as he focused on my face. "What was that for?"

"It was for luck. You're gonna need it." I smiled and quickly got out before my father made it off the porch.

My father had spent an entire summer building a wraparound deck that surrounded the entire house. The house was recently updated, but its shell is an old country style home, with a tri-level layout, a huge finished basement and a massive gourmet kitchen surrounded by a great room with every kind of hanging plant imaginable. It's perfect for entertaining and is decorated in warm earth tones.

"You're early as usual. Good girl." He gave me a warm kiss and wrapped his arm around me in a proprietary fashion. "And you must be Angie's friend, Scot." My father was about the same height as Scot, probably the same build too, but I don't look at my father's butt like I look at Scot's, so I hesitated to compare them any further. "I'm Mitch Harrington, glad you could make it."

"Scot King."

He shook my father's hand with a wide smile and didn't waver as my dad narrowed his eyes. It takes a strong man to not buckle under the narrowed eyes of my father. His blue eyes were piercing and years of being in his federal positions kept him fairly apprehensive around new people.

"The place looks wonderful." I said as I surveyed the surrounding area. Dad always planted a few more trees every summer and this year was no different. I think the flowering plum trees are the prettiest and they give the large backyard just enough color.

Scot was kind enough to pull my bag out and toss it over his shoulder. "I can get that," I said, attempting to take it away.

"I got it." He smiled.

He followed me and my dad up the hill toward the house. The grass was cut and trimmed nicely along the edge and just past the porch, the party rental workers were setting up a large dance floor just beyond the row of new yellow and pink roses. New cedar bark mulch added the finishing touches. Everything looked pristine and perfectly placed.

My mother met us on the porch with a smile, dressed in her favorite white frilly apron.

"Shoot," I grumbled from beside Scot just as he stepped onto the back deck with me. "Mom knows nothing about... *you know*."

"Got it." He smiled, winked and made his way to Mom.

"Mom, this is Scot King. Scot, my mother, Katherine," I said in a delicate voice, mimicking my mother.

"Well," she said once we were inside and out of the hot sun. "I've made up the guest room downstairs for you and Scot can bunk in the basement."

I knew that was coming and I had failed to warn Scot. His face drooped slightly, but he held it together for the sake of the church lady. "Mitch, can you show Scot his room, please?"

"No, Mom. I'll do it."

It had only been ten minutes and I wasn't ready for my father to get Scot alone yet. I wanted to have a few glasses of wine in me first. Grabbing my bag off his shoulder, I dropped it on the couch and grabbed his hand. We went down the three flights of stairs, opened the door of the basement, and then went down another flight.

"This house is huge," he said as we entered the dark basement. It wasn't dirty and musty. It was a finished basement that mostly housed my father's exercise equipment and his collection of Sports Illustrated Magazines that he'd started collecting as a teenager.

"Sorry," I said, plopping down on the queen-size Murphy bed that was pulled down from the wall. She had even pulled back his covers and left him a note saying, "God bless you." I picked it off his pillow and sneered, "I should have warned you."

"This is fine. I didn't expect to shack up with you at your folks' house," he said, looking around at all my trophies that lined the top shelf around the room. "Soccer, crew, softball, bowling, archery... and shooting?"

"Look at those," I said with pride. I stood up to get a closer look at my former accomplishments. Every single one of my karate belts was still hanging on the special holder my dad made for me in junior high years. "Never got my black belt though. I decided to go out for volleyball and quit karate my first year of high school."

"Is there anything you can't do?"

I was pulled into his arms as he dropped his black duffle at his feet. His heartbeat was just as erratic and deafening as mine.

"They're going to send down a search party if we don't get back up there," I muttered softly against his lips. "And well..."

"I know," he bit down on my lower lip and nibbled it softly before breaking away and slapping my butt. "But if you ever kiss me like you did in the car again, I'm taking that as a signal to ravage you."

"Is that a threat?" I snickered and raced up the stairs like a horny teenager.

***

We both did our best to keep busy with our hands so we weren't tempted by lust. I had changed into my afternoon gala attire and was wearing the blue polka dot sundress, the one that showed a touch of cleavage, just to torture the man and keep him interested while I continued to torment him by saying no all the time. *Why the hell am I doing that, by the way?* Oh yeah, something to do with celibacy rocks and I'm not ready to lose myself again. That makes perfect sense. *Not!*

The jazz band was setting up near the dance floor, the invited guests were still milling around, waiting for the party to get under way and Bull had just pulled up in his big black Hummer.

Scot stilled beside me and watched as dad and Bulldog did their ritualistic handshake thing. His hand was hot on my lower back and I don't think he was quite aware that it was slowly moving closer to my butt. Either that, or he's incredibly brave, because my mother was a mere three feet behind us, telling the caterer where to put the ice sculptures.

I cleared my throat loudly and he flinched, taking his hand off my butt just as Bulldog and my father approached. I never told my father that Bull and Scot had met and I had a sneaking suspicion that neither had Bulldog.

"Scot, this here is my oldest and dearest friend, Bulldog Mathers."

Scot looked at me, I looked at him and then he shook hands with Bulldog.

"Nice to meet you."

"Likewise." Bulldog nodded graciously, and then released Scot's hand to pull me into a big bear hug.

"This little lady right here is our *baby*." He pulled on my cheek with his thumb and knuckle and made a goofy face at me. "We don't like to see her sad." He bowed his smile into a frown and then scowled at Scot.

I felt Scot shudder, and then the men stood and sized one another up for what seemed like an eternity before I decided to break the ice and cut through the fog of bullshit testosterone. "Scot's a Portland Police Officer and a former Marine."

"Well, well." Bulldog's smile returned. "How about that, Mitch?"

My father chuckled and then ran off to tell the band to "hurry the fuck up and start playing. I'm not paying you to stand around and sip wine." Then he smiled, returned to his former nice self, and said, "Do you like it? It's my newest Pinot. I think it's a tad too bitter, but it's a big hit with the locals."

I think my father really tries hard to fit into his new life as a quiet, happy-go-lucky winemaker. It suits him, but every so often his alter-ego rears its ugly head and he can be quite demanding.

We still had many preparations to make and Scot held up nicely under the pressure of being under the watchful eyes of Aunt Rita, my father and Uncle Bulldog. My mother had already held Scot's hand a number of times and introduced him to Father Ashley seven times. I was on my second glass of Merlot when one of my favorite songs began to play.

I think I may have been swaying to the music a little too much because before I knew it my new friend was hauling me onto the dance floor.

The feel of his hand on my back was almost as nice as being smashed up against his front. He seemed rather stiff, but not in that way… get your mind out of the gutter.

"You okay?" I asked against his jaw. I gave it a quick kiss because it was clenched tightly.

"I'd feel better if I could relax."

I don't know if he meant it the way I took it, but I had to laugh and hold him closer.

"What exactly are we waiting for, anyway? You obviously find me attractive, or you wouldn't be groping me every other minute and I want *you*, so what's the big deal?"

"I'm groping you?" My head shot off his shoulder. "I beg to differ." I chuckled and he clutched me closer, taking the opportunity to caress my ass again while his back was toward the spy trio at the center table. All three of them were sipping wine and staring at us nonstop. "Case in point. Are you crazy?"

"I don't think I can wait another minute, let alone another day." He nuzzled my neck and sighed. "Do you know what you're doing to me? It's like I have this massive weight on my chest, making it hard for me to breathe. All I think about is your cute smile and your great lips and if you'll just tell me what we're waiting for, I'll fix it. I can do that, can't I?"

"Actually you can't fix it. No one can fix it." I said, keeping the pressure on his back to keep his body exactly where it was because, my God, it felt so good to be that close. "You wouldn't understand, even if I tried to explain it. Besides, you said you'd wait until I made my move. That you were cool, remember?"

He twirled me around a few times when the music changed. Soon, we were practically doing the mambo. "I said I'd wait, yeah..." I got flung around his backside and then back to where I could see his eyes again. "But we're out here in the most amazing place I've ever seen. I'm drinking wine for Christ's sake and the smell of caramelized brie must make me horny because I feel like a damn teenager and I'm afraid my dick is going to explode."

He actually said all this through clenched teeth. Like he was in serious pain. That incited a burst of giggles to spill from my lips.

"It's not funny, Ang. I'm not kidding."

"I'm sorry," I said as I slowed and moved toward him. I didn't care if the music was moving faster, I slowed and held him tightly, wrapping my hand with his and leaning forward to give him an innocent kiss. "You're a wonderful man, Officer King."

I was going to say something else, but my father interrupted us by cutting in.

"Sure," Scot said as my father asked his permission to dance with "his Pumpkin." "I'll be back."

I moved in my father's arms just in time to see Scot dancing with my mom. *Oh boy.*

"So, how's my girl?" my father asked with a cocked brow.

"Good," I said. "I'm still working on who killed Walter, but I'm feeling much better and, again, thanks for your help." I kissed his cheek and smiled. "Actually, I'm feeling much better about everything lately. I think I was a little out of it for a while. It's good to be back."

"It's good to have you back. What's with the cop?" He nodded toward Scot who was dancing the waltz with my mom. "Is this serious?"

I wanted to say, "As a heart attack, or more like as a *heartache*," but I didn't. I just blushed and looked away. My father had changed into his fancy chinos and gotten out the big guns by actually wearing a button-down white oxford just like the good old days.

"Bull seems to think you want some career advice. Is this true?"

Damn Bull!

"I don't know yet, but I'm keeping my options open."

"You say the word and you'll have a job tomorrow. They'd be lucky to have you," he said with pride.

"I know, Dad, but if I do it, I want to do it on my own. I don't need agency nepotism."

With one eye on Scot, I kept my other eye on Bulldog who was slowly converging on him and my mother. "I better go save..." I started to say, but Bulldog already had Scot by the elbow with a bottle of wine in his hand. They were slowly walking down the hill and soon...out of sight. *Double damn.* God help him!

I ate some crackers, nibbled on a bite or two of gourmet cheese, and then sat down beside Rita. "How's business?"

"Same old, same old," Rita said. "What's new with you? You never mentioned you were in love again."

"Is it that obvious?" I groaned and planted my chin in my palm. "I hate admitting it to myself, let alone my best friend... or even him, but, boy, I'm hooked," I said dreamily. I think it was the wine talking. Either that or Aunt Rita had slipped me a truth serum cocktail. "How do you go about being in love and keeping your identity intact? Huh?" I slurred. "Answer me that." My hand slammed down on the glass tabletop.

Rita just laughed and she gave me her best advice and then we talked about old times, old lovers, and why she was looking at Bulldog the way she was.

***

Scot and Bulldog had come back into view, arms wrapped over each other's shoulders, laughing and having a great old time. They'd been gone for nearly an hour and my guess is that the bottle of wine was gone.

"Ladies," Bull crooned, and then grabbed Rita by the hand and twirled her onto the dance floor.

"What'd you two talk about?" I asked Scot, trying to stay casual about the fact that I was tipsy and, while intoxicated, had actually admitted my true feelings about this man who seemed to be staring into my soul.

"Homework," he said seriously. Scot wasn't drunk, or the least bit off his game. He was sitting close, nudging his knee against mine, and wrapping his fingers into the hem of my dress. "Are you drunk?" His tone was slightly husky.

I may have accidentally dropped my cracker into my wine, which was a good thing, because I'd had enough wine. "No," I said haughtily. "I have a high tolerance."

"Yeah, right," he grinned and pulled me closer. He kissed the tip of my nose, and then slid his hand up my inner thigh. I felt a white-hot sensation warm me instantly, but I didn't flinch, and therefore, he smiled smugly and backed away. "You're drunk all right."

We sat in silence, while he continued to caress my thigh and, yeah, I contemplated dropping my face into his lap and doing something completely nasty. The music kicked up a notch and Scot stopped groping me and leaned toward my ear. "What's up with those two? Looks like they're hitting it off."

I looked in the direction of his gaze. Bulldog was casually caressing Rita's behind with his large hand. "They've hit it off before," I hiccuped loudly. "But then they got divorced."

"What?" he all but knocked me out of my chair, by turning around so fast. "So, then he was your uncle."

"For about eight months." I was really feeling the air around me electrify. "She got reassigned to D.C., he got sent to Central America and they split. I know they still love each other though. She looks just like me, huh?"

"It's uncanny," he said with a questioning appraisal. "You and him never…"

"Gah-ross," I bellowed and stood up, wobbled a bit then fell back down in my chair. "I think we better go for a walk before my mother catches me."

The long way down the hill was the path we chose. The summer sun had just dipped behind the horizon and I was toting a couple bottles of water and a bag of pretzels. Scot was doing his best to keep me from tripping over vines. I wasn't that incapacitated, but it was getting dark and my legs were a bit rubbery.

"Here is good, don't you think?" I grabbed the blanket off his shoulder and dropped it beneath the grapevines, yet far enough away that I could see all the stars in the sky. I loved that time of night. When the sun was down and the first stars started to twinkle. The air had cooled, but Scot had brought his denim jacket for me to wear over my shoulders.

"You know, I don't know a thing about you. Why don't you ever talk about yourself? Do you have parents, sisters, brothers, an ex-wife, illegitimate kids?" I closed my eyes, leaned back against his chest and felt his arms wrap tightly around my waist. This was the closest thing to heaven I had felt in years. Yes, there I said it. In years, not a year since my Ray left, but years. It was nice. It was comfortable and my mind not once tried to talk my body out of relaxing completely as his hand moved toward my breast. It was like second nature to have his hands on my body. I loved it!

His breathing grew labored and when he finally found the underside of my breast with his fingers, I felt his breath catch in his throat. "Is this okay?" he whispered in my ear and massaged my breast from the outside of my dress.

I did one better and moaned, quickly unbuttoning my dress to give him access to what he obviously wanted.

"You're sure sending me mixed signals," he complained.

"It feels good." I gasped when his flesh touched mine. I felt a ping of tension between my legs, letting me know it had been a long, long time since I'd felt climax or anything even remotely close to climax. I've been too damn angry with myself. Well, no more. I'm done. *What's in the past stays in the past and now, right now is the only thing I was going to concentrate on.* "Your parents? Where do they live?"

He groaned, taking his fingers off my nipple, leaving it taut and erect from his caresses and the cool air. "I'd rather not talk about my parents right now."

"Oh," I giggled and rolled over to face him. I was on my knees, nudging myself closer into the V of his legs. "How awkward. I wasn't thinking."

I leaned down and closed my eyes, ready for a passion-induced kiss of epic proportions. A million stars were now twinkling, the frogs were singing and a coyote was even serenading us with its howls at the full moon.

Nothing happened. Well, except that I felt a gush of air on my lips when he growled. "You're drunk and we're not doing this."

I blinked in confusion a couple of times and sat back on my heels. "I'm not that drunk. I'm just a bit... uninhibited."

"Exactly, Ang." He shook his head and looked deep into my eyes.

After I stopped groaning we heard a meowing sound in the distance. Inky was on the prowl. We listened for a minute and then Scot turned his attention back to me.

"My parents, Dave and Jennifer, live in San Diego. I have a younger sister named Allison, an older brother named Jack, three nephews and they all live in and around Seattle."

"What do they do?"

"Jack's an attorney, his wife Emily stays home with the boys. Allison works in Seattle and my father's a police captain in Everett. Mom's... well, she takes care of my dad, redecorates the house every couple years and makes the best chocolate chip cookies in the universe. They've been married for nearly forty years. Any more questions?"

I tugged his jacket closed around my chest and sniffled. His tone was snippy at best, and could I blame him? I'd been telling him no for so long and then I have a little wine and I'm letting him touch my boobs. *What the hell is wrong with me?*

"Please don't cry," he said, cuddling me close, kissing the top of my head, and gently rocking me from side to side. "I can't believe I'm actually going to say this out loud, Angela Harrington, but I happen to respect you."

I dried my eyes on his shirt and tried to smile. "Really?"

"Really." He kissed my nose. "That and I'm afraid your father has us under satellite imagery right now."

We laughed and then we sat in silence while I begged myself not to fall even harder than I already had. You really never know what's going to happen in the vast unknown of what we call "the future." Now I knew that he was raised by a stay-at-home mother who makes wonderful cookies. His brother has a stay-at-home wife and she probably cooks the best meatloaf in Washington. I will not and I repeat, will not, become someone I'm not – ever, ever again. What if he expects that of me? What if? Oh gosh, what if I just shut the hell up and get over myself.

***

We crept into the house at nearly one a.m. I was sober by then, had a horrible headache and felt like a stupid putz for pulling my boob out for Scot to touch. He probably feels the same about touching said breast and that's why we walked back to the house in silence.

"I'm sorry I got drunk," I said as I gave him his jacket back. "I'll explain everything to you someday… when I'm ready."

He grabbed the back of my neck, bringing me closer to his lips before giving me the mind-bending kiss that I had wanted in the vineyard. He seized my waist with both hands, pulling me hard against him. When he broke from the kiss, he looked down at me with lazy eyes. "When you're ready, you won't have time to explain. You'll be busy for like... I don't know... three or four days at least."

"Huh? Now that I'm sober, the heat has returned." I kissed him before pulling away. "I see how you are."

"I want you focused. What's wrong with that?" He pulled me closer and brushed his lips against mine. "No regrets, Angie." And then he embraced me warmly and held me in his arms for a good couple of minutes. It was nice. Friendly. Confirming what he had said in the vineyard – he respects me.

"Thanks." I waved and watched him walk down, down, down, the flights of stairs.

Knowing Dad and Bulldog were sleeping on the floors between us made my decision to follow him that much more enticing.

I changed into my sweats and pulled my hair into a ponytail before brushing my teeth three times and then checking my breath again. I just wanted to be close to him, anyway I could.

The downstairs steps squeak in various places, but I did a good job managing to get past them before opening the basement door and giggling like a twelve-year-old.

"Are you completely nuts?" I heard him whisper loudly. His voice hit a high note and the light flickered on.

"I'm lonely. Please, I promise I won't touch you and no one will know."

"That's no fun." He patted the bed and grinned. "I can't believe I'm doing this." He pulled back the covers exposing his naked legs. He wore black tight boxer briefs and nothing else. *Lord have mercy.*

"Stay on your side and don't make any of those cute chipmunk noises, or I'll be forced to take drastic measures."

"Goodnight," I said, keeping my eyes on his fine physique until he shook his head and flicked off the lamp.

At four a.m. I still hadn't fallen asleep, but Scot was already in deep breathing mode, shivering every so often and sometimes even mumbling things in his sleep. I'd never done this sort of thing before; slept with a man I hadn't just made love to. It was sort of erotic in a way and it was good practice for when I was ready and was certain that I'd remain in control. That was the scary part. Could I love him and be in love with him and still do things under my own volition. Not be sucked into some sick twisted vortex of passion that made me incapable of making sane choices. Choices good for me, not just for him. Would I be able to say no to him if he wanted me to make him dinner every night? Could I lovingly tell him that I don't particularly feel like rubbing his stinky feet at any given time? Could I assert myself and still let him know that I loved and respected him.

Oh boy! I analyze crap to death, don't I?

I rolled over and stared at the side of his face as he slept. Then I wondered how Dale was sleeping, if at all. Was he scared about spending the rest of his life in a state prison with men who ate little boys like him for breakfast? A knot quickly formed in my stomach and I had to get away. Sleep was eluding me and my mind couldn't be shut off, so I headed upstairs, grabbed my father's quilt from the couch, and curled up at the bay window, staring out at the vineyard with tears in my eyes.

I'd suffered from insomnia in the past. Mostly in college when I was worried about papers being due, or whether or not I was going to get A's on my finals, but never like this. I was deeply exhausted, but was nowhere near being at peace. Perhaps, I'd finally gone over the edge and lightning had struck, but I'd been drunk when it happened so I didn't feel it. Whatever the reason, I let the tears stream down my cheeks and cried because I'd fallen in love with the man in my parents' basement.

Ten

I heard voices before I was fully cognizant to the fact that I was asleep on the porch swing. The coffee I had made was already cold and tipped over on the deck.

"Morning," I said with a dramatic yawn. "I couldn't sleep."

My mom sat down beside me and brushed the bangs from my eyes. Dad stretched in the doorway, still dressed in his dark blue robe and fuzzy slippers. He waved as he closed the sliding door and disappeared into the kitchen.

"I heard you pacing. Is everything okay?"

"Fine, Mom." I leaned over and gave her a kiss on the cheek. She looks wonderful for her age. Not that fifty-seven is very old, but still she's not getting any younger. Her eyes looked saddened by my standoffishness toward her question. "It's nothing really. I'm just having a hard time with something."

She opened her mouth to say something and I cut her off with a scowl. "And saying a prayer won't help me now. It's something I have to figure out on my own. It's something inside me that I need to fix, Mom, and unfortunately, God can't help me now."

"I wasn't going to say anything," she huffed and closed her robe around her bare knees. "Do you want to know why your father and I are still very much in love?"

I was beyond stunned. When Ray and I divorced, my mother said, "Go to church and God will bring you strength." I kid you not.

I wiped the sleep from my eye, and then pinched myself to see if I was still dreaming.

"Your father and I are completely different people in our outside activities. Lord knows I never wanted to hear the details of what he did and couldn't imagine the kind of world he lived in while he was on assignment or attempting to fix giant holes in the government's law enforcement agencies, but the minute he would walk in that door, we would drop our outside differences and see each other for the people that we are on the inside. I'm a woman, he's a man, and that strong bond between us has never died," she paused for a short moment. "He cries a lot. Did you know that?"

I wiped the tears from my eyes and shook my head.

"He hasn't had an easy life. He's seen things that nightmares are made of, but he's a strong, brilliant man with a heart of gold and enough compassion to coddle a small country. I see a lot of him in you, Angela. When you find someone who you truly want to share your life with," she emphasized the word share knowing full well that mine and Ray's marriage was a disaster, "then you have to look at that person with wide eyes and see them for who they are on the inside. Don't let the outside world distort your visions of people. Trust your heart, darling, and don't give up on happiness. Scot's a man, Angela, and by goodness, he's not going to be perfect, but if you look at him as just a man first, then you can't go wrong. Don't put him on a pedestal like you did with Ray. Shut out the world, shut out the past and just see him for who he is and if he's truly a good man, then he will do the same."

I wept hard against her shoulder and couldn't believe how incredible she was. Telling me this now, at this crucial juncture in my life, when usually she just skitters on the surface of major issues. "How do I get past the fear that I'll lose myself again?"

She caressed my face in her hands and smiled. "That you have to take up with God." She winked and met my dad at the door. He handed her two cups of coffee, and then gave her a sweet kiss. I cried even harder.

We made pancakes together; just the three of us, just like old times. Scot finally made it upstairs, fully dressed, showered and all. I was still sporting my smeared mascara look. My hair was probably standing on end, my big sleep tee shirt had coffee spilled on the front, but there I was, flipping pancakes with a big ol' grin on my face.

"You want some coffee?"

He nodded, sunk down at the kitchen counter, and watched me with a smile. I flipped, I flopped, and then I cracked a couple dozen eggs into a big blue bowl. Moments later, Bulldog emerged from his room down the hall, hand in hand with Aunt Rita.

The room stilled for a couple of awkward moments, then Rita gave us all the riot act about how they're grownups and what's the big deal?

I didn't know how to react. Boy, I knew they still loved each other, but after the divorce, Dad and Bulldog had it out one night about the split, so I thought it was pretty ballsy of them to fornicate under my father's roof. Thank goodness, I had more sense than that.

Scot and I took a walk around the vineyard after breakfast. I had a hard time articulating my words, but he just held my hand and listened to the lame explanation I had for sneaking out of his bed in the middle of the night.

"I couldn't sleep," I said again. "We should head back. Lily and Chad will be here soon."

The big party was actually scheduled for that afternoon. Yesterday's function was solely for the benefit of the buyers and restaurateurs who had come from out of town. Today is when my father will announce his new Select label and thank his close friends and family for their support. Most of the people who will be attending are financial analysts or had been at one point or another.

"You didn't answer my question." Scot slowed to a crawl and tugged me back to him when I tried to escape.

"I think I don't really trust myself to say no to you. Okay, that's why I can't get naked with you."

He laughed and pulled me closer. "We don't have to go all the way. I just want to see you naked and besides, it's getting hot out here." He nodded toward the pond, which did look incredibly refreshing. "Chicken?"

"I don't think you're supposed to be getting your stitches wet, are you?"

"I didn't say I was going swimming. I just wanted to watch you." He bobbed his brow at me and then slid his hand up the back of my shirt. I felt a tingle, a prickle of heat somewhere below the waist, and then I jumped out of my skin when I saw my father's head bob from the top of the hill.

"Saved by Daddy."

"Ha, ha."

My father trotted over to us, and then asked me if he could borrow Scot. I guess my father had to do it. It wasn't enough that Bulldog had just done it the night before, my father had to get his digs in too, I suppose.

"Be nice," I said as I kissed my father's cheek and smiled sweetly.

I stood there and watched as they disappeared up and over the hill. My skinny-dip with Scot would just have to wait. No big deal. I wasn't prepared anyway. I had Dale on my mind, a murder to solve and my best friends were due any minute.

***

"Geez," I groaned and plopped my butt down on the top step of the deck. "It's been over an hour. What the hell is taking them so long?"

Bulldog and Rita were helping my mom with a basket of fresh roses she'd just cut. I heard snickers, but nobody would acknowledge my angst.

"Bulldog tells me that you've just about got this case wrapped up,"

Rita said as she took a seat beside me and handed me a bottle of water. "I've been waiting for this for a long time. It's about time you got in the game."

"I'm not in the game... not yet anyway," I said haughtily, giving her a bump to the shoulder and returning my gaze to the field. "There they are." I stood up to get a better look. "Does he look okay? Is he limping?" I shaded my eyes and listened to the laughter behind me. "Hey, lots can happen out there on the back forty. There are snakes and creeping vines, cougars and over-protective ex-special agents." It was I who snickered that time.

Dad and Scot stopped at the back of the yard and my father actually hugged him. Scary on so many different levels. I stared in awe and was completely speechless as they finally ascended the steps and met us on the deck.

Scot smiled sweetly, then immediately engaged in conversation with Chad and my father pulled me aside with a frown. "I don't like him, Angie. Not one bit."

At first I couldn't tell if he was joking or not, but then Bulldog put his arm around my father and added. "Snake in the grass, Ang. The guy has no values, no moral code of conduct. I'm actually ashamed to be a Marine right now."

My skin crawled with tiny prickles and my jaw tightened on the verge of tears. Dad and Bulldog knew people well. They saw things that the naked eye does not. I clasped my hand over my heart and Bulldog furrowed his brow. "Do not and I repeat, do not marry this guy Angela Reese."

Then the two men that I trust most burst into chuckles and enveloped me in a giant bear hug. I tried to keep my hands free to pound both of them in the gut, but they out-manned me and I surrendered.

"Thanks." I brushed a tear from my eye. "I will get both of you back for this someday."

"All kidding aside, Pumpkin. I know you could care less about how I feel about your potential suitors, but watch out, this guy means business."

I swallowed hard and looked over my shoulder at Scot entranced in conversation with my two best friends...just like he belonged there all along.

***

I pretty much stayed glued to Lily's side for the next couple of hours, afraid that I'd be dragging Scot down to the pond for that long awaited relaxing swim if I was left alone to think about it too long. My father's *walk-slash-interrogation* must have gone well, because Scot seemed more at ease around Dad and Bulldog than he did the day before. He was smiling a lot and every once in a while would corner me near the buffet table.

"Are you dodging me?" he asked, dipping a shrimp into the red cocktail sauce and lifting it to my lips. I'd never been one for saying no to jumbo prawns, so I opened up and accepted the appetizer between my lips. I was still mesmerized by the way he was staring at my mouth when he tipped his head forward and kissed the excess sauce from my lips. I gasped, almost choked to death, and then swallowed. He just smiled and reached for my hand. "Let's dance."

Romantic? I think Scot wrote the book on sensuality. He unnerved me with his smile and sent my skin ablaze with his warm touch. I melted into his arms and felt a surge of blood rush through my veins and sing in my ears.

"Are you having a good time?"

He nodded, but kept his eyes locked with mine. "Are you doing okay? You seem distracted today."

I shrugged innocently and was willing to only divulge one of my worries. "Just worried about Dale, I guess. I wish there was something else I could do."

"I think your quest to find out who killed Walter and clear the kid's name is enough, don't you? What is it about this kid, anyway?"

"He's brilliant," I said. "I've been teaching for eight years and I've never met another kid like him. He's focused and ambitious and he doesn't deserve any of this. He should be hanging out at the river, making love to his girlfriend and planning his life, not sitting in jail, taking the wrap for something he didn't even do." I sucked back a tear and leaned my head against his shoulder. "His father died when he was only eleven and I just want what's best for him. If his mother did do it—which I still doubt—then he's going to be all alone."

He lifted my chin with his gentle fingers and kissed me lightly on the lips, slowly breaking away. "You're the most amazing woman I've ever met," he said a bit breathlessly. "And I'm sorry for being such a big baby about not getting you naked. I know you have a lot on your mind and that you think you're not ready for me and I know I haven't made it easy on you. I'm really sorry and from now on I'll try harder, because I'm not letting you get away."

My shoulders dropped from their tense position and I kissed him back. "I don't want you to think it's anything you've done. It's not. I have something I need to sort through and, of course, it would help if I knew who killed Walter."

"Uh-uh." He smiled against my lips. "We're done talking about it now. Tomorrow you can give me all your harebrained scenarios and I'll help you as much as I can before I go back to work, but we have..." he paused to look down at his silver watch. "Three more hours before we leave and I'd rather be having fun. Do you want some wine?"

I stuttered, stammered, and then was cut off by his kiss again. "Sure, just one glass."

He laughed and retreated to find me a glass of Pinot Noir. I liked watching him walk away, but then Bulldog slung his burly arm around my shoulder, and I was busted.

"Wham... like lightning." He winked playfully and left me alone.

Maybe I don't want lightning. Perchance, I had lightning with Ray and that's the reason for my nine-year brain-fart. I like Scot, a lot. I'm attracted to him and I enjoy his company, so who needs lightning. All I need is time. Time to find out who killed Walter and time to know for certain that I'm truly back from outer space. I wish there was a way to test myself.

"What's up? You look weird," Lily said from beside me. I hadn't even heard her approach me. She looked at Scot, then back to me. "Don't you want to ask me why I look weird?"

"What?" I peeled my eyes off Scot King and looked at Lily. She didn't look weird. She was smiling, but that's normal. Her eyes were alight with cheeriness, but that's normal too and she was wearing black shorts and a tank top just like me. Again, not weird. I narrowed my eyes and saw her lift her spoon to her lips. "You look fine."

It took me a minute to realize what the green lumps in her ice cream were and then I just started screaming like a girl and bawling my eyes out. "Oh my God!"

That incited a dirty look to be sent by way of my mother, but I cared not. Lily also burst into tears and then we were hugging and kissing and I was rubbing her still-flat belly with my palm.

I swiped the salty tears from my cheeks and stammered helplessly like I always do. "When... I mean... How... Oh my God!"

She hugged me again and Chad joined her by my side. "We found out yesterday morning. I'm only three days late, but I had to know... so he ran and got a test and it lit up right away. A bright pink double line... oh my God, Ang. I'm really doing it. I'm having a baby."

Scot made his way toward us and handed me a glass of wine.

"Congratulations," he said with a smile and lifted his bottle of water to Chad's glass of wine. "Way to go, Tiger."

"So, how are you? Do you feel different? Are you sick or anything? Tell me everything." I pulled Lily by the arm and sat her down on the comfortable padded porch swing. I know I was treating her like an invalid, but I couldn't help it. I was excited and more jealous than I'll ever admit.

***

"You okay?"

I heard his deep voice, but I was still so zoned out that I didn't comprehend his words.

"Ang, you okay, babe?" He squeezed my hand to get my attention.

"Sure," I sighed heavily and turned my head to look at him. I'd relinquished my control and let him drive home. The pale wheat fields were just a blur as I stared out the window.

I'd said goodbye to my parents, reminded Bulldog that we were due to interview Dale and Madeline first thing in the morning, and then we had tossed our bags in the back and headed for Vancouver. We were already halfway home and it was the first time either of us had spoken. I guess I was a little pre-occupied that my best friend was having a baby. It was weird to imagine. I've known Lily since I was two years old and she's having a baby. We were supposed to be doing this together. Just like we planned since we were twelve. We'd get married in a double wedding and then we'd have babies at the same time, so they could grow up together and be best friends like we are. I was just feeling sorry for myself, but it made me think of Ray and his baby for just a short minute. Then I snapped out of it and realized that his son will grow up just like him. A controlling, self-centered sexist pig, and I don't want to raise a son to be like Ray. I want my son to grow up to be a good, kind chivalrous man. A man like... *Scot perhaps.*

"Isn't that great about Lily and Chad?" My lips actually quivered as I said it.

Scot pulled over on the side of the highway and put the car in park, turned off the ignition and reached for me. "It's great," he said. "Are you okay though? What's with the tears?"

"I don't know." I sniffled and looked into his eyes. I was practically in his lap, which wasn't a bad thing, but there was a steering wheel in the way and I wanted a hug. A big hug; a hug that said, "I love you, I want you and I'll give you my sperm someday, so don't fret. You're right behind her."

I struggled to get closer, which incited him to grin and lift my torso off his lap. He struggled to move out from under the steering wheel, but kept me close. He hugged me tightly and began kissing my neck once he was situated... my God, we were necking in the front of my SUV, on the side of the highway no less. I didn't care. It felt wonderful. My nipples puckered tightly and I was smiling like I've never smiled before.

"God, you're beautiful." He bit my lower lip just before suckling it and then he parted my lips with his tongue and delved deep into my mouth, igniting a searing, pulsing sensation between my legs. His hand moved to my breast and I gasped from the pleasure of it.

It took a minute of squirming and moaning, but I finally got myself straddled in his lap and moaned when he lifted my blue tank top and moved under my bra, forcing his hand up under the silky fabric. He looked into my eyes with his hand hot on the back of my neck. I felt very sexy as he narrowed his eyes and lifted my shirt, just enough to get a peak at my naked breasts. My bra was pushed up over them and he couldn't stop staring.

"Oh man," he growled like an injured animal and bent his head, lightly suckling my taut nipple between his lips.

There was lots of moaning, mostly by me. While keeping his lips on my breasts, he wrapped his other hand around my butt and pulled me closer to his more-than-obvious erection. I'm somewhat inexperienced with making-out in cars. I think I'd done it maybe three times in my life, all in college, all before I lost my virginity and that same amazing feeling of anticipation was causing me to breathe extra heavy and press myself against him tightly.

"Angie," he said, looking up to meet my gaze.

I cut him off with a kiss. I kissed him the way he deserved to be kissed. No holding back, no thoughts in my mind other than how good he tastes and how much I'd like to feel him hard inside me. Our bodies meshed together in the heat of the moment and the next thing I knew, my hand was actually caressing his groin. Kissing him passionately and breathlessly, I made my way up his chest and began unbuttoning his shirt as if I had no control over my fingers. My lips were swollen and engorged with blood, my eyes heavy and drooping slightly from the rush of desire.

Out of nowhere, I heard honking, saw headlights, and then froze in place when I saw Bulldog sauntering toward the driver's side door.

"Shit," I yelled and all I had time to do was pull my tank top back into place and remove my hand from Scot's hard-on.

His eyes were also dazed and lazy from arousal, but boy, they sure shot wide open when he too saw Bulldog's face in the window.

Bulldog turned, like the considerate man he was, while I hurried off Scot's lap, banging my head on the sunroof, inciting a long line of obscenities to roll off my tongue. Okay, the obscenities were mostly due to the fact that I had just been interrupted in the midst of unadulterated passion.

I rolled down the window and gave Scot a small smile. "What's up, Reese?" I asked, leaning out the window.

"Nothing," he said with a smirk. "Just saw your car here on the side of the road and thought you might be in trouble."

Oh, I was in trouble all right. Another minute later, I would have lost my mind and demanded to Scot that I was ready and we didn't need to wait another minute longer. Who cares if we were in a car on the side of the highway with no condoms? I was ready... Okay, so I'm not; I was just weak for a moment.

"No." It took a minute for me to swallow. "Things are just fine."

"See you in the morning," he snickered and ambled back to his Hummer, clearly chuckling all the way.

I tucked my head back inside and found Scot shaking his head with a grimace.

"I'm sorry," I said, trying to shake the horror of it all.

"For what? Getting caught, or making me crazy?"

"Both," I said as I bent forward and gave him a quick kiss on the cheek.

***

Monday morning, I woke up cranky. Mostly because I had stayed awake most of the night analyzing my life and feelings like I always tend to do. It was seven a.m. when my alarm went off and it took everything I had not to throw it against the wall. I have to admit that I was also cranky because Scot was so damn nice. He had dropped me off the night before around six, after we stopped for a quick dinner and then had walked me to my door, where he gave me a sweet kiss and wished me luck with Dale.

Ah. Is that not the sweetest damn thing you've ever heard?

I analyzed that to death too. Perhaps he was going to try harder and as long as I behave, then he will too.

I made coffee, got dressed in shorts and a yellow tee-shirt, slipped on my tennis shoes, and met Bulldog on the corner of Fremont and 158th Street just a block from my old house on Cherry Blossom. I looked down the block to the tall brick home where Dale and Madeline lived. Both the cars were in the driveway, so we glanced at one another and I again told him what to ask Madeline. I don't think he liked me telling him what to do, but for some strange reason, he was letting me take the lead.

I knew exactly how I was going to get in Dale's head. I was going to use love.

Before we could even get to the door, it opened and Dale looked out at me, looking sullen, dehydrated, and perhaps a little happy to see me.

"Hi," I said, gathering him into my arms for a warm embrace. Dale was just a few inches taller than me, but I outweighed him with my female girth. Not that I had a lot of girth, but he was a rail. "How are you?"

He shrugged and looked over my shoulder at Bulldog. "Nice to see you again, Mr. Mathers." Then he looked back at me. "What's going on?"

"Can I come in?" I looked over his shoulder and saw his mother sipping coffee. Still wearing her slippers. There was an old, ratty couch, one side table, and not another damn thing in the front room. No fancy art on the wall, no television, or stereo. Just a couch, which I sat down on and gestured for Dale to join me, all the while, giving Bulldog the signal to occupy Madeline.

"Would you like coffee?" she asked nervously.

Bulldog was good. He wrapped his hand around the small of her back and offered to help. That a boy!

"So," I didn't know if I should just get right to the point, or beat around the bush. "Why are you doing this?" I chose the direct route.

"I'm sorry," he said, all the blood rushing from his cheeks, leaving him paler than normal. "Doing what?"

I sighed and placed my hand on his. I did my best to become one with my mother and channel my inner spirituality. All I could come up with was love and understanding.

"I know you're worried about your mom, but think of your future. Have you thought about what this is doing to poor Ella? She's worried out of her mind and of course she knows that you would never do anything like this... just like I know you wouldn't hurt anyone. She loves you and so does your mother, but this isn't right, Dale. I know what you're trying to do."

His eyes shot open wide, on the verge of tears, so I continued with my assault. I knew that a couple more minutes of sweet talk and he'd be singing like a canary.

"You have a brilliant future, a full ride to a wonderful prestigious school, and you're blowing it. You worked hard to get where you are and I know you did it to make your father proud." I stopped when I hit that note because he began to cry. By God, I had done it. Not that I'm proud of myself for making him cry, but I know I got through to him. I placed my hand back on his and gave it a squeeze. "Don't throw your future away. I don't think your mom is guilty any more than I think you are."

He sniffled and stood up, pacing the floor in front of me. "I'm so sorry that I let the cops think it was you. I should have said something sooner, but I was scared, Mrs. Shirpa." I know now was not the time for me to hound him for calling me that, but boy it sent my hairs standing on end hearing my former name – I haven't used that name for awhile now. "I don't know what I'm doing. Ella's a wreck. She's even thinking about not taking her scholarship so she can stay here with me and..."

"Why? Why do think it was your mom and why are you protecting her? Isaac is in jail. He can't hurt you anymore. You have to stop this before it goes any further."

I stood up and planted my hands on my hips. "The cops are going to see the hole in your case before it ever goes to trial. They aren't stupid…" I had to bite my tongue there for a minute. "They're very good at what they do and they'll put it all together eventually." I at least hoped they would. I mean just because the kid confessed shouldn't take away from physical evidence and the fact that his motive sucked shit.

Dale raked a hand through his unruly hair and sat back down. "They had a fight. A big one. She was screaming that he wasn't going to get any more money for whatever it was he was doing and that she'd find out what he was up to and then she threw a plant at him. I've never seen her so mad in my life. Not even when I destroyed the bathroom with my chemistry set."

"So, they fought. That means nothing."

"Yeah, but after the fight, I saw her out front, gardening with your shovel. The one she killed Walter with. She always pulls weeds when she's upset, but after I thought about it, I remembered that she was using your shovel."

"How… I mean…"

"I borrowed it a couple days after you yelled at Walter. Ella's sister's gerbil died and we had a funeral out back. I'm sorry, I never told the cops that but I couldn't. My mom had the shovel."

"But her prints weren't on it," I said under my breath. But he heard.

"She was wearing her garden gloves," he said in rebuttal.

I still wasn't convinced she was guilty.

"What happened then, after you saw her gardening?"

"I was packing some things to take with me. I'd had enough, so I was going to Ella's that night. I didn't come home until eight-thirty the next morning. I saw Mom drive down the street just as I was coming home, so I just kept driving because his car was in the driveway and I didn't want to see him. I wanted to run away and never see him again."

I paced some more and clasped my sweaty palms together. I re-thought every single detail of the report that Bulldog had given me. The one describing every detail of the house. The fact that the sliding door was unlocked, that Walter was naked and that there was no forced entry seemed to point to the wife. But why? Like Bulldog had said, this was a crime that took rage and anger in the moment. Could they have fought again the next morning and she had killed him and then casually driven off down the street? Nah. She would have run. Unless she was that cunning and ruthless and, come on, Madeline wasn't very bright. Dale got his smarts from his father, God rest his soul.

"Okay, so you have to go tell this to the police. Let them do their job, because it makes no sense to me that your mother would commit murder."

"He was having an affair," Dale said sternly. "And he told her the night before he died. Said he was going to leave her for a woman named Laura. I also saw him hit her a couple weeks before. I'm not saying anything to the cops."

Wow! I felt a gush of air escape my lips. "But you can't do this, Dale. It's not your job to protect her. You don't see her running for the police, surrendering and admitting that she did it to save your ass, do you?" I think I may have sounded a bit pissy, but I was upset and when I'm upset, I yell. "Goddamn it, Dale. This isn't up to you to fix."

Bulldog and Madeline came back into the room, probably when they heard my shouting.

"We should leave you two alone now." Bull pulled my elbow and moved toward the door.

"Think about what I said," I cautioned Dale and then I don't know where it came from, but I found myself glaring at Madeline. "Don't let him do this, Madeline. Please."

Then Bulldog yanked me out the door, where I barreled down the street in tears, kicking up dust and leaves in my wake until I was safely in my SUV, pounding on the steering wheel and saying *fuck* every other word.

"*That* was playing it cool?" Bulldog sounded disappointed but gave me a weak smile. "I think the kid might be guilty after all, hon. I'm sorry."

I didn't say anything, I just hurried home so I could splash cool water on my face and hear the bad news that Bulldog was so eager to give me.

It started raining before I pulled into my driveway. It rarely rains in July, but it was a downpour. I got out and slammed my door, my hair was already matted to my forehead by the time I got inside and shook the droplets from my face. "He's not guilty. He's protecting her. But I don't understand why she's not protecting him. If she did it, she wouldn't let him take the bum rap. Would she?" I dropped my shoes onto the floor and padded into the kitchen in my soggy socks. "You want coffee?"

He nodded and sat down at the table. I still had my theories about who killed Walter splayed out on the light oak. "You're obsessed," he said, looking over my pile of theories.

"I'm trying to be thorough," I said as I sprinkled coffee grounds into the filter. "Sorry I interrupted, what were you saying?"

"The kid took the shovel. She saw him just days after you screamed at Walter, taking the shovel from your bucket."

"Yeah, I know. So what?" I snapped. "He needed it to bury a gerbil." I filled the coffee machine with water and flipped the switch.

He gave me a funny look and continued. "She also said that after that day, when Walter hit him and you threatened death, she found him muttering to himself about how he'd give him what he deserves and that it was the last time he'd ever lay a hand on him. She said he looked possessed."

"So," I said with hands on hips.

"She also said that Dale witnessed Walter hitting her a couple weeks before the murder and it scared her that Dale might do something to Walter in retaliation. He kept muttering to himself that Walter would pay."

"So…" I felt a twinge of pain behind my right eye. "Wait a doggone minute." I shouted and put my hands up to stop him from saying anything further. "She honestly thinks it was him. That's why she's not coming forward, because she's innocent too, but she thinks he really did it. That's it, isn't it?"

"Why, what did the kid say?" Bull asked just as the coffee machine blipped. He poured himself a cup and then poured one for me in the mug he gave me for high-school graduation. It was a special mug that had my name on it and what my name meant. It was a bit spiritual for Bulldog, but he is also my godfather, so it seemed fitting.

"He said that after their fight, he saw her with the garden shovel and that she knew about the affair and that Walter was leaving her."

"That's a better motive than the kid's," Bulldog said. "But what about the fact that she saw him coming home the morning that Walter was murdered. She said she saw him driving down the street on her way to work and that's about the time that the police said he died."

"So, she could have killed him and then left him to bleed on the floor while she got ready for work," I said arrogantly, again with my hands clasped around my hips. "He didn't do it."

"I don't think she did either. So where does that leave us?"

We finished our coffee, talked some more about Aunt Rita and then when he got too uncomfortable with my line of questioning he stood up and stretched. "I should go. I'm way behind on something and I can't play detective with you anymore. You're on your own, baby girl."

"Thanks," I said with a small wave. "I appreciate your coming with me. I owe you one."

"Then take my letter of recommendation and dare to live your dream. Pretty please."

I narrowed my eyes. "I'll think about it."

***

Two hours later, I woke with a start, peeling my face off my pillow and glancing at the clock. I had just laid down to stop the pounding in my head and really had no intention of napping. I haven't taken a nap since I was four years old, so it unnerved me slightly that I was that exhausted – to the point where I had actually wasted two entire hours sleeping when Walter's killer was still at large.

"Angie?" I heard Scot's voice just outside my bedroom door. "You in there?" he asked as he peeked his head in.

I sat up and smiled, pretending that I hadn't just been napping. How pathetic am I?

"Little afternoon catnap?" He leaned against the doorjamb and crossed his arms at his chest, looking sexy as hell. It had been a while since I'd seen him in Levi's. *Yum!* His dark blue rugby was tight across his chest and his hair was damp from the relentless rain. "You want company?"

"I'd say yes, but I have so much to tell you. What did you find out?" I said as I swung my legs over the side of the bed and stood up. "Dale didn't do it. He actually admitted it right to my face. I know I can't take that to Jessup, but perhaps he'll be willing to listen. What do you think?"

"I think you look adorable with sleep lines on your face." His gaze dropped to my breasts. I looked down and had completely forgotten that I had taken my shirt off and was just wearing my white lacy camisole. I crossed my arms over my breasts and whimpered like a chipmunk.

"Concentrate, please."

I got really nervous and suddenly flushed when he started toward me with *that* look in his eyes.

The first thing I felt was his finger snagging the spaghetti strap of my camisole, followed closely by his hot lips against my collarbone.

"How can I concentrate when I know how amazing those boobs feel?" he said with a sensual snarl. "Want to do something fun and exciting?" He kissed up my neck, over to my ear and then began tenderly nibbling my lobe.

"No," I moaned helplessly. "I mean... maybe... no. I mean *no*, damn it." I pushed his shoulders and looked at his devilish smile.

"So you don't want to come with me to Laura Moncrief's apartment?"

"Really?" I grabbed his shirt and curled my fingers into the cotton. "Are you serious? You'd take me with you?" Now I was panting like a dog that gets to go bye-bye.

He winked and I got dressed.

***

Not more than half an hour later, we were questioning the apartment manager about the last time that anyone saw Laura.

The man was short, bald and was cross-eyed under his horn-rimmed glasses much like the ones my grandmother used to wear. His pants were denim, but his pale yellow bowling shirt was one-hundred-percent polyester and I think he may have borrowed his tattered shoes from a hobo.

"Laura's been gone for quite some time. Haven't seen her in weeks, but her rent's paid through August 'cause she and her man-friend signed the lease and then they were supposed to be moving, so they just paid it all up front when they signed. I got it right here, if you want to see." He shuffled through his desk, narrowly spilling his half-drank bottle of cheap scotch. "Right here." He handed it to Scot, who perused it quickly, then held it up for me to see.

The co-signer was Walter A. Dobbs. *Interesting.*

Scot held up a photo of Isaac Moncrief. "Have you ever seen this young man before?"

"Sure, that's her kid. He comes and goes, but hasn't been around in awhile."

"What's awhile?" Scot asked impatiently. "I'm looking for specific dates. When did you last see her?"

"Look man, I work days. She worked mostly nights. I'd see her take off in her car around four and then she'd usually come home sometime around three a.m., but like I said, I'm usually sleeping." He hiked up his jeans and sniffed loudly, kind of proud like. "Unless I have company." He winked at

Scot, who cringed and looked down at me. I was biting my lip, trying not to burst into laughter.

"Thanks," he said, handing Mr. Happy a business card. "Call me if you think of anything or if you happen to see her."

"Will do." He grinned and then turned back to his television.

When we got safely out the front door of his apartment-slash-office, the rain had stopped and Scot looked perplexed.

"What is it? Gut feeling? Cop's hunch?" I asked.

"Hunger," he snorted. "I haven't had lunch. You hungry?"

How can he think of food at a time like this? Laura Moncrief, a.k.a Sheila The Stripper, is missing.

"Sure, I could eat."

Who cares? She's probably just upset about Walter's death and is too depressed to take off her clothes on stage. Or, perhaps her son is right and Madeline killed Walter and Laura and hacked her up and put her in her freezer behind the Lean Cuisines.

"Wait." I grabbed Scot by the back of the arm and looked up to the third floor where Laura's apartment was. "What if?"

"What if?" He cocked a brow. "You're nuts. Cute, but nuts. Let's eat."

"No, what if Isaac is onto something? What if her disappearance is connected somehow, or..." I gasped for a dramatic effect. "What if she's dead in her apartment?"

He looked up and winced. "I think someone would have smelled the stench by now. Let's eat."

"You're impossible," I said, clearly outraged by his lack of humanity. "What if she had a stroke and is laying in a pool of her own feces and urine and can't get up?"

He actually laughed at me. "Again, neighbors have noses, honey."

"Don't call me honey!"

"Darling." He wrapped his bulky bicep around my neck and hauled me toward his truck. "I'm hungry and since I can't have you yet, I need food."

My knees felt like Jell-O at the near mention of his hunger for me and have I mentioned how great his truck is? It's navy blue metallic that shimmers in the sunlight. It has an amazing front grill and when I see him behind the wheel, my vagina goes into spasms. *Like it's doing right now.*

"Are you coming?" he asked, turning the key. The hum of the engine caused my insides to rumble. *And my God, is he reading my mind?* "Angela Reese Harrington, get in the damn truck right now."

"No!" I stood my ground and looked up to the third floor. "What if I just go up there right now and bust the window? You can call the cops on me and they will go in to investigate."

"And I'll have to arrest you for B and E and therefore will have to wait eight to ten months longer before getting what I want. It's not going to happen. Not right now." He sent me a long look of warning, and then exhaled loudly. "Look, if you let me grab a sandwich, I'll bring you back here and you can peek in the window all you want."

"Can I break it?" I climbed in.

"Not a chance."

***

After Hungry Man was finished inhaling a foot-long turkey sub, he did what he promised and took me back to Laura's apartment. I knocked on the door, looked in the dingy window, but unfortunately, I couldn't see through her curtains and then saw one of her neighbor's unlocking their apartment just two doors down.

"Excuse me, have you seen Laura?" I hurried down to the woman before she could enter her apartment.

"Laura's gone, dawg."

I know my hair was pulled tightly behind my head, tucked into a baseball cap because of the earlier rain, and I was in jeans, but come on. I thought dawgs were men, but whatever.

I continued on. "What do you mean *gone*? When was the last time you saw her?"

"Weeks. I know that 'cause she borrowed money from me right before she left and that was weeks ago." Then the tall woman slammed her door in my face.

"Nice going, dawg," Scot teased me and leaned back against the railing. "You seen enough yet?" he asked with his head cocked to the side, clearly bored to tears. I think he was checking out my ass as I walked by. I too look very good in Levi's. In fact, I think everyone looks good in Levi's. They're just the most perfect jeans ever made.

"No," I said and just as I went to grab the doorknob, he yanked my hand backward. It sort of hurt. "Ouch!" I shouted. "What the..." I looked down at him; he was bent down, surveying the underside of her doorknob. "What is it?" I knelt down to have a look. "Blood?"

"Probably just paint," he said, but kept my hand held tight in his. He fished his cell phone out of his pocket and called 911. *Paint, my ass.*

Needless to say, I was shuffled downstairs, into his truck and told to stay – like I was a dog.

"But..."

He slammed the door in my face and met the police cruiser that had just pulled in beside us. I saw them chitchat for a moment, then they both looked up at the second floor landing, and then another call was made on the walkie-talkie and I was still furious with being told to stay put. What else is new? I hate being told what to do.

Ten minutes later, I recognized one of the plainclothes detectives as Tony Little.

"Hey," he said through the window that I had just rolled down. "You're quite the detective I hear. Let's see if you know what you're doing."

I saw him snap a latex glove on his hand and he was gone with a wink. He marched up the stairs with Scot and another band of officers. They did their thing, and then Mr. Happy walked by with a long string of keys. *Yippee.*

At that point, I was tired of waiting, but I had no choice. If I went up and got in the way, Scot would be mad. If I went up and saw a dead body, I would pass out, so I stayed put and waited and waited and waited.

Forty-three minutes later, Scot came back and slid in behind the steering wheel. The sun had returned in full force and I was sticky from the humidity.

"So," I said excitedly. "What happened?"

"She wasn't home."

"And that's it?" I felt my jaw drop. "What's going on?"

"It's a missing person case now. It doesn't concern you."

"Come on." I grinned and moved closer. "What does that mean? I'm the one who found out who she was and that she was even missing."

I had moved so close that I was practically in his lap. He chuckled and grabbed a handful of my breast. "Are you willing to bribe me for information?"

"Uhhh," I stammered and flushed slightly as he kept massaging my boob. "You're a pig!"

Eleven

Tuesday night, I had road rage class again. Tony was once again at the head of the class. I had four more classes to go and then I was a free woman again. Our first assignment was to take a personality profile that tests how we handle stress, conflict, and aggression. I think I told the truth for the most part. At least I didn't do what Biker Andy did, which was color in all the B's down the page. He leaned back in his chair and smirked at me when he was done.

"B personality," he said with an obnoxious chuckle.

I ignored him, then wandered up front to see if I could weasel any information out of Detective Little.

"What's on your mind?" He dropped his Nikes to the floor and pulled a chair up next to his desk.

"I was just wondering if they found Laura yet." I sat down beside him.

"Not that I know of. Why? Is she missing?"

My jaw dropped and he laughed.

"I can't tell you any of this and you know it."

That wasn't going to stop me from trying though. I was still fairly peeved at Scot for ignoring my questions and I think he was peeved at me for slapping his hand off my boob. "Please. I just need to know if they found her...dead or alive."

He looked around, as if to make sure no one was watching. I felt my pulse rocket and my hands got clammy so I wiped them on my khaki shorts. He leaned even closer, put his finger to his lips, made a shushing sound, then when I drew in a breath, he grinned wickedly. "She's either dead... or alive."

"And you're a big...ugh." I stood up and stormed back to my desk. I didn't think it was a wise idea to tell my road rage awareness instructor that he was a big horse's ass. Even more importantly, I knew Tony would be a very close friend of mine someday, so I cooled my jets and kept my big mouth shut for once.

After class, he wrapped his lanky arm around my shoulder and walked me to my car.

"Look, I know you think the kid is innocent, but there has to be some sort of proof of that."

"Yeah, but..." I gave up. Unbelievable, isn't it? "Goodnight, Tony."

***

Thursday morning, I was still dodging Scot's calls and had made plans with Lily to go baby shopping. It was a good thing too, because my mind could not be stopped. All I thought about the past two days was blood, murder, crimes of passion, Scot's penis, Scot's butt, Scot's lips, and poor Dale. Shopping could not have come at a better time.

"You're losing it," Lily said as I broke into tears for the third time. Babies R Us tends to do that to me. Little bitty baby clothes in pink or light baby blue, it mattered not. I was having a full-on meltdown.

"I think I love him." I sniffled and held up a tiny little dress with pink ruffles and tiny red bows. "And I've been miserable the past three days without him and that sounds so incredibly stupid because I miss him and yet I'm dodging his invitations to dinner and his many phone calls. What the hell is wrong with me? I'm doing it all over again, aren't I?"

"You're not!" she said, pulling out a package of onesies that would fit a newborn bundle of joy. "Scot is not Ray. He's not going to tell you how to style your hair, or what clothes to wear or that he'll be disappointed if you don't devote your life to teaching." She paused momentarily to ponder her choices. "What do you think? Pink and yellow, or green and blue?"

"I think you should wait until you know what the sex is, don't you?"

"No," she said adamantly. "I don't want to find out. I want to be surprised, so I'll just get all of them." She tossed them into her cart and continued on. "Anyway, Scot loves you and now you know you love him. It's okay to miss him and want to see him every day. It's called being in love and it's fun. Enjoy it while it lasts because it will wear off slightly and you'll be happy to see him just once a day, then after three years, you'll just be happy to see him every other day and so forth. That's life! But if you really love him, then... well, I just know that he's nothing like Ray. I wouldn't lie to you, Angie, and I'm sorry that I didn't pull you aside when you met Ray and slap the living shit out of you." She took her attention off the designer line of strollers and turned to me with a sparkle of tears in her eyes. "I should have. Lord, how I wanted to, but you were so happy and so excited that you finally fell in love. I'm sorry, sweetie."

"You did fine. Besides, you were away at school and I wouldn't have listened to you because I was brainwashed and completely gaga over the man. And you're right, Lily. Ray reminded me of Bulldog." I rolled my eyes and groaned. "So, how should I handle this?"

"Tell him."

I dropped the Diaper Genie, narrowly missing my toe.

"Tell him that I love him?" I squealed. "Are you high?"

She glared and wrapped her hands over her flat stomach. "Not in front of the baby. No, I'm not high. Sheesh," she said. "What's so wrong with that, you know he loves you."

"No," I began, carefully placing the Diaper Genie in Lily's cart. "I know that he wants me for sex. That doesn't constitute love. He's never said love. I think he said "crazy about" once, but not love."

"He loves you."

I think I smiled and I know my stomach did a back handspring. *He loves me?*

***

After returning Lily to her home and unloading her mass quantities of baby goods, I said goodbye, grabbed a red apple off her counter, and headed to road rage class. This evening Tony was the instructor, but Scot was sitting on the edge of Tony's desk sipping coffee in fine form, I must say. I love that uniform on him and I was happy that he was able to return to the job he loves so much.

He smiled when he saw me, then he went back to his conversation and laughed a lot.

I tucked in behind Biker Andy and twiddled my thumbs waiting patiently for class to start. At seven fifteen, Scot finally got up and abruptly left the room. My heart sank into my stomach and I felt bewildered and incredibly sad.

"Miss Harrington," Tony said sternly from the front of the classroom. "Officer King would like a word with you in the hall – now!"

The entire class, which was now just four of us, mumbled under their breaths, but I couldn't help the smile. I got up and sheepishly walked out the door and down the hall. Scot was nowhere to be seen.

"Scot," I called and looked around the corner by a long row of overturned chairs. It was dark except for a couple of flickering fluorescent lights near the classroom. "Hey." I practically yelped when he caught me from behind. I would have turned in his arms, but his hold was strong and I liked his hand on my breast and he was in uniform. That alone almost made me squeal in delight. "You wanted to see me?" I clutched his hand and kept it right where it was, massaging my left breast.

"Where have you been? Are you still mad at me?"

"Uhh," I moaned and closed my eyes, trying to shake the erotic fantasy that was transpiring in my mind. I pressed my butt against him and wiggled a bit, until he grunted and turned me around to face him.

His chest was heaving, much like mine, up and down in a ragged fashion.

"I'm not mad, in fact I… I…"

"You were right," he whispered against my neck before kissing it softly. "They found blood on Laura's kitchen counter and the blood on her door." He kissed me again, this time on the lips, taking his time tasting me with his roaming tongue. He broke away and smiled against my lips. "They're analyzing it right now."

"No way!" I shouted and pushed away from him. "Are you serious? Why are you all of a sudden telling me this?"

"Because I'm proud of you and I knew once I slipped you some info, you'd fall into my arms and we'd finally get to *relax.*"

"Is that all you think about?" I said, trying to escape, but come on, I wasn't trying very hard. "What is this to you, some sort of game?"

"Jesus, woman." He raked a hand through his dark hair and grimaced. "When you know you want to make love to someone, then every day seems like…"

I cut him off at that point. I'd heard that line before. "Why? Why do you want me?"

"Because you're cute?"

"Nice try," I said and turned on my heel to head down the hallway in the opposite direction. He caught up with me and took my hand.

"That's not what I meant," he said sincerely, entwining his fingers with mine. "What exactly do you want from me? You tell me you're not ready. What exactly does that mean? I've been very confused and frankly I'm getting annoyed."

"You're annoyed?" I looked down at his pants and scowled. It looked to me like he was aroused, not annoyed. But hey, what the hell do I know?

"Come home with me. Let's talk about this."

"I have class, remember?"

"Tony said he'd cover. Come on, I have dinner waiting in the truck. Please Ang, I miss you."

What could I say to that, other than, *Wow!*

I followed him back to his place and helped him gather his bags of groceries from the deli. He had a lemon cake too. The man is a god.

"What else did they find?" I was eager to keep the subject on something I felt comfortable with. Talking about feelings and love, and sex and relationships was still scary business. I think even more so now that I know I'm completely and totally in love with him. *Love is scary.*

"Not much," Scot said, lifting boxes from the brown bag and opening them on the counter. He took out two plates, a couple of forks and handed me a bag of rolls. "They found a bunch of moldy food. Garbage everywhere and clearly she had left in a hurry. The gals at Dancing Beaver say she hasn't even come in for her latest paycheck. Not that it's all that much. Those women live off their tips."

I unwrapped the rolls, grabbed the butter from his fridge, and helped him carry our plates of Italian food to his table. It wasn't oak like mine, but it was a nice white wooden table with matching chairs. Well, three of them matched and the fourth was a folding chair. I sat down, grabbed my fork, and looked over at him. At that moment, I felt as if I'd known him my entire life. Like we were meant to be. Needless to say, I was trembling.

"I'm scared."

He finished the bite he was chewing and swallowed with difficulty. "I'm sure she's fine. They didn't find a lot of blood; just a few drops here and there. Some spattered on a shoe. No decaying body parts lying around."

"That's not what I meant." I paled slightly thinking about the blood.

He set his fork down and planted his elbows on the table. "I think you're analyzing this to death aren't you?"

"That's such a *man* thing to say."

"It's true." He took another bite, and then pointed his fork at me as he spoke. "Men are easy. We have simple tastes and we don't think shit to death like women do. I like you. You're

very pretty, I love your laugh, and your smile drives me crazy.
Case closed."

I sat in wonderment waiting for him to continue.

So, that answered my question from earlier today. No,
there's no love. He just said it, he likes me.

"I think you haven't gotten over your pig husband leaving
you for a bimbo and now you're taking your crap out on me. Is
that fair?" He pointed at me again before digging back into his
lasagna. "I don't think so. I'm not blaming you for shit that Jill
did. Get the hell over it. I'm not Ray."

I was speechless, but boy, I wanted to throw my multi-
grain roll at his big head.

"You are so wrong!" I shouted and stood up. I guess I do
have a bit of rage in me left, 'cause I felt it boiling in my veins.
"You know nothing about it. You don't know... anything!"

"Oh yeah," he said with a piercing gaze. "I *do* know
something. I know that you're not ready. What the hell does
that mean anyway? You're not ready for what? For sex? Fine.
We'll wait. Not ready to go steady? Is that it?" His eyes
narrowed slightly. "Or is that what you want? You want to
know there's a commitment on the horizon before you fall into
bed with me. Fine, Ang, do you want to go steady?" He pushed
back from the table and slammed his hands down beside his
plate, causing his silverware to do a little dance.

"Can you go a whole minute without referring to sex?" I
yelled. "Sex is not love, big guy!"

He shook his head slowly from side to side. "Is that it?"
He growled. "Is this what this is really about. Are you trying to
get me to tell you that I love you before we make love? For
God's sake, Ang." His plate jumped again when his big hand
slammed down on the table. That's when I tried to retreat. "Get
your ass back here!"

"Go to hell!" I shouted, two steps from the front door.

He was fast. So fast that I didn't stand a chance. Not a
chance in hell. He must have been on the mend, because he
lifted me onto his shoulder and carried me down the long, long
hallway before flipping me onto his bed. I bounced a couple of

times and stared up at him, astonished and honestly, a bit turned on.

"I love you! Is that what you want to hear?" He shouted, pacing the floor in front of me. "My God, I think I've loved you since you cried on the crab at the Crab Shack. Don't you get that by now?"

I started crying, placed my hands over my eyes and curled my knees up. "Go away."

"No," he chuckled. "It's my bedroom."

I snorted, and then sniffled loudly. "You're a horse's ass." So what if he does love me, he's still a horse's ass.

"You're a lunatic!" The bed bounced lightly when he fell beside me. He watched my eyes for a moment and then kissed me like a man in love.

What did I ever do to deserve a man like Scot King?

"Sex is not love," he balked. "That sounds like something your mother would say."

"Hey, she's a smart church lady," I said with a quick slap to the chest.

He caught my hand and tenderly kissed the palm.

"I meant what I said. We can wait," he replied. It was like an arrow to the heart. I warmed instantly… everywhere.

I shook my head slowly and brushed the hair from his eyes; they were narrowed slightly as I said it, and then he kissed me again and I felt the room spinning. Everything was a big blur. For the next couple of minutes I probably felt what a man feels, just an unrelenting need for release. I tried to think like Scot and make it simple for a change. I love his smile, his scent drives me wild, and he makes me laugh. Case closed!

My muscles were clenched tightly, my toes were curled, and I felt tiny prickles licking my skin. My shorts seemed to be sliding down my thighs without any effort and then his mouth was hot on my naked breast.

Oh my God! I whimpered and moaned and covered my head with his pillow as he worked a couple fingers into my panties. "Scot," I said, my voice hitting an octave above normal. "Scot."

"Huh," he said, looking up from my breast and into my eyes. "What?"

"I…"

"Shhh." He kissed me again and pressed down hard with his lips, creating a seal over my lips with his entire mouth. His fingers worked faster and more rhythmic and thirty-nine seconds later, I felt a shot of pleasure rip through my body like a bullet. Hard and fast, and when it was over and the orgasmic spasms stopped, he smiled at me with the devil in his eyes. "You're not ready."

"I beg…*ohmygod*…to differ." I was still breathless and waiting to be pounced on.

"I appreciate your opinion on the matter, but something's missing. I don't know what it is, but you still seem distracted." He bent and kissed my breast, then removed his fingers from my purple panties. He snapped the elastic a couple of times and watched my expression go from orgasmic to bewildered.

"I thought this is what you wanted. It's all you ever talk about."

"I'm a guy." He shrugged and helped me with the chore of adjusting my bra. "We're supposed to talk like that. We're supposed to be obsessed and nag our women folk about our sexual frustrations – that way you know we're still interested." He tugged my shorts back up, gave my navel a little kiss, and entwined his fingers with mine.

"You could just buy me flowers." I felt my breathing steadily return to normal. I have to admit; I really, really needed that for my sanity. Now I can focus, find out who killed Walter and then when I'm no longer distracted, I will jump his bones and tell him how much I love him. It's perfect. I felt *Grrr-eat*!

He tweaked my nose playfully. "And your job as a woman is to keep me in line. What the hell were you thinking? If I wasn't a noble man, I would have ravaged you just then, even though you were crying and clearly weren't thinking straight. You know that, right?"

"Your nobility is appreciated. I have too much on my mind and you deserve better. You deserve fireworks, sexy negligees and..."

"A blowjob?"

I snorted with laughter, rolled into his chest to hide my blushing cheeks, and gave him a little slap. "You're a guy all right."

***

I love the feeling of being in love. After I got over my embarrassment about fellatio, we talked for hours and then played Scrabble and ate cold lasagna and lemon cake. I should just say that I'm probably a bit old-fashioned. I've been with two men in my life. My first was my college boyfriend Darwin. Dar and I had sex three times before I decided it wasn't good for me to be in a sexual relationship. I was nearly twenty-one years of age and it was all about my education and my quest for a career. I met Ray about eighteen months later. We didn't do it until he all but told me I was his soul mate. We were married a few short months later. So, there's my sexual history up 'til now. Now, I want it to be perfect and Scot deserves excellence. He deserves my undivided attention, so now I'm even more determined than ever to free Dale and get on with my soon-to-be-great sex life.

***

Friday morning, I woke with the sunrise, after getting the best night's sleep of my life. *Orgasms are better than sleeping pills.* I felt so good and invigorated that I walked four miles, and then sanded my deck with the belt sander that my neighbor Brett had loaned me. I borrowed it a month ago, but I've been a bit busy lately trying to clear my name.

I thought about Dean, I thought about Laura and then I thought more about Scot and the magical things he did with his fingers. That incited me to drop my sander and call him.

"Hi," I cooed into the phone. My whole body went into convulsions just hearing his sweet voice. "How are you?"

"Good," he answered. "How are you?"

"Did they get the results back from the blood? Have they found her, did you get a hold of Dean Hopper and…"

"I'm at work," he said flatly. "I'll get back to you about that as soon as I can."

"Oh," *Duh.* "Sorry," I said and then I hung up and bawled like a baby. Okay, so not ready for this! What is my problem? So, the man couldn't drop whatever he was doing and rush to my side. *I'm obsessed…I'm deranged…I need…chocolate and caffeine.*

***

When I reached the coffee bistro, Lily was sipping lemon water, with a look of peril on her face.

"I think I'm going to be sick."

"Really?" I said. "Morning sickness? What's it like?" *Can I have some please?*

She tried to smile. "What's the big emergency? Did you get laid?"

"Almost," I said sternly. "Sort of, but not technically and that can wait." I told her all the details of Laura and the blood in her apartment and how my gut said the two were connected somehow.

She in turn ran for the bathroom while covering her mouth with her hand.

I took her home, made her some tea and handed her a box of saltine soda crackers. "My mom swears by these," I laughed. "They may even cure cancer someday."

And then I left and did a completely off-the-wall thing. I drove straight to Dean Hopper's office and demanded an explanation. What I got was attitude, as you can imagine.

"I'm beginning to think that you're hiding something from me." I stood with hands on hips, full of false bravado and painful gas cramps. "Did you know he was shacked up with his ex? Isaac's mother?"

His beady little rat eyes narrowed on me. "Yeah, who the hell didn't? It's been going on for months. What about it?"

"Do you know she's missing?"

He looked even more slitty-eyed. "Watch your back, teacher."

I don't know what the hell he meant by that, but it made my skin crawl. "I'm just trying to find out who killed Walter so Dale can go to Stanford."

"That's kind of you, I'm sure, but don't go poking your pretty little head around where it don't belong. Capice?"

"Whatever," I said and then turned to leave just as a tall, uniformed officer stepped inside the front door. The bell chimed a number of times as he held the door open for me.

I felt his eyes burrowing right through me and sheer panic made my knees wobble.

"Were you leaving, ma'am?" Scot said deeply. A lot deeper than his normal voice, which is still fairly deep.

I nodded and ran out to my SUV and paced the parking lot until I was grabbed from behind and pressed up against the side of my Expedition.

"You are nuts, aren't you?" I felt his hot breath on the back of my neck. "Stay away from Dean Hopper. In fact, go home and... plant something."

He let go of my arm and stood in front of me much the same as the day he arrested me for poking him in the sternum. I couldn't help the feeble grin.

"What?" he growled. "Don't be thinking just 'cause you're cute and I love you that I'm letting you off easy. This is officially a re-opened murder investigation and you're not invited." He pulled me out of sight of the street and kissed me hard. "I'm not invited either, but I promised you I'd ask this joker some questions. He didn't want to answer them so it's over. You're out. I'm out and that's all we can do for the kid."

"Officer," I said sweetly. "You're nightstick is poking me in the thigh."

"Sorry," he backed off and helped me into my SUV. "I'll come over later and tell you all the good news, but I have a poker game that I can't miss."

"Okay, how late?"

"Depends on how long it takes me to win back all my money." He kissed me and was gone.

Goody. Good news and the murder investigation has been re-opened. That's just the kind of news I want to hear.

I went home, showered, changed into my black negligee, and lay in bed. I waited and waited and then dusted my bedroom with an old sock. At midnight, I showered again, because I was sweating from also rearranging my drawers and closets and vacuuming the guest bedroom.

At two, I ate a piece of leftover lemon cake that Scot had given me and fell asleep on the couch.

The phone rang at ten the next morning, waking me from my murderous dream of how I was going to hunt Scot down and gut him alive.

Being in love *is* fun!

"What?" I barked grouchily.

"What, *what?*" he said. "I'm sorry. It got really late and I figured you went to sleep."

"Whatever," I said. There's something about him that I find so damn endearing. I know I'm disappointed because if he had super duper good news for me last night, I was going to thank him with my body over and over again. But I like him as well as love him, so I truly wasn't all that angry about being stood up. But on the other hand, I was dying for some super good news. "What happened? Did they find Laura? Is Dale off the hook? Tell me!"

"Good morning to you too, honey."

"Sorry, good morning, Scot. Now tell me!"

"What are you wearing?" he asked, clearly teasing me with his husky voice.

"Sweats, my father's old Marines tee-shirt and dirty, smelly socks, why?" I lied with a chuckle. "You would have seen for yourself if you had brought me good news last night."

"Oh," he said smugly. Then I heard my doorbell chime. I knew it was him, so I ran in and threw on my oversized chenille robe.

Just as I suspected, Scot was at the door, dressed in khaki shorts and a navy-blue Polo. I opened the door and leaned against the doorjamb. "Tell me now!" I flipped the phone shut and was hauled into his arms, right where I wanted to be.

"I have time for one cup of coffee," he said. "The blood matched Walter's. She's now a suspect and Dale's confession is being scrutinized. You're an amazing woman, Ang."

"So that's it. It's over, Dale gets to go home?" It seemed so anticlimactic.

"Not exactly. Laura's just wanted for questioning, but they are talking to Isaac and it's still entirely possible that Madeline went to Laura's apartment right after she killed Walter and she's the one who left the blood on the door and counter. There's no indication saying that Laura did it. She's just going to be questioned."

"Like I was," I said under my breath and took a moment to rein in my severe disappointment. "So, she could be dead. Is that what you're saying—but not saying?"

"Did I say that?" He grabbed my hand and pulled me to his lips again. His kiss was soft and inviting. "I've had fantasies about this."

"Oh yeah," I whispered while he continued kissing up the side of my neck.

"You making me coffee… in your sexy robe."

That sent my shivers a halting. "Not funny," I said and stepped back. Ray used to like it when I dressed up for him while making him dinner. I shivered, but not in a nice way and I felt myself involuntarily retract from his grasp.

"What'd I say?"

"Nothing." I tightened my robe and stepped back even further. "Help yourself to coffee. I'll be in the shower."

He tried to reach out and grab me, but I too can be fast when I want to. I locked myself in the bathroom and wept quietly. Ten years under the demanding, controlling hand of Ray Shirpa apparently had left deeper wounds than I had suspected.

When I finally finished my bout of tears under the hot spray, I got out and waddled into the kitchen to find a note from Scot saying sorry and he'd be gone at a golf tournament until Sunday night. *Great! That's just great!*

***

My weekend consisted of planting new trees in the front yard. I weeded my entire backyard and then sat back and enjoyed the fruits of my labors by nibbling on my fresh strawberries. I love gardening more than anything, more than teaching, more than bowling and definitely more than cooking. It's not that I loathed doing domestic chores like laundry and cooking; it's that when I was married, I did it non-stop. The house was always in pristine condition and I was berated for imperfection. I think what Ray did to me could be construed as anal abuse. No, that sounds disgusting. I was not anally abused; I was verbally abused by an anal man. Big difference.

Sunday night, I had dinner with Lily and Chad and ended up sleeping in their guest room, surrounded by baby clothes, cribs, and gifts that were already pouring in from her relatives and four sisters. I lay there half the night and stared at the cute baby on the Pampers box and wondered where I had gotten off track. Just five short weeks ago, I was in "Celibacy rocks!" mode with a plan to get pregnant on my own. Okay, it wasn't really a plan as of yet, but it was an idea about a plan. What went wrong on my quest to keep men at bay and just use one for his sperm?

I sighed and rolled over to face the lime green wall. Needless to say, Lily hadn't gotten around to repainting that guest room yet and I think she may have considered it for the nursery because it was far from the noise of the kitchen and shaded by the tall elm tree in the backyard. Anyway, I think it's time I told Scot the God's honest truth and sat him down for a little honesty-among-friends-chitchat. That might scare the bejeezus out of him, but then again, he loves me, so maybe not.

I rolled back over because the wall was ugly and then I thought about Dale and Madeline some more. *God help the boy and if there's any justice in the world, may you strike down*

Dean Hopper just for being so nasty. I fell asleep shortly after saying three Our Fathers and seven Hail Marys for wishing such a thing.

***

Tuesday night was road rage class...*again.* One more to go and I am forever cured of wanting to run down Barbie wannabes and beat them senseless with a cell-phone. Six weeks had passed since I'd first come to class. Six weeks in which I had learned to breathe and count to ten before blowing my lid. Six weeks in which I've been obsessed with who killed Walter Dobbs and literally six weeks that I've been head over heels in lust with Scot King.

He, thankfully, was not at the head of the class this evening. Nor was he lurking around the hallway, waiting to touch my boobs. I missed him, but time apart was a good thing because I don't want to compare him to Ray and I don't want to feel bad for not being ready. Ready for what? I still did not know. *The lightning perhaps*, or perhaps just the idea of having someone in my life that I had to consider. I'd done a good job just concentrating on myself for the past year. *Was I ready to share myself again?* Yada, yada, yada. I even bore myself with my analytical nightmares.

"What happens if you find yourself angry and behind the wheel of a car?" Tony's voice boomed in my head, bringing me safely out of my analytical nightmare. "Anyone?"

There were only three of us left. During the coffee break, Tony told me that eight of us were now in jail and the others still haven't surfaced. Andy, me and the googly-eyed guy with thick glasses were the only survivors. We were taking bets on whether or not Biker Andy and Little Luke were going to make it to graduation on Thursday night.

"Do you think it worked?" I asked Tony when the boys retreated out the door for a smoke break. "This class I mean. Did we give them what they were looking for?"

"What do you mean? Who?"

"The bureaucrats. I mean when I was offered this class, Sergeant Leo said it was a new program that the city was trying to implement."

"I think you've been a wonderful guinea pig," he said with a chuckle. "I think the class overall failed because most of the people never returned and they will look at that, but you and Andy have shown a great deal of improvement and even I see a difference in you. You're not snarling anymore. In fact, if I didn't know better, I would think you were actually happier. Did it help you? Do you feel a difference?"

"Yes and if I get the chance, I'll have to thank Officer King for doing me such a service. I hate to admit it, but I did learn a lot. I really enjoyed those exercises and papers. Sometimes it helps to write things down." I looked at him and almost let a tear escape. "Did you read last week's?" I had written a paper about how I was angry with myself for being such a fool in love and how now that I'd found it again, I was scared I'd fall into the same trap. Tony's Scot's best friend, but it felt good to let it out and I didn't name names. Tony knew though. He'd become a friend, someone I could really talk to.

"I won't tell Scot," he said sweetly. "I'd never break that confidentiality, but I would like to give him the one you wrote the first night. I think he'd want to put in on his refrigerator and have a good laugh about it."

"That's fine," I chuckled. I remember that first night, when I was still so angry about everything. My life, my marriage, Ray and the El Salvadorian slut. About how I was going to remain celibate and alone until I'm sixty. Ha! I couldn't wait to see the look on Scot's face when he sees my fine essay about how I will never poke another cop for the rest of my life. I know he'll laugh. He loves to laugh and that's one of the things that I love about him.

***

Wednesday afternoon, I got a call from Detective Jessup of the Portland Police Bureau. I felt my stomach clench just hearing that deep raspy voice of his.

"Can we talk? Off the record?"

"I don't know? Can we?" I said, holding the phone tightly, so it wouldn't slip from my sweaty palm. "I don't really trust the men who were trying to bushwhack me with a murder wrap. Why should I tell you anything?"

"Because you know Dale didn't do it. Come on, Ang. Talk to me."

"Ang?" I just about screamed. "Did King put you up to this?"

I heard him chuckle a couple of times before clearing his throat. "He actually warned me not to call you, Ang, but I wanted to see what happened when I pissed you off."

"That you did. What do you want?"

"I want you to tell me everything. Scot can't do it without turning the heat on himself, so that leaves you. He said you had it figured all along and that I'd be a fool not to listen to your story."

"He said that," I whimpered. "Really? What else did he say?"

"That you're intelligent and probably the most wonderful woman he's ever met." It was sounding a bit rehearsed, like he was reading it right from his little black notepad, but it made me smile anyway. "And that you have amazing insight into the miniscule details and that you sure can analyze stuff to death."

"Anything else?" I quipped casually.

"Your smile drives him wild, he likes the way you hold his hand and he's miserable without you, etc. etc. Please don't make me read the rest."

"That's very sweet. Where is he?"

"He's at McFadden's waiting for you to rescue him from all the sorority girls in tight tee-shirts."

"I bet he is." I giggled and hung up after agreeing to meet the detective for coffee in the a.m.

***

I liked that Scot was already sentimental about our first outing together. When I arrived, he was still in uniform, sipping a cola and munching on French fries at the end of the row of booths. He looked sullen until he spotted me, and then his eyes lit up like a kid's in a candy store.

"Detective Jessup says hello and good luck." I sat down beside him in the booth and ordered a beer. "You didn't have to go to so much trouble. I happen to like you and you could have just asked me out for a burger."

The place was packed with college students, talking and screaming obscenities at the baseball game on the wide screen television. The lights were dimmed, but I could still tell that something wasn't right with Scot. He seemed nervous, despite his bad-ass police uniform and serious scowl.

"I don't know how to make this better for you." He fidgeted with his fries and turned to look into my eyes. "I'm at my wits' end, Ang. I love you, but it's not getting any easier. What did I do? What is it that you can't get past?" He shook his head and dipped his fry in a puddle of runny ketchup.

I squirmed a bit and hadn't thought of how I was affecting him, other than causing his balls to ache every time I said, "I'm not ready." I felt like a cad. A selfish, horrible person who had hurt the one person who didn't deserve it the least bit.

"I love you too," I admitted breathlessly.

His eyes popped open and he leaned over and kissed my lips tenderly. He moved away with a smile and seemed a tad more relaxed.

"Then what are we waiting for?"

"It's complicated."

"Then after I get off work tomorrow night, we should talk about it."

"Tomorrow night?" I said. "Why not tonight?"

Why did I care? I wasn't particularly looking forward to having this damn conversation, but I knew it needed to be done and I guess I was feeling bad for tormenting the poor guy.

"I'm on tonight and most of the day tomorrow."

"Oh, I have class tomorrow night. I graduate. Yippee," I said cheerfully, but didn't feel much like smiling. "I could come over after, if you want?"

I saw something in his eyes change. Almost fright, or perhaps apprehension.

"No," he said. "It'll be too late. How about Friday morning? We could meet for breakfast."

"Sure."

He got up, kissed me goodbye and walked out the door.

***

I met up with Detective Kevin Jessup at Waddles just before nine a.m. on Thursday morning. He had a cup of coffee in hand when I arrived and a series of files strewn out on his large corner table.

"Sit, please." He was all business. "Start at the beginning and don't leave anything out."

"Sheesh," I grunted. "Good morning to you too."

"Sorry," he said, rather sincerely. "The baby kept me up most of the night. I'm a little grouchy."

"Baby?" I asked as the waitress filled my coffee cup. I guess I never imagined Detective Jessup as a human being, let alone a husband and a father. "I had no idea."

"Three months old. Her name is Shea Lynn."

"Sweet," I said then got right to work because my uterus was rhythmically clenching again like a time bomb. "The beginning was when I went to the Dancing Beaver and talked to the girls. I had no idea that Isaac Moncrief was his son; they just said that Laura was his mother and she was connected with Dobbs. It wasn't until I asked Dean Hopper that he told me Isaac was his son. Madeline and Dale didn't even know about him."

"Oh no," he said, easing back in his chair. "Madeline knew Moncrief. Moncrief stole her car about three years back and Walter begged her to cover the kid's ass. She said she would if he severed all ties with his son."

"How did you know that?"

"Got a tape of it from the car theft unit. They were in the interview room and the whole thing got recorded. She's not as innocent as she seems."

I was dumbfounded. "So she knew about Moncrief. Why would she lie?"

"Embarrassed probably." Jessup sipped his coffee and forked his eggs. "Doesn't really matter. What happened next?"

Yes, I think it did matter because if Madeline found out all his money was going to Laura and Moncrief, there would be hell to pay, perhaps even death. My spine tingled for a moment. I went on and on about how I and this un-named person (Bull) had gathered this information and come up with the conclusion that Dale was protecting Madeline. I didn't tell him anything that Dale had confided in me, because I knew he was still being charged. Jessup seemed half relieved and half annoyed that I had found out more about these people than the police had.

"Just got lucky, I guess," I said with pride. He paid for breakfast and said thanks again. He'll be in touch if he has more questions. Blah, blah, blah!

***

I graduated Thursday night from Road Rage Awareness 101 as Tony calls it. We had sparkling cider and huddled around the three cupcakes that Tina had made for the only ones left standing. Actually two more idiots showed up on the last night, thinking they were going to get away with it, but Tony told them to get lost and they better pay their fines or they were in big trouble. I thankfully had no fines to pay. No big insurance premium that would go through the roof and no official repercussions for poking Officer King in the sternum with my index finger. I was once again a free woman. For my celebratory last essay, I wrote an apology letter to Officer King and told him that I was sorry for my behavior that day and that I was in fact acting like a deranged meth-head. I signed it with love and asked Tony to make sure he gets it.

Twelve

Friday morning, I postponed my breakfast with Scot and, in turn, Saturday morning he postponed it again. All weekend, I was busy dodging him and it seemed that he was busy dodging me, but I didn't know why?

Okay, so I did know why. *I make him crazy!*

Finally, on Tuesday night, just as I had finished popping my microwave popcorn and had The Usual Suspects cued up on the DVD player, there was a light rap on my door. I was snuggled into my comfortable, yet unattractive fuzzy slippers and even more unattractive giant tee shirt that says *Bite Me* on the front.

"Hi," I said, opening the door as wide as I could.

He was casual in Levi's, white Nikes and a white tee shirt, but he made it all look good. "Can I come in?"

"Sure." I shuffled out of the way and closed the door when he stepped past me. "I was just about to watch a movie. Do you want to watch with me?"

He sauntered past me without a word and sat down on the edge of my sofa. My favorite blanket was laid out on the sofa, awaiting my arrival.

I didn't know where to start. The funny thing was that I just wanted to throw my arms around him and snuggle with him all night. And then after that, I wanted to take him to my bed and do pleasurable yet naughty things with my tongue. It was nice that the snuggling part was thought of first though.

That gives me hope that I'm not just infatuated with his great lips and tight butt. Snuggling goes deeper.

"I don't even know how to be around you anymore, Ang. I've lost my mind."

"And I've lost mine apparently because I should have told you this stuff a long time ago. I shouldn't have wasted so much time. I'm sorry for that, I really am."

"So, you're ready to explain."

"Somewhat," I said with a wince. I scooted back against the couch and crossed my legs at the ankles. Best way to do it is like ripping off a bandage. I'll just come right out with it and say it really, really fast. "I don't know if I can love you and still manage to keep my own identity. I'm afraid of losing myself again."

"That's it?" he groaned and dropped his head into my lap. I chuckled nervously and wound my fingers into his dark hair. "Oh man, my mind has been going non-stop for a week. Baby, that's nothing."

"Well, it's everything to me," I said, still massaging his scalp. He liked it, I could tell by his lazy smile and the way his eyes were drooped closed. "I had a really hard time even realizing that's what I was so scared of. I have deep wounds that are far from being healed. And yeah, I've been horribly distracted with my quest to find out who killed Walter. You just happened to meet me at a very difficult time in my life."

He exhaled and opened his eyes to look up at my face. "Tony gave me your paper."

"Really?" I said with a smirk. "I really think you did me a favor. I had no idea how out of control I really was and it was actually a blessing that you cuffed me and tossed me into the back of your police car. I thank you for that."

"You're welcome, but that's not what I was talking about."

I know I paled slightly because I felt all the blood pool in my toes. "What...I mean...he did not...oh hell!"

"He did, but I don't think he meant to. He handed me a folder and said you'll get a huge laugh out of this and that I should hang it on my refrigerator."

I swallowed with difficulty. "So it didn't say I will never poke another policeman for the rest of my life, over and over again, like a chalkboard mantra?"

"No, it was a love story with a very unpredictable ending and it wasn't funny."

Oh God help me!

"Was all that true?" he asked. "Do you really think that I would do something like that or that I'd make you become that unhappy person again and do you really love me that much?"

I felt the familiar sting of tears as I nodded and dropped my chin to my chest. "I never ever meant for you to read that. I just had to get it out and I'm sorry if I hurt your feelings with anything that I said. But yeah. That's why I'm so scared. I think I have a tendency to love too much and I wanted to make sure I could handle it before things... well, got intimate, I guess."

He eased up on his elbow and met me in the middle for a small, innocent kiss. "I love you." He kissed me again, this time with more meaning. "I get it now, but I'm still going to bug you for sex every chance I get because, my god, I can't wait. I'm so horny right now, I probably wouldn't even make it inside you."

My tears spilled at that point because I loved him that much and he's so damn cute when he's playing the sex-starved martyr.

We watched The Usual Suspects in silence and then cuddled in my bed until he crept out at four in the morning. It was again, one of the most amazing nights of my life. Intimate acts are fairly over-rated when you have a true connection like Scot's and mine.

I'm so damn full of crap, aren't I? I once said "Celibacy Rocks!" Ha!

I'm happy to say that we spent the next week having dinner, making out on my couch, and sneaking off to have coffee and donuts while he was on duty. I had lesson plans and organizational duties up the yin-yang and had to go to the high school a number of times during the week. I mapped out a plan of my career and decided one more year as a teacher would not kill me. I get to torture yet another senior class. It was an easy decision to make because having a new man in my life was just about enough drama, all I could handle at once. Small steps. That's what I was doing to change my life for the better. Lily and I had time for tea a couple of times and she's not enjoying the early stage of pregnancy like she thought she would. Morning sickness is a myth. It's more like all-day sickness in her case.

I had just dropped my car keys in my bowl and finally tossed those horrible over-ripe avocados in the trash when I got a call from Detective Jessup.

"Well, I hope you have amazing news, because I need some amazing news today." I sounded rather chipper, because Scot was due any time and I had even prepared homemade tamales. Wow, I cooked for him, can you believe it?

"I took all the information you gave me and dug a little deeper. They found Laura Moncrief at her sister's place in Prineville. They towed her car, took some samples of some blood on the seats and it matched Walter's."

I sat down hard on the couch and bit my lip, trying to halt the tears. I don't know why I was so relieved that she was alive. I guess I just needed to know that Madeline was innocent and Dale would still have one parent to lean on in life. I know I couldn't have made it through my life without either of my parents, or Bulldog, so I was so happy that I felt a tear trickle down my cheek.

"And," I said when he apparently stopped to light a cigarette. I heard a lighter flicker, then a deep inhale. "What's happening? Did she do it?"

"Yes, she did," he exhaled loudly and rambled on while I sat and listened and wept for Dale. "After we talked to Madeline and Dale together, and then spoke to the strippers at the Beaver, they all confirmed different important details that we used to get her to talk. She ended up confessing. Dale will be just fine. I just thought you should be the first to know, because we'd have figured it out eventually, but you helped speed it up and we appreciate the help."

I asked him tons more questions about the details, which he answered fully and then I asked him if Scot knew yet.

"I haven't been able to reach him, so go ahead if you want. You didn't hear any of this from me though."

"Of course," I said and disconnected for a good cleansing *Hallelujah.*

***

Twenty minutes later, I pulled my black tank top over my head and pulled my hair into a ponytail. I opted for khaki Capri pants and went barefoot into the kitchen to wait for my man and grate cheese for the nachos.

He arrived ten minutes later with a bouquet of flowers and a bottle of champagne. Without a word, he lifted me into his arms and kissed me madly. His hand covered my butt and he grunted like Tarzan. "I just heard. You're the talk of the station... unofficially of course."

"I can't believe it myself. I wanted to call Dale, but Jessup said I had to be cool about knowing."

"I want to hear all the details, but first things first." He popped the cork, sending it into the living room. I pulled out two champagne glasses, that I had to rewash because I hadn't used them in ten years, and he poured us each a glass.

"To Dale's freedom and my super sleuth Angie." He kissed me with lots of tongue and hands that weren't content by his sides. I was bent over backwards, nibbled on and caressed on the breasts by his hot mouth. "What time is dinner? Do we have time?" He bobbed his brows while I slapped his chest. "What? No more distractions. What's the big deal? I love you. I love you. I love you!"

"And I love you, but it's not a good time." I was sure that super cop dude would be able to figure that one out without me actually having to mutter the word "menstruation" out loud. But he just furrowed his brows and readjusted his package. It was a nice package and it was growing bigger. I felt for him, I really did.

"Damn it, I'm gonna DIE!" He grabbed my hand and brought it down to cup his bulging erection.

"You're so dramatic. What's two more days?"

"What's in two more days? Why not now? I love you and I don't want to wait two more days."

I think I once called him a big overgrown baby. Well that's exactly how he was acting. It wasn't sexy, even on a guy like Scot King. Whining for sex is not sexy. It's amusing and somewhat hilarious, but not sexy.

He helped me with dinner once his profuse sweating stopped.

I sat down and poured my father's latest creation, a nice Riesling. "Are you working Thursday night?" I asked between bites. We'd become a comfortable couple, sitting in silence at the dinner table, but in reality, I think he was still sulking over not getting laid. But I love him anyway.

"Thursday?" he replied, knocking on his forehead a couple of times. "No, but I think I'm supposed to be doing something." He looked confused.

"Okay," I bit down on a hot tamale and then sipped some wine. "So, when they questioned Laura, she caved and she admitted all of it."

"What happened? Did she catch him in bed with his wife or something?" he chuckled.

I loved hearing him laugh.

"How'd you know?" I felt somewhat perturbed that he guessed. "She went over to meet with him and found him in bed with Madeline. She was so mad that she grabbed my shovel off the back porch and killed him right after Madeline left. Crime of passion, all right. Got pissed off that he was actually fucking his own wife." I shook my head and Scot choked a couple of times. "What? I've said fuck before. Get over it," I quipped and took another bite, watching his coloring go back to normal. "Afterwards, she freaked out, ran home, packed a bag and took off for Prineville. Unpremeditated crime of passion. Dale will be just fine. I'm sure the D.A. will cut him a break for lying. Don't you think?"

"Sure, he did it to save his Mom. I think he'll be off to Stanford in no time."

After dinner, Scot helped me with the dishes and then right before I was going to ask him to stay the night, he got fidgety and yawned.

"I should just go. I have an early shift tomorrow." He kissed me and smiled. "I love you and thanks for dinner."

"I love you," I said. "You can stay."

He backed up as if being drawn by a magnetic field. "No, I... I have to go."

I waved and then ran out to his truck before he got away. "You're not mad are you? I just want it to be perfect."

"And I appreciate it, but I'd kind of like to get it over with so I can see straight again. You're causing me considerable unwanted and unneeded stress."

"You're such a man!" I shouted and stepped back. My mother had said appreciate the fact that he's a man. Well, I was having a hard time doing that because I wanted him to stay and cuddle with me. I stuck my tongue out at him and went back into the solace of my home. "MEN!" I shouted as he left, and then called my best friend, for emotional and mental health support.

***

Two days later, I had been to Dale's celebration dinner, had finished planting the shrubs in the front yard and my legs were freshly shaven. "Now what?" I said to my reflection. Like I didn't know. I was just hours from making my move and taking the man I love to bed. Sure, I was nervous, but I was also prepared. I had a box of condoms, my negligee was being pulled down over my naked breasts and for the sake of shocking the crap out of him, I had decided to go without panties and had every intention of driving to his house dressed only in a sexy black negligee and my long black overcoat. When I decide to do something, I go all out. My makeup was perfect, I had done my hair down so the curly tendrils tickled my shoulders, and I was on a mission. I'd checked his schedule, he was off at eight, and I had Trojans in my pockets and a bottle of wine under my arm. *Watch out, baby, here I come.*

I had serious anxiety about driving around wearing this getup, but what are the odds that I'd be in an accident tonight. I'd never been in an accident in my life and if by chance I did this evening, it would just be an omen from God telling me that I still wasn't ready. I think I am. Or at least I was sure enough that I was ready. Things had been wonderful with Scot. I thought of him as a friend, an equal, and just a man like my mom had said. We have similar interests and he has never tried to tell me how he prefers my hair down as opposed to pulled into a comfortable ponytail. Scot is wonderful; he's kind, respectful and doesn't ogle women when we're in public. Most men are oglers and, therefore, can't be trusted, but I trust Scot completely. I love him!

I pulled into his driveway and his truck was in the garage. It was open, so I figured he had just gotten home. *Perfect.*

I rapped a couple times on the door and took a deep breath. I felt like a thirty-three year old virgin. I knocked again and then when the door opened, a very attractive, young brunette smiled at me. "Can I help you?" she asked.

My jaw dropped and I nearly dropped the bottle of wine. You don't want to know all the dirty names I called him under my breath. For a moment I thought I was dreaming. Time stood still. The tall trees and shrubs seemed to be spinning and I was standing in the doorway of my beloved's house, staring at the perky breasts of my worst nightmare come true. She was unbelievably gorgeous. Long curly dark hair, cascading down her *skinny-ass* back and she was wearing a tight white camisole, a tight, black skirt, black nylons and four-inch-god-damn-heels! Making her at least two inches taller than me.

I stuttered and then leaned back to make sure I had the right house. "Scot?" I managed to stutter.

She finished her bite of toast and said, "He's in the shower. Do you want to come in?"

No, I didn't want to come in! I wanted to bash his brains in with the bottle of wine I was holding.

"Allie," I heard his deep voice before I had time to run. "Who's..."? He stopped short and looked at me through the screen door. He fumbled with his words. The damn bastard was wrapped in just a white bath towel.

"YOU!" I shouted and felt the sting of tears. I backed down the stairs and nearly tripped on his garden hose. "You bastard!" I screamed when I saw him lurch for the door.

He stammered and tried to say something, but all I could hear was the pain in my head, radiating down my spine and causing even my toes to ache. Not to mention my heart.

"You stupid mother-fucking-son-of-a-bitch!"

I actually dishonored my father by throwing the bottle of wine at his head. It missed and shattered on the patio, leaving a pool of burgundy liquid seeping into the concrete. Everything seemed to blur together as in slow motion. He was reaching out to me and I think I was screaming in pain. I looked to my right, getting ready to bust-a-move and haul ass down the driveway and that's when my vision cleared for a brief second and I saw Tina and Tony standing in the street holding their hands over their son's innocent ears.

"Bastard." I turned to Scot muttering more quietly now that I had an audience. "You couldn't wait two more days for me. I was on my period, you big jerk!"

That's when he forcefully grabbed my arms and held me in place.

The slut was still on the patio, cowering behind the screen door.

"Jesus, Ang. That's Allison... my sister." He motioned to the door with a nod of his head. His hands clutched me tighter as I relaxed in a heap of tired bones.

With steady hands and a bewildered smile, he chuckled and held my trembling body as I wept and sagged. I felt like a stupid putz, to say the least.

"Glad to see those classes paid off." I heard Tony chuckle from across the yard, but I was still busy weeping and shaking my head against Scot's bare chest.

"I'm so sorry," I moaned. "I'm, I'm not...ready." I mumbled against his shoulder and held onto him as tight as I could. His naked back felt exquisite and for a split second, I contemplated running, but I guess I was already too comfortable in his arms.

"Yes, you are!" He kissed me sweetly and brushed the tears from my eyes with his thumb. The man was so understanding yet seemed to only be interested in the slight opening of my black trench coat. "What are you wearing?" It came out as a half whistle. He eased back to take a look at my ensemble. I was trembling in my four-inch heels, but he didn't seem to notice. He just growled and took a peek under my overcoat. "My god, I love you and I'm willing to wait another..." he paused to moisten his lips, "ten minutes for you, but that's it." He kissed me again with more passion and deeper meaning. We broke momentarily and I grinned as best I could at feeling his urgency.

"Okay, maybe nine minutes," he chuckled.

I laughed along with him and then felt the most amazing sensation roll over me. It damn near felt like a bolt of lightning.

***

Scot went inside, probably afraid of exposing himself to the crowd of neighbors who were milling around, interested in our squabble, while I shared a good laugh with Tina and Tony in the middle of Scot's driveway. I apologized repeatedly for my outburst. I now had even more stories to tell our children someday. I walked inside and was greeted by Allison King, who laughed and gave me a huge hug, then buttoned her double-breasted jacket over her pretty camisole and kissed her brother goodbye.

"I hope it's what you were looking for," she said, handing him a manila envelope, grabbing her keys off the counter. "It was nice meeting you, Angie." And then was out the door.

Scot met me from behind, still draped in his towel, which I felt drop and puddle at my ankles. My coat soon followed, drifting down my bare legs, crumpling on the floor. His warm hands on my skin made my heart flutter in my chest. He whispered some fairly enticing things in my ear, dimmed the lights, closed the blinds and we didn't leave his house for three entire days.

***

Monday morning, I was ready for real food and some natural vitamin D. We did get fresh air the night before around two a.m. when we cuddled naked on the porch and watched the meteor shower, but I was ready to become one of the living again and feel the sun on my skin.

"Morning," I bent down and gave him a kiss, then handed him a cup of coffee. "My father's probably worried sick. I usually call every Sunday."

His eyes fluttered open a bit wider and he patted the bed. "Come back to bed, I have a surprise for you." He rolled over and hopped out of bed with coffee in hand and an outrageous.... well, you know. He was naked. I couldn't help but look.

"What is it?" I slunk back under the covers and waited rather impatiently for him to return from wherever he had snuck off to. I couldn't help the nervous giggle and began kicking wildly under the covers. I love surprises.

He came back into his bedroom with a bagel between his teeth, his coffee cup in one hand and a manila folder in the other. With little effort, he knelt beside me on the bed. I grabbed the bagel from his teeth and gave him a quick kiss right before he gave me the folder.

I didn't know what I expected. Perhaps breakfast in bed, or freshly cut roses from his garden. But a folder?

"What is it?"

"Your homework," he said with a smile and eased down under the covers with me. I felt his toes on mine and my breath had suddenly caught in my throat. "Well, open it."

I looked from the folder to Scot's loving eyes, and then back to the folder. I sucked back a tear and opened the seal with my index finger.

Inside was a classified document, a couple photographs and an agency report on the agent-involved shooting in Miami,

Florida. I read down the page while appreciating the small kisses that Scot was planting on my bare shoulder. I'd been naked with the man for three days, but his kisses still set my skin ablaze.

"I can't believe you did this. How... I mean, who did..." I then remembered what his sister had said when she left Thursday night. "Your sister?" My head tilted to the side like a curious puppy. "How did she...?"

Scot's warm kiss melted away the rest of my question. He moved closer and met my gaze with his stifling dark eyes. "You're not the only one with family agency connections."

"I can't believe you did this for me." I couldn't wait to read the entire file, from beginning to end and learn all about why my father was in Miami and how it connected to Colombia 1986 and how Dad had saved Bulldog's life and, my God, it felt like I was cheating on a mid-term. "I don't know what to say."

"How about... you love me?"

"I do love you," I said. "You have no idea what this means to me...this is like – I don't know, worthy of..." My eyes pinched together at the corners and the blood began to flush my cheeks. I kissed him hard on the mouth and pressed him down onto his back. Then I continued on my oral exploration of his body and moved down his throat with miniature French kisses. I didn't stop at his chest, but I did spend a fair amount of time suckling his nipples, while he moaned and warned me that I better not be teasing him. Oh, I was teasing him all right. It took me another three minutes to reach my final destination and then... *I thanked him.*

Scot and I are an amazing team. I thanked him and then he thanked me and then we both *relaxed...* together. I was still hungry because the bagel he brought to bed had gotten jostled to the floor when I was being thanked, multiple times I might add.

"I need food," I muttered against his naked chest. "Do you want me to make you some breakfast?"

Cohabitating for three days was easy when the clothes remained on the floor, but life doesn't quite revolve around being naked in Scot's bed. I wasn't delusional in thinking that all my angst and nervousness about the future were just going to disappear because we'd made love. I was just more peaceful about it.

He brushed the hair from my eyes and kissed my forehead. "I'll do it. You just get your homework done." He made a move to get up, but I pulled him by the hand and gazed into his eyes.

"By the way, I know I'm naked and lying in your bed, but let's take things slow."

"Take all the time you need," he said with a smile and wiggled his naked butt at me as he left the room.

Epilogue

Who knew I only needed a year? One year and I was walking down the aisle on my way to becoming Scot's wife – partner – best friend for life, and I couldn't be happier. I still maintain my own identity, but now I just do it with an amazing man by my side.

It was fun to read all about my father's life, that morning in Scot's bed. A life that I really knew nothing about. Apparently, after Bulldog had finished his mission in Colombia and the dust settled, a cartel member had survived and was out for revenge. Years after Colombia 1986, a mole was discovered within the organization and my father was informed about the mole's connection with the cartel member. That's why he was in Miami that day, to set up a sting and save Bulldog's life. I guess when you love someone that much and they mean the world to you, you will just about do anything to keep them around, so my father took a bullet and thankfully lived to tell about it. I guess reading that bit of information just gave me the extra nudge I needed to take the plunge and change careers.

I gave up my life as a schoolteacher after tormenting the seniors at David Douglas High one more time. I currently have a very interesting job. I contracted with a top government agency doing what I do best. I'm a special research analyst and it feels good to get paid to analyze shit to death. I didn't even have to use my father or Uncle Bulldog as a reference, although it was suspicious when the director slipped and said that jobs like mine were few and far between and you usually have to know someone, or perhaps be the niece of someone special to get it. I guess I'll just have to say thanks to Aunt Rita when she gets back from her honeymoon. She took the plunge and again made Bulldog my legitimate uncle. Unlike us, they got married on a private sandy beach in Belize. Scot and I had a long Catholic ceremony at the vineyard, surrounded by hundreds of law enforcement officials, one fire fighter, one schoolteacher, and their four-month-old baby girl.

It's nice to be Scot's wife, although, this time I became Angela Reese Harrington hyphen King and I don't do laundry. I got smart and hired a housekeeper to do it.

Scot is still happily fighting crime on the street and rarely gets shot at anymore. I work from my wonderful home office in our house, formerly my house. Yes, Scot demanded that we live in my house, because he loves me that much and knows how much of an effort I put into my garden.

Right after the wedding, we talked about kids, but I needed to make sure I didn't lose myself in my marriage first. That lasted about four months in which I spent hours upon hours with Lily and her adorable baby, Emily.

Now that I feel completely capable of keeping a straight head about love, marriage and household chores, I have another challenge to conquer. I'm going to try very hard not to lose myself to the baby that is taking up residence in my womb, but the little bugger is already calling the shots and telling me when to eat, when to pee and that I no longer like to eat salmon and avocados. *Lord, help me*!

Printed in the United States
131402LV00001BA/24/P